THE TRUE LOVE BOOKSHOP

ANNIE RAINS

FOREVER

New York Boston

Copyright © 2022 by Annie Rains
Reading group guide copyright © 2022 by Annie Rains and Hachette Book Group, Inc.

Cover design by Daniela Medina
Cover art by Allan Davey
Cover image by © Evelina Kremsdorf / Trevillion Images
Cover copyright © 2022 by Hachette Book Group, Inc.

Forever
Hachette Book Group
1290 Avenue of the Americas, New York, NY 10104
read-forever.com
twitter.com/readforeverpub

First Edition: July 2022

Forever is an imprint of Grand Central Publishing. The Forever name and logo are trademarks of Hachette Book Group, Inc.

The publisher is not responsible for websites (or their content) that are not owned by the publisher.

The Hachette Speakers Bureau provides a wide range of authors for speaking events. To find out more, go to www.hachettespeakersbureau.com or call (866) 376-6591.

Library of Congress Cataloging-in-Publication Data
Names: Rains, Annie, author.
Title: The true love bookshop / Annie Rains.
Description: First edition. | New York : Boston ; Forever, 2022. | Series: Somerset Lake
Identifiers: LCCN 2021053694 | ISBN 9781538710050 (hardcover) | ISBN 9781538710074 (ebook)
Classification: LCC PS3618.A3975 T78 2022 | DDC 813/.6—dc23
LC record available at https://lccn.loc.gov/2021053694

ISBN: 9781538710050 (hardcover), 9781538710074 (ebook)

Printed in the United States of America

LSC-C

Printing 1, 2022

PRAISE FOR ANNIE RAINS

For my kindred spirits, the booklovers

Chapter One

"No," Tess Lane said, maybe a little too forcefully for her new employee at Lakeside Books. "It's not a romance if it doesn't have a happy ending." Tess pointed at the book in Lara Dunkin's hand. "The hero dies at the end of that one. That novel can't be categorized as a romance." Tess gestured at another shelf of books with a sign overhead that read ROMANTIC FICTION. "It can be shelved over there."

Lara dutifully took the book and placed it where Tess had directed her.

But maybe a book where the hero died wasn't even considered romantic fiction. Tess stood there thoughtfully. Perhaps that book belonged in the Horror section. Or the Nonfiction section because real life heroes died all the time. She should know.

Her heart squeezed, and emotions tumbled over each other, spilling out messily inside her while she worked to maintain a composed demeanor. She'd learned that it was comfortable for others if she played the role of the grieving widow for only about a month after Jared's death. Now, when people asked how she was doing, they didn't really want to hear the truth, that some days were harder than others. Or that she still had to give herself pep talks to make it to work some days, especially ones like this.

No. People wanted to know that Tess was doing well. That she was running a successful bookshop in her quaint little hometown of Somerset Lake, North Carolina, complete with a book club of her closest friends. That she had taken up hiking and was considering getting a dog to join her on the trails. And that she was journaling because some self-help book she'd read last year said it had changed the author's life.

That's what well-intended folks wanted to hear, so that's what Tess told them when they asked how she was doing, three years after Jared's death.

The bell above the store's door chimed, announcing a customer. Tess headed in that direction and froze. Even the breath inside her stilled. Then she folded her arms over her chest, hugging herself tightly. Of all days, why was River Harrison standing in front of her today? "You're not welcome in my store."

He looked calm, as always. That was the thing about River. Nothing fazed this man. He'd been Jared's best friend once upon a time. They'd served in the military together. Then River had betrayed Jared in an unforgivable way.

Tess pointed toward the front door, her body shaky. "You can leave now. Get your books somewhere else. The library maybe."

"Actually, I was hoping to use your bathroom," he said, his words coming out slowly.

"If my bathroom was the last one on earth, and your bladder was about to explode, I wouldn't let you use it." Tess was vaguely aware that her new employee was watching and overhearing every word. Tess really hoped she didn't quit. Lara was Tess's first full-time employee for the bookstore and would allow Tess more free time for all the hiking, journaling, and dog walking she'd be doing when she finally got herself that dog. Lara didn't know the history between Tess and River. If she did, she'd understand the animosity.

River took a step forward, and Tess noticed that he was limping a little. "Can I just use your phone then?"

"Where's yours?" she asked, vaguely aware that he looked pale. The scar under his right eye was a deeper shade of pink against the pallor of his nearly translucent skin. She couldn't remember if she'd ever been told the story of how River got that scar under his eye. She'd asked Jared about it once, but he had given her some vague answer that really didn't tell her anything. That was one thing about living with an ex-Marine. Marines had secrets, and she'd had to accept that she wouldn't know certain things about the man she'd pledged to live the rest of her life with, short as Jared's had turned out to be.

"I've been camping in the woods, and my phone is dead. I drove this far, but I can't make it home...I thought you might put your feelings toward me aside for just a moment."

"Feelings?" Tess asked. "Oh, I have feelings about you. And I don't think I will ever put them to the side. Maybe you need to walk down to Sweetie's Bake Shop. Darla might be willing to help you out."

River turned to leave, stumbled, and caught himself against a shelf, knocking a book to the floor.

Tess's mouth dropped open. "Are you drunk?" she asked, hurt and anger funneling at the center of her chest.

"I wish," River slurred.

"You *are* drunk. You have some nerve coming in here, today of all days." Tears collected in her eyes. She blinked them away, choosing to focus on her anger. "I bet you don't even know what today is, do you?"

"Yeah, I do," he said quietly, his back toward her, his hand still clutching the bookshelf for support.

"Somehow that makes it even worse then," Tess said quietly. "I don't know what Jared ever saw in you."

River stopped, straightened, and turned to face her, his skin even paler under the low lighting of her bookshop. "I could say the opposite about you. I always knew what he saw."

Tess stiffened. It was too late for niceties. Her gaze dropped to a large, dark stain on his T-shirt, and a gasp escaped her mouth. "Is that blood?"

"Just a little."

"You're injured?" The sight of blood had always triggered a surge of adrenaline through her. Even a tiny drop from a paper cut. This was way more than a droplet though.

He looked down as well and then stumbled again, this time failing to catch himself as he fell right over in the middle of the aisle.

"Lara, call nine-one-one!" Tess rushed to River's side and crouched beside him in the aisle. She patted his cheek gently at first and then a little harder. "River? River, are you okay?"

He moaned, his blue eyes cracking open to peer up at her.

Her breath caught as she looked down at him.

"Tess?" he asked.

"Yes?"

"Don't call an ambulance. I hate hospitals."

"Sorry," she said, "but I'm not going to allow you to bleed out in my bookshop today."

He chuckled quietly and then closed his eyes again. "Because of the mess, right? Not because you want me to live."

Tess glanced at the large blood stain on his shirt. "I do want you to live, okay? And you *are* going to live because Lara called an ambulance. You're going to Magnolia Medical, whether you want to or not."

River's smile faded.

Panic shot through Tess. She leaned over his face again, hoping he wasn't dead. "River?"

He cracked open an eye. "Yes, Tess?"

"Just don't die, okay?" Her breaths were shallow as nerves bound her chest.

"One condition," he said.

She frowned. "You're in no position to make conditions."

"My dog is in my truck. Can you watch him for me? Please."

Tess hesitated. River was the last person she would ever do a favor for. But he was kind-of-maybe dying right now, and his dog was apparently helpless and alone inside his truck. "Fine."

"My keys are in my pocket."

Tess gulped. Okay, he was asking a lot. She hesitated before reaching quickly into his jeans pocket, grabbing the keys, and yanking them out. "What's your dog's name?"

"Buddy."

"Is he aggressive?" she asked, hearing sirens grow louder as they approached her store. Thank goodness they were almost here.

River's eyes shut, and his head fell to one side.

"River?" She slapped his face. "River?"

He didn't respond this time.

A few seconds later, two paramedics rushed through her front doors, spotting her immediately. Her heart jumped into her throat. Many times, she'd had the thought that she wished this man in front of her would just drive off a cliff. She didn't mean it, of course. She didn't really want any harm to come to River Harrison. Once upon a time, she'd thought he was a nice guy. One of the good ones. All that changed on her wedding day, however, when he'd told her husband-to-be that he was making a huge mistake.

The paramedics, a male and a female, took over. Tess stood and moved away, feeling breathless and upset.

Lara stepped up beside her. "Don't worry. He'll be all right," she said gently.

Tess nodded again, tears burning the backs of her eyes. "Oh, I'm certain. He's a former Marine. He's tough." But then again, her late husband had been too. Tess looked at Lara. "Please tell me you're not quitting. The bookstore isn't usually this...active."

Lara smiled. "You're stuck with me. I need this job."

"That's good. Because I need you." Tess watched as the paramedics wheeled River out on a gurney. Then she took a deep breath and jingled the keys in her hand. "I need to get his dog from his truck. Can you watch the store?"

"Of course."

Tess didn't recall ever seeing River with a dog. She hoped it wasn't massive or hyper. Or a biter. She headed out the front door of the store just in time to see the ambulance disappear down the street. Then she realized she didn't know what kind of vehicle River drove. He'd said a truck. That's all she knew to look for.

She scanned the street where there were several vehicles parked nearby. One was parked haphazardly, like maybe someone had rolled in while bleeding from their left side. Tess headed in that direction and saw a large hound dog's head pop up from the driver's seat. He watched her as she approached. He didn't bark or growl, and he wasn't foaming at the mouth, which were all good signs.

She reluctantly opened the driver's side door, ready to slam it shut if the dog's behavior changed. It didn't though. "Hi. I'm Tess. River's, um…Well, we're not friends. Definitely not friends," she told the dog, immediately feeling silly for talking to it. "But I'll be watching you while he gets better."

The dog looked at her with an almost bored expression. Then it hopped down from the truck's seat and stood beside her, looking up as if to say, *Lead the way.*

River despised nothing more than being in a hospital.

His eyes weren't open yet, but he could already feel that's where he was based on the steady sound of a *beep, beep* in the room and the cold, stale air he was breathing, unlike the fresh mountain air he preferred.

Not that he had much of a choice in coming here. He'd made a foolish mistake while he'd been out in the rugged wilderness beyond Somerset Lake. He liked to go off on the weekends sometimes and test his survival skills in the mountainous terrain. Well, this weekend, if there was a pass or fail to survival skills, he would have flunked with flying colors.

Everything had been going fine until the unexpected summer storm hit yesterday, sending temperatures dropping and rain pelting his makeshift shelter. That's when everything had fallen to pieces. Such was how true survival situations went. The unplanned happened. True skills were challenged. And sometimes people got hurt.

River was a trained Marine. He was careful—always. But a distracted mind was dangerous. He'd needed the weekend getaway after running into a former buddy from his old Marine unit when he was stationed at Camp Lejeune. Jared Lane's name had come up, of course. Back in the day, River and Jared had been best friends. That had all changed after they'd gotten out of the Marines, but River wouldn't expect this guy to know that. Then the guy had mentioned Ashley Hansley, another former Marine they'd all been close to.

"I ran into her the other day," the guy told River.

"Yeah? How's she doing?" River hadn't seen Ashley since an awkward situation three nights before Jared's wedding. Walking in on two people who were hot and heavy was awkward to say the least.

"Ashley seems to be doing great. She got out of the Corps as well. Guess none of us were lifers. She's living in Morrisville these days."

Morrisville. That town name had plagued River for years. There was nothing in Morrisville as far as River knew. Why would Jared have been there on the night of his car accident? River prided himself on being a good private investigator, but he hadn't a clue until that chance meeting with his Marine Corps buddy last week.

The implications had occupied River's mind while he'd been

camping over the weekend. His thoughts had been muddled. And while trying to sharpen the tip of a stick that he was using to tamp his shelter into the dirt, his knife had slipped against his rain-slick hands, sinking the blade into River's left side.

It was just a superficial wound. River had cleaned and sewn the small gash up himself. But the hike back to the mainland the next day had busted open the stitches, and River had realized too late that infection was setting in. The river was flooded from the earlier storm, so he'd been forced to backtrack and take the long way to his vehicle.

River's intention was to drive himself home to complete his own wound care and assess whether the situation called for something more. But he'd started seeing stars on the drive toward Mallard Creek. He'd pulled off on Hannigan Street for safety reasons, and that's when he'd spotted Tess's bookstore like a beacon of hope in his rearview mirror.

Beep. Beep.

River groaned softly, resisting the harsh fluorescent lighting in the room as he opened his eyes. *Still alive.* That was always goal number one in every emergency situation. Survival.

"Good news, Mr. Harrison. You're alive," a nurse confirmed.

River shifted around under the paper-thin blanket.

She laid a hand on his shoulder. "Try to take it easy, Mr. Harrison. The bad news is that you'll be here for a couple days."

"A couple days?" In a hospital. If the woods were his paradise, this was his anti-paradise. "You sure I'm not in hell?" he asked gruffly.

The nurse chuckled, the sound as high-pitched as the monitor's beeping. "Very sure. Do you need me to call someone?"

River's father was in Weeping Willows Assisted Living Facility. River would need to call Alice, the director there, to tell his dad not to expect him for a visit for a couple of days. Other than that, his dog was his family. "Is my cell phone around here?" River asked, looking for his clothing. He didn't want to even think about how his clothes had come off.

The nurse pointed. "On the bedside table. We located a charger for you to borrow and plugged it in for you."

"Thanks. I need to check on my dog." He reached for his phone, feeling the pinch of pain in his left side. And that was no doubt blunted with medication. He hesitated, wondering just what he would say to Tess. Asking her to care for his dog might be too much of a favor even for a friend. And Tess had made it clear they weren't friends.

River supposed he could ask one of the men he'd recently started hanging out with at the tavern. His dog, Buddy, was a loner like River though and preferred not to be around other dogs. Miles and Lucy had a French bulldog. And Jake had a lab mix. All of River's friends had dogs, come to think of it.

River didn't have Tess's phone number programmed into his phone so he brought up the website for Lakeside Books. Tess's picture came up on the contact page. He studied it for a moment. He'd been jealous when his best friend, Jared, had first started dating her. He'd met Tess briefly just before he'd realized that she was the same girl his friend wouldn't stop talking about. In that one chance meeting, River had thought he might try to get to know her better.

It was her eyes that grabbed him first. They were the brightest brown he'd ever seen against the backdrop of soft brown skin. Tess's eyes seemed to always be dancing. It didn't matter if she was amused or irritated or looking at someone with complete loathing—which was how she looked at River—the dancing was always there.

What made River most envious when Tess was with Jared was the way her eyes had looked at his best friend with love. River regretted that he'd ever wanted her to look at him that way. It was wrong. Probably despicable. Definitely not best friend behavior. But that wasn't the reason he'd objected to their wedding six years ago. Nope. And the only thing River regretted about his actions that night was that he hadn't told Tess what he knew. Instead, he'd urged Jared to confess. It was Jared's truth to tell after all, not River's.

River searched for the phone number for the bookstore and tapped the digits into his cell phone, saving it as a contact. Then he connected the call and waited for Tess to answer.

"Lakeside Books. How may I assist you?" a woman's voice answered.

It was too soft-spoken to be Tess's voice. River cleared his throat. "Tess Lane, please."

"She's, um, busy right now," the woman told him.

"It's important," River said. "She has my dog."

"Oh. Yes. That's what she's busy doing. Your dog, um, chewed up her books."

"Chewed her books?" That didn't bode well for Tess agreeing to keep Buddy. Buddy needed a chew toy, especially when he was stressed. Otherwise, he was likely to gnaw on everything in sight.

"It was just one book," the woman clarified. "And it didn't have a happy ending anyway, so I'm sure Tess doesn't mind."

River chuckled. "I see. Well, I'll pay for the damage."

"Would you like me to have her call you back?"

"Please." River gave the woman his number and then disconnected the call, looking around what would be his home for the next two days. He felt claustrophobic in the small room, even though it was mostly empty. His cell phone lit up on his bedside tray, and Lakeside Books scrolled across the screen. He took a breath and then answered, wishing he could look into Tess's dancing eyes as she turned him down. Because there was no way she wouldn't be turning him down. For one, his dog was ruining her books. For another, if River was the last person that Tess would allow to use her store's public restroom, he highly doubted she'd agree to dog-sit for him while he recuperated.

"I'm glad you're not dead," Tess said when he answered.

Well, that was a good start. "If I am, this hospital room is not my idea of heaven. Listen, I hate to ask, but I kind of need a favor."

"You've surpassed your limit of zero with me," Tess said flatly.

He imagined her dancing eyes with that quick comeback. She was no doubt proud of it, and she should be. Her wit and humor were two of the things he admired about her. "I'm going to be here awhile longer than expected. It seems I have an infection."

She was quiet. No quick comeback this time. "I'm sorry to hear that," she finally said in an almost sincere tone.

River cleared his throat. "Buddy won't chew up your stuff if you give him something he's allowed to chew. He has anxiety. You can go to my place and get his ThunderShirt and chew toys to help."

"Why would I do that?" she asked, but he noticed that her voice was softening. The hard edge had disappeared.

"Because I need help, and I don't have anyone else to ask." River didn't like feeling vulnerable. He prided himself on being independent.

"I care about this because...?"

River knew he was one of her least favorite people. Maybe he was the very least of them. There'd been a time when she'd rolled out the hero's red carpet for him though. "Because I saved Jared's life once, if you remember." He must be desperate to bring that up. Jared had gotten caught in enemy fire during what was supposed to be an uneventful deployment to Iran. River had risked his life to bring Jared to safety. When Tess had heard about his actions, she'd called River in tears, thanking him profusely. Even so, Jared had died just three years later. River had only delayed destiny, if one believed in that kind of thing.

Tess released an audible breath on the other line. "Fine. I'll need your address."

River felt himself relax as he exhaled. "I recently moved into the last house on Mallard Creek Drive."

"Right. I heard you bought that place," Tess said. "Miles Bruno was thinking about buying it last winter until he decided to keep living in The Village with Lucy."

"That's the house," River confirmed. "The key to the front door is on the keyring for my truck."

"Got it. Anything else?" she asked.

"Yes." River shifted, trying to ease the discomfort in his left side. "Thank you. I owe you."

"You already owed me for saving your life earlier today," she said before disconnecting the call.

13

Chapter Two

An hour later, Tess turned into River's driveway. So this is where River called home these days. The place suited him better than it would have Miles. The address was the last house on a dead-end street. Quiet. Closed off and close to nature. It backed up to Mallard Creek, which was undoubtedly the appeal for a guy like River.

Buddy barked beside Tess, as if to say, *Let's go inside.*

Tess reached over and patted the top of the dog's slick head. "We're here to get you something appropriate to chew on other than one of my books." She eyed the dog, who, if she didn't know better, looked a little sheepish. Did he realize he'd destroyed something of value? Did dogs feel remorse? She wasn't sure, because she'd never had a dog before. It was on her list of things she wanted, but before delving into the role of pet owner, she intended to read every book in her store on how to care for a dog appropriately. She might even look into dog-sitting Lucy's or Trisha's furry friends before making the leap.

She curled her fingers to scratch behind Buddy's ear. *Or dog-sitting my enemy's furry friend.*

Pulling her hand back, she pushed her car door open, stepped out, and closed Buddy inside the car behind her. She wouldn't be gone long. All she needed to do was collect a few things from River's house and be on her merry way. She was looking forward to snuggling up with a book and reading a chapter or two. She still hadn't read the required chapters for Thursday's book club meeting.

She headed up the front steps and unlocked the door. She wasn't sure what she was expecting to find when she stepped inside, but it wasn't an immaculately clean and orderly place. River was former military though. As such, he'd been trained to keep his things neat and tidy. Tess remembered that about Jared. When he was alive, her home had been much more orderly. There hadn't been stacks of books in every corner, ready to distract Tess at a moment's notice.

She spotted one of Buddy's chew toys where River had texted her that it would be and placed it inside a large Ziploc bag that she'd carried in with her. Then she located the ThunderShirt folded neatly on top of Buddy's kennel near the back door. She'd had to Google what a ThunderShirt even was. She'd had no idea that compression garments helped pets with anxiety.

River had also texted earlier to let her know that Buddy's bed was in his bedroom and that Buddy would be most comfortable if she grabbed the blanket there as well. Tess glanced down a dimly lit hallway and started walking. Going into a man's bedroom felt weird on a lot of different levels. She hadn't entered a man's bedroom in years. Hadn't been with a man since her late husband.

There were a couple of bedrooms down the hallway. Tess

glanced inside each, trying to determine which was River's. One had a framed picture on the bedside table that made her think she'd hit the jackpot. She stepped inside and walked over to the picture, absently picking it up. She expected to see a photograph of Buddy or maybe of River's father, Douglass. Instead, she nearly dropped the frame when she saw the photo. Beneath the thin glass protector was a picture of River and Jared smiling next to each other, sunglasses shielding their eyes and reflecting a woodsy setting in their lenses.

Tess was surprised River would even have this photograph on display. River and Jared hadn't been friends for a long time before Jared's death. That was River's fault, of course. She set the frame down with shaky hands, rattled mostly by seeing Jared's face in an unfamiliar picture. She'd thought she'd seen every picture he was in, had them all in a scrapbook that she looked at less and less often these days. She hadn't seen this photograph though.

Tess felt the familiar uneasiness that came with moments like this. After Jared's accident, the officers had given her a box of things that they'd collected from his totaled car. It'd taken a year to even go through them, and when she had, she hadn't recognized a lot of the items. At first, she'd even wondered if the officers had given her the wrong box. They were little things that mostly didn't matter, like the unfamiliar shirt in this picture of Jared and River. But Jared was her husband. She'd thought she knew all the details of his life. Realizing that wasn't necessarily true hurt in a way she hadn't expected.

Tess sucked in a breath and looked around to locate Buddy's blanket. Her gaze snagged on another photograph on the opposite bedside table. This one wasn't framed. Instead, it was lying flat on the table's surface along with a neat stack of papers. Walking over to look at that picture and those papers would be snooping. She should *not* go over there, she told herself, even as she moved in that direction.

She stood over the picture, not planning to pick it up. Then she realized who was in it, and she couldn't seem to help herself. There were three people in this photograph. River, Jared, and a woman whom Tess had never seen before. She was a white woman with brown hair and light-colored eyes, and she was laughing in the photograph. Jared stood in the middle with one arm around River and the other draped around the woman's shoulders, squeezing her tightly against him.

Who is she? Jared was looking at this woman in the photograph, a smile curving his lips as he watched her laugh. Had he said something funny to her? There was something about his gaze on the woman that made Tess's stomach turn. Jared was only supposed to look at Tess that way.

Tess put the photograph down and glanced at the papers on the bedside table. A letterhead for Linton Security was at the top. That was where Jared had been working in the years leading up to his death. Why would River be in contact with them? Was he looking for a job there too?

Tess nibbled her lower lip and closed her eyes. It was none of her business what River was doing or if he was seeking employment with Jared's old employer. She was here to get Buddy's belongings and get out. That's all.

She turned and searched the room again, locating Buddy's blanket and draping it over her forearm. She gave one final glance at the photograph and papers before forcing herself to turn and hurry into the kitchen to collect a large Ziploc of dry food. She locked up the house on the way out and returned to Buddy, who was lying lazily across the passenger seat of her car. She handed him a chew toy that was shaped like a hot dog, noticing that Buddy looked especially apologetic. She inspected her surroundings more carefully. "You chewed on my purse strap, didn't you?" It was shiny and slick with dog drool. There were also a few canine impressions in the leather. "That's gross, Buddy." She tapped the hot dog–shaped chew toy. "No more excuses."

When she arrived home, she tapped out a quick text to River.

> **Tess:** I retrieved Buddy's items from your home.
> **River:** Thank you again.

Tess wanted to ask about the picture of him, Jared, and the mystery woman, but then River would know she'd been snooping through his stuff, even though those things were in plain view for anyone to see. She kind of thought that River didn't have a lot of people over to his place though. He hadn't been such a loner when he and Jared were buddies. River was always quiet, but she'd never pegged him as a recluse the way he seemed to be now. Things changed though. People changed. She'd done a lot of changing since Jared had passed away.

She'd once been an eternal optimist. She used to have this confidence that everything would work out the way it was supposed to. Since that call three years ago, however, she was more of a glass half-empty kind of girl. A Chicken Little waiting for the sky to crumble. Not to say she was Ms. Negativity. She wasn't. She was just well-acquainted with reality.

Tess poured some dog food into a bowl and put some water in a second one for Buddy. Once Buddy was all set up, she poured herself a glass of rosé muscadine wine—her favorite—and sat at the dining room table with her laptop. She wished she didn't visit Facebook as often as she did, but she enjoyed seeing what her friends and family were up to, even if the appearance of their happy lives always left her feeling a little void inside.

What was she supposed to put on Facebook? *Hi everyone! I'm still a widow! Here's a picture of what I plan to read alone in my bed tonight. Here's another of my wineglass. Yes, I'm drinking alone.*

She was sulking, but it was her right. Today was Jared's birthday, and it wasn't enough that River had crashed her wedding six years ago, he'd also come crashing in on this day as well—literally.

She took a gulp of wine as Facebook showed her memories from four years ago that she'd posted. They were pictures that only she could see. She'd made Jared a three-layer birthday cake that he'd referred to as the Leaning Tower of Pisa. They'd been too scared to even put candles on the top because it was tilting too heavily to the right side.

Tess frowned at the message from Facebook above the memory asking her if she wanted to share it with her followers. "No Facebook, I don't care to share that memory all over again." She was about to exit out of the page altogether when she got a notification of a message on the right-hand side of her screen. Maybe it was a reply from bestselling author Jaliya Cruise.

Jaliya was the author of one of Tess's favorite books. It was a memoir called *A Woman's Journey to Joy*. After losing her husband, Jaliya had traveled the world all by herself, determined to prove that she hadn't died along with the love of her life.

It was a remarkable story. One that had inspired Tess the first time she'd read it. And the second time. And the sixth. Jaliya strongly encouraged everyone to take up journaling, especially those who were going through some form of grief. After reading the book for the first time, Tess had gone out immediately and gotten herself a journal. Then she'd decided to sell journals in the bookshop. Tess had also taken up hiking to be like Jaliya in some small way—since there was no likelihood she was ever going to travel the whole world.

One night a couple of weeks back, Tess had gotten brave and contacted Jaliya to invite her to do a signing at Lakeside Books. It was a ridiculous request. Jaliya's book had been on the *New York Times* list for seven consecutive weeks. She'd been on news shows. Why would she say yes to Tess's small request? Tess knew that Jaliya lived in North Carolina though, and she was scheduled to do several signings at some of the bigger cities in the area over the next couple of months. That might bode in Tess's favor.

In her email, Tess had also mentioned that her aunt, the shop's previous owner, had been named Minority Small Business Person of the Year in 2009. That award had shone a light on Lakeside Books and helped to create a loyal customer base that Tess was sure would come out to meet such a prestigious author. At least she hoped they would.

Tess didn't have an email address for Jaliya, so she'd sent the author a private message as a fan through Facebook to tell her how much she'd loved the book and how much Jaliya's words had meant to her. Jaliya hadn't responded yet—until now.

Tess held her breath as she clicked to open the message.

Dear Tess,

Thank you so much for your kind words. I'm glad you enjoyed my book, and I would love to do a signing at your bookshop. I'm doing several signings in North Carolina next month. Maybe we can slip yours in while I'm in your direction? I'm attaching my signing schedule for you to peruse. Perhaps the afternoon of June 23rd would work? Let me know!

Love and Peace,
Jaliya

Tess squealed, making Buddy lift his head in alarm. "Sorry, Buddy. There's nothing wrong." Instead, there was something right. Tess reached for her glass of wine and took another gulp. Then she closed the page without answering just yet. She would need to look at her calendar to see if the twenty-third would work. She'd do that tomorrow. Right now, she just wanted to celebrate with wine and a hot bath. And forget about the photograph on River's bedside table, the one of her late husband holding a beautiful woman who wasn't Tess.

River had woken every hour on the hour last night, either because a nurse had wanted to check if he was okay or because the machine he was hooked up to had somehow become disconnected and was beeping obnoxiously.

Now he was tired. He just wanted to go home, where he could relax and heal in private. Where he could make sure that Buddy was all right.

Buddy was family after all. Not blood-related, but neither was River's father. Douglass Harrison was the man who had raised River from the time River was two years old. Douglass was the only father River had ever known, but they weren't related by blood. Not that River had ever cared about that.

When he was thirteen, River's parents had sat him down to tell him that he was adopted. He didn't even bat an eye. At that point, it had become somewhat obvious to him anyway, given that Douglass was Asian American and Julie was of Irish descent with red hair and fair skin. With his brown hair and blue eyes, River didn't look like either of them. He didn't mind, and he'd never once considered looking for his real parents. His stance had always been, if they didn't want him, he didn't want them either.

This latest case River was working, however—another reason he needed to leave this hospital—was somehow making him look at things differently these days. When Ella Peters had enlisted his private investigation services to help her find her real parents, River had agreed. He made his living hunting down missing people, finding lost items, and solving minor *Hardy Boys*-type mysteries. After leaving the

Marines, someone had asked if he could work a case for them. River hadn't set out to become a private investigator, but he'd quickly discovered that he had a knack for it.

He guessed that's how fate worked. Maybe fate had also brought Ella Peters to his doorstep, wanting to find her birth parents. Now the seed was planted in the back of River's mind—not for the first time—and some part of him wanted to locate his roots as well. Especially since his family had whittled down to Douglass and Buddy.

Being in this hospital bed was not a date with destiny, however. It was a date with disrupted sleep and frustrated days that River was ready to say goodbye to.

The door to his hospital room opened, and a nurse with a friendly face walked in. Her name badge read BETH.

"What are the odds that I can go home today?" he asked hopefully.

The nurse glanced down at the clipboard in her arms, her frown deepening. Finally, she shook her head and looked up at him. "Not very good, Mr. Harrison. Not unless you decide to check yourself out, which would go against doctor's orders."

River didn't have any qualms about going against the doctor's orders. He wasn't arrogant enough to think he knew better than someone with a medical degree. He was just stubborn. "Just show me where to sign," he said. "I can promise you that I'll follow up with my regular doctor first thing tomorrow." He raised two fingers to show off his Boy Scout's honor.

The nurse looked like she wanted to argue, but River really hoped she didn't. Now that he knew it wasn't an impossibility, he was going to fight for the chance to go home tonight. His dog was counting on him.

"I'll talk to the doctor. I really think you should stay until she decides you're ready to go home though," she urged.

"Noted. But I still want to check myself out."

An hour and a half later, River was seated in a wheelchair outside the front of the hospital waiting for his pal Miles Bruno to pick him up. River had just started hanging out with a couple of the guys in town at the tavern on Thursday nights. It was good for him. Miles was a deputy sheriff in Somerset Lake and an overall good guy. Even if he was running later to pick up River than he'd promised.

River tried to stand, but Nurse Beth stood behind him and laid her hands on his shoulders to press him back down into the seat of the wheelchair.

"Not on my watch," she scolded. "My orders are to leave you in this chair until I hand you off to a proper caregiver."

River was never going to live this down among his friends at the tavern. He turned his head and looked both ways down the street for a deputy cruiser, prepared to jump up from the chair and beyond the nurse's reach as soon as he saw it heading in his direction. River had been out here a little over twenty minutes and had started to wonder if his ride was even coming.

The thought had just entered his mind when a car pulled under the carport. It wasn't a deputy cruiser so River assumed it was for another patient. The driver stepped out and looked at him. River was still under the influence of pain medicine, antibiotics, and whatever else the doctors had given him since yesterday so he thought maybe he was hallucinating at first, or just confused.

Why is Tess here?

He was so taken aback that he forgot how embarrassed he was.

"Are you here to pick up this patient?" Nurse Beth asked.

"I am," Tess said.

River's mouth fell open. "Where's Miles?"

"He got called to a fender-bender on Hannigan Street so he asked Lucy to contact me, because he knew I was watching your dog. And now that I have help at the bookstore, I have a little more freedom to run errands. Or pick up alpha men who go against doctor's orders and check themselves out of the hospital." Tess lifted an eyebrow. Then her expression softened just a touch as she seemed to take in the image of him sitting in a wheelchair. "Are you okay?"

"Good enough to go home," he assured her. "And take care of my own dog."

A smile flickered at the corners of her mouth, making her even more beautiful, if that was possible. How was it fair that the only woman to ever catch River's eye hated his guts completely?

Okay, it was completely fair. He *had* tried to stop her wedding.

"Do you need me to help you up, sweetheart?" Nurse Beth asked, still standing behind River.

He glanced over his shoulder and looked at her. *Ah.* There was that all-consuming mortification that he'd been expecting to be overcome by. "No. Thank you. I got it." He braced his hands on the armrests and pushed himself up to stand quickly. The blood drained from his head, making him dizzy, but he tried not to let the two women hovering nearby notice. He just hoped he didn't black out and fall on his face. If that happened, Nurse Beth would be rolling him back inside the hospital.

River's vision returned to normal and so did the feeling in his head. He stepped away from the chair toward Tess's car, noticing that Buddy was waiting for him inside. River headed around the front of the car toward the passenger door, opened it, and gave his dog a great big hug. "Hey, big guy. I missed you."

Tess laughed from the driver's side as she dipped into the seat behind the steering wheel. She grabbed a pair of sunglasses from the dash and slid them over her eyes as she spoke. "There is no friendship like the one between a man and his dog. You know, I've never seen you greet another human being with that much enthusiasm. And yet you just practically kissed your dog on the lips."

River shifted around uncomfortably, his side wound already giving him grief. He reached for the seat belt and pulled it over his body. "I didn't kiss Buddy on the lips. Lip-kissing is only for women."

Tess glanced over, her mouth dropping open just slightly. And since they were talking about lips, without thinking, River glanced down at hers. It was just a millisecond of a glance, but when he returned his gaze back to hers, her eyebrows were lifted above the rim of her sunglasses. He cleared his throat and offered a blanket excuse for everything that might happen between one minute ago and the next twenty minutes that it took for Tess to take him home. "I'm on pain medication," he explained. "I'm, uh, not thinking clearly."

The corner of her mouth twitched in an almost-smile. "Is that why you just kissed your dog?"

River shook his head. "I didn't kiss Buddy."

Tess put the car in drive and headed away from the hospital. "Oh, you totally did."

Chapter Three

It had been three hours since Tess had dropped River off at his house, but now she was worried about him. She knew he didn't have family or close relatives to check on him. He'd left the hospital early, like an alpha male, and she doubted he'd go back if he needed to. Like an alpha male.

He could be lying on the floor of his home right now, in need of help, but being too stubborn to ask for it. Or in his bedroom, where the picture of him with Jared was prominently displayed on his nightstand. Where the picture with Jared and the mystery woman was lying on the opposite nightstand.

Tess reached for her mug of hot tea, taking a long sip while thinking about that photograph now. She had never been the jealous type, but something akin to the feeling had been gnawing at her since she'd seen it. There'd been times in her last year of marriage when she'd wondered if Jared was still attracted to her. His lingering looks had stopped. Cuddling before bed had fallen to the wayside. But that was normal in a marriage, right?

On a sigh, Tess grabbed her cell phone and pulled up her text messages, retrieving the thread between her and River. Then she tapped off a quick message.

> *Tess:*   Just checking to make sure you're still alive.

She didn't send that message. It sounded a little harsh so she deleted it and tried again.

> *Tess:*   Hi! How are you doing? Feeling okay?

She deleted that message too. It sounded too friendly to send to someone she didn't even like. On a sigh, she tapped out a third and final attempt at checking on River.

> *Tess:*   Hi. Just checking in on you. Do you need
> anything?

She hit SEND before she could second-guess whether that was harsh or friendly or anything other than what she wanted to relay. If he responded, she'd know he was alive. If he didn't, then she might need to worry.

The dots started bouncing within a few seconds. That was a good sign.

> *River:*   I'm good. All I needed was to be home
> with my dog.

Tess somehow thought River Harrison needed a lot more than that, but maybe he didn't even know it.

Tess: You can call or text me if you need something.

It took all her willpower to press SEND on that offer, but she'd feel like a horrible human being if she didn't. She did not need to like someone to help them.

She set her phone down and reached for her mug to take another sip of her tea. Then she startled when her cell phone buzzed beside her. She blew out a breath and picked up her phone to read the text.

River: You can call or text me if you need something too.

Her first thought: Such a man. Her next thought: She did need something from River Harrison. What she needed, more than anything, were answers.

Tess unlocked Lakeside Books and stepped inside, greeted by the delicious smell of books. Her friend Jana had a thing for sweet aromas and thus owned Choco-Lovers down the street. Tess, however, could always be found in a library when she was growing up. Sometimes, when no one was looking, she would literally have her nose stuck in a book, breathing in the pages.

Right after college, her aunt Sheila had given Tess a job at Lakeside Books while Tess looked for work that aligned with her business degree. Tess had never left the bookshop though. When her aunt was ready to retire, she'd signed the store over to Tess. Tess had never seen herself as a full-time bookshop owner. She'd thought she would use her degree to build her own business from the ground up.

Tess had always looked up to her aunt though. Sheila was one of the first minority business owners in town, paving the way for many more. Taking on Lakeside Books left Tess with big shoes to fill, but she thought she was doing a good job most days and that Sheila would be proud to see the changes she'd made. Tess was making the business her own and, if sales numbers were any indication, business was hopping.

Tess flipped the sign on the front door to OPEN before heading down the aisle toward the front counter. Lara was coming back this morning. Hiring an employee was one of the best decisions Tess had made in a long time. For a while, Tess had thought having an employee would feel suffocating. Tess enjoyed working alone. She liked having complete control over everything. What she didn't like was not being able to leave if she needed to. Like this morning. There was a tiny, nagging voice inside her head telling her to go check on River to make sure he was okay. Technically, he should still be in a hospital bed.

She'd texted this morning, but he hadn't responded yet. Plus, her curiosity was getting the better of her and she wanted to discuss the picture she'd seen in his bedroom. She wanted to ask him in person, not over the phone or by text. She considered herself a good read of people. She wanted to look in River's eyes when she brought the photograph up. Not that Tess suspected Jared of any wrongdoing. Her late husband had been a good guy. The whole town had loved him. Jared had been the kind of guy who would volunteer his whole weekend to help people move out of their house. He would also be the first to sign up for any kind of charity run.

Tess and Jared had started dating right after high school. They'd been an item when he'd signed up for the Marines, making their relationship a long distance one for a while. Jared hadn't met River until he'd joined the Corps. The photograph must have been taken at that time.

The front door to the bookstore opened, and Lara entered with a large bag on one shoulder and a steaming Thermos of what Tess guessed was coffee in her opposite hand.

"Good morning," Lara said cheerily.

"I didn't scare you off yet? This is good news," Tess teased. If she was going to share her space with someone, she was glad it was Lara. Lara was quiet, but not shy. Always smiling and agreeable. Lara could hold her own in a conversation about practically anything, which Tess appreciated. Tess also appreciated that a conversation wasn't necessary at all times. In a lot of ways, Lara reminded Tess of Jared.

Did Lara have secrets like Jared had too?

Tess blinked and felt her smile flatline. Since when did she doubt that her late husband was anything less than a saint? A photograph was not evidence of anything seditious.

"You okay?" Lara asked as she approached the counter.

Tess waved a dismissive hand. "Yeah, I'm fine. I just had a random thought. Hey, do you think you can run the shop alone this morning while I step out for an hour?"

Lara placed her bag under the counter. "Of course. Take your time. I think I've mastered the register. I'm still acquainting myself with where the books are shelved, but I'll work on learning that system this morning."

Tess offered a grateful smile. "Thank you. Feel free to call or text with any customer questions. I'll have my phone on me."

"I will," Lara said.

Tess grabbed her own bag from under the counter and draped it over her shoulder. The smell of Lara's coffee had her longing for one of her own. Maybe she'd stop into Sweetie's Bake Shop a few doors down and get one for herself and another for River, as a bribe of sorts. She didn't know how he liked his brew, but if she had to guess, River seemed like the type to drink his coffee black.

"See you before noon," Tess promised Lara on the way out of her store. The little bell overhead jingled as she stepped out into the breezy morning. The air was warm against her skin, and she breathed it in, turning right toward Sweetie's Bake Shop.

Darla looked up from behind the counter as Tess opened the door and stepped inside. Darla was in her fifties and had long red hair that she kept smoothed back in a low-hanging ponytail most days. She was the mother of one of Tess's closest friends, Moira. "One grande caramel latte?" Darla asked as Tess approached the counter.

"Yes, please. And a grande black coffee to go as well."

Darla straightened with a stumped look on her face. "Who is that one for?"

"River Harrison," Tess confided, placing her hands on the counter. She didn't wear her wedding band on her left ring finger anymore. She'd worn it for the first two years after Jared's accident, but then she'd taken it off one day while cleaning out her garage. She'd placed it in her jewelry box and had never slipped it back on. Her fingers were bare except for the gray nail polish she'd painted on the other night.

"River Harrison?" Darla looked at her with interest. She'd been one of the guests at Tess's wedding, and she, no doubt, remembered River's grand entrance. River was supposed to be Jared's best man, but he'd backed out a few days before. River wasn't even supposed to attend the occasion, but he'd shown up, dressed in a dark navy blue–colored suit with a little carnation tucked in his lapel. Tess and Jared were facing each other at the end of the aisle with the preacher in front of them, prepared to exchange vows.

"*Wait!*" River had called from the back. "*I have something to say.*" He looked at Jared. "*You know this is a mistake, Jared. You can't go through with this.*"

Tess had looked back and forth between them. River standing at the back of the church. She and Jared standing at the front. Then the church broke out into a commotion.

"*Jared?*" River had said. "*You know—*"

That's when Jared's newly minted best man had charged down the aisle and escorted River out.

What had River meant by those words? When she'd pressed Jared, he'd told her that River didn't think he and Tess were a good match. He'd explained that River thought they were too different, the great outdoorsman and the bookworm.

She wasn't the stereotypical bookworm though. Tess liked adventure as much as the next person. How dare River judge her when he barely knew her?

"Here you go!" Darla slid two cups of coffee in front of Tess, interrupting her memory.

"Thank you." Tess inserted her debit card into the reader beside the register and paid.

"I'm sure you have your reasons for bringing River a cup of coffee. That reason is none of my business. Unless you want to tell me." Darla winked.

Tess adored the bakery owner, but she didn't want to disclose anything on her mind right now, especially with Reva Dawson sitting at one of the nearby tables. Tess slid a glance over to the woman with rose-toned hair as big as her nosy personality. Reva ran a blog about the town that covered the A-Z of local gossip in Somerset Lake. "Another time," Tess told Darla. "But for the record, I'm going to see him on business, not pleasure."

"I would have guessed as much. Although I always did have a tiny crush on that man." Darla reached into the glass display case and brought out a blueberry muffin. She wrapped it in a parchment paper sleeve. "I've told Moira many times that, if I were younger, I might try to catch River Harrison's eye. My daughter isn't interested in him though. Or in any of the men I suggest." Darla sighed and laid the muffin down. "Take this to River and tell him it's from Darla with well wishes. I heard about his injury."

News traveled fast in Somerset Lake.

"I will. I'm sure he'll appreciate it." Tess collected the muffin and the coffee and waved at Darla. She also waved at Reva as she passed by her table, walking faster so she couldn't be roped into conversation. Tess didn't have time for any more chitchat. She was on a mission, and she had caffeine and sugar to soften River up.

She headed back out to the parking lot, got into her car,

and drove to Mallard Creek Lane. She slowed at the end of the dead-end street and turned into the driveway of River's one-story yellow home. His truck was parked in the same place as yesterday, which meant he at least had the sense to stay put and rest as the doctor ordered.

Tess grabbed the coffees and muffin and headed up the porch steps. She rang the doorbell and waited. And waited. Then she heard his voice call to her from the creek side of the house.

"Around back!"

Tess left the porch and walked around to find him seated on the back deck of his home in a yellow Adirondack chair with his feet kicked up on a stool.

"Morning," he said in an easy tone.

He seemed so relaxed that he didn't quite look like the man she knew. The River Harrison she knew was a serious private investigator, former Marine, and former best friend of her late husband.

He glanced to the two cups of coffee in her hand. "Is one of those for me?"

"It is. I took a guess that you drank your coffee black." She climbed the deck steps and placed his cup on a piece of furniture beside him.

"And you'd be correct. Thank you."

"You're welcome. This muffin is from Darla. I think she has a tiny crush on you." Tess sat down in the second Adirondack chair. Buddy immediately raced toward her, propping his paws on her thighs. She scratched behind the dog's ears and down his back, realizing that she'd missed this adorable canine.

"Maybe if Darla were twenty years younger, I wouldn't

be destined to be a single man living alone on the creek," River joked.

Tess rolled her eyes. "Oh, come on. I'm sure there are a lot of Somerset Lake women who would love to make the town's Lonesome Dove a little less lonely."

River looked over at her. "I don't read Reva Dawson's blog, but I hear that it's her I have to thank for the nickname. I don't get it. I'm not lonesome, and I'm not a cowboy."

Tess leaned back in the chair and sipped her coffee. "It's better than being known as the town's youngest widow," she said quietly.

Silence floated between them. For her, it was full of Jared's absence. For River, she could only guess at what he was thinking. The fact that he had Jared's photograph by his bed made her wonder if he missed her late husband a fraction as much as she did.

Tess looked at Mallard Creek, admiring the view from River's deck. It really was gorgeous back here, with a good amount of shade from the oaks along the water and a section of sunlight beyond their reach. A small pier jutted away from the creek bank with a two-person swing at the very end. She'd love to sit out there and watch the sunset. Not with River, of course.

Turning, she took a breath and decided to ask the question that had been plaguing her since yesterday. "Why do you have that picture in your room? Of Jared, you, and a woman I've never seen before."

River didn't even flinch. "He was my best friend. The only one I've ever had, except for Buddy."

Was that true? She didn't think River had ever replaced

Jared in his life after Jared had disowned him. Jared had replaced River though. Jared had quickly found a new pal to hang out with, and had never looked back. It was as if River was completely disposable.

Tess swallowed and returned to looking at the creek. There was a white egret walking gracefully along the bank now, its head lifted high and with seemingly not a care in the world. She envied that egret.

She sipped her coffee and summoned her resolve.

"Something more on your mind?" River finally asked.

Tess felt River watching her. "The three of you had your arms around one another. I've never seen the woman in the photograph before."

River didn't immediately answer.

"It wasn't framed. It was lying on your nightstand with papers from Linton Security," Tess continued.

River expelled a breath. "Are you sure you're not the private investigator here?" he asked, a hint of teasing in his voice.

Tess was too on edge for humor. "Who is she, River? The woman."

He shifted around as if trying to get comfortable, reminding her that he was still injured. "Her name is Ashley Hansley. Jared and I served in the Marines with her."

Tess exhaled softly. Of course. That's all it was. They were Marines together. "What about the papers from Linton Security? Why do you have those?" she asked.

River gave her a long look. "I had some questions. I sent them a written inquiry, and they replied."

"What kind of questions? Questions about Jared?"

River's gaze swept toward her and then moved along

the creek. "Yeah. I've always wondered why Jared was in Morrisville when he died. It never made sense to me."

Tess shook her head. "I don't know the reason either. He never mentioned that town to me." And the not knowing had always sat wrong with her as well.

"Linton Security confirmed that Jared didn't have a job in that area on the weekend of his accident," River said. "But he told you he was working. I read the police report."

Tess found this piece of information interesting. "Are you investigating Jared?" she asked.

"Not officially, no. I ran into an old friend last week though. He told me that Ashley, the woman in that photograph, lives in Morrisville."

The missing puzzle piece clicked into place in Tess's mind. "You think he was there because of her?" she asked, remembering how Jared was looking at the woman in the picture. Tess trusted Jared. She loved Jared. He would never hurt her. Even so, she felt uneasy. "Why would he want to go see her?"

River shook his head. "I don't know, but I'm a private investigator. I leave no good clue unturned. It's not in my nature."

"There must be a good explanation. What is it that you think you'll discover?" Tess asked.

River's gaze was steady. Hers moved to the scar below his right eye. It was jagged and uneven. There was nothing beautiful about it, but somehow, on River's face, it was attractive. It added an element of mystery and ruggedness, like the man himself. He sipped his coffee and finally said, "I don't like to speculate. I prefer facts."

Tess sucked air into her lungs as her mind whirred with possibilities. It had always bothered her that she didn't know why Jared was in the town where his accident occurred. It felt unfair that he was taken so soon and she didn't even know why he'd been in Morrisville. If this Ashley person was the reason, why was Jared going to see her? Tess took a breath and nodded. "Okay, let's do this."

River frowned back at her. "Do what?"

"Investigate why Jared was in Morrisville. I had resigned myself to never knowing, but if you can tell me the reason, I think it would give me some element of closure. I need to know the truth."

River shifted again, looking uncomfortable. "Hold on now. This is just something I'm looking into, on the side."

Tess was sure River was expecting to prove some wrong-doing of Jared's. She wanted to prove otherwise though. Her hands shook as she set her cup of coffee down on the plastic deck table beside her. "What if I hire you and move the case to the forefront then? The way I see it, you owe me. And this is how you can repay me for saving your life."

"I'm sorry?" River asked.

He had just taken a sip of his coffee when Tess said she wanted him to investigate Jared. He almost spewed it all over his fresh T-shirt. Nothing like a coffee stain on the front of your shirt to spoil a morning.

"You heard me correctly."

Tess's posture was poised and graceful. The way she held

herself had always reminded River of a ballerina. She kept her back straight and held her head high. He'd wondered before if someone in her past had insisted on having her walk around with books on her head as a young girl. Or, knowing Tess and how much she loved books, maybe she'd done that on her own.

"You're a PI, and you're good at your job. I know you are," Tess said.

"How do you know that?" he asked, pleased that she would say so.

"Because Della Rose hired you last year when she suspected Jerome was having an affair."

River shifted uncomfortably. He'd forgone pain meds today because he didn't like how they slowed his mental processing. "Della told you?" Della Rose was one of Tess's good friends. For that reason, River had initially turned her down. The bubbly real estate agent had been adamant though. And she'd cried. River could never say no to a woman with tears in her eyes. Della had been so distraught when she'd come to see him, asking him to dig into her husband's extramarital activities. "That was supposed to be private."

"Well, I'm sure Della doesn't want you to tell others that she hired you, but it's different if she told me and the other book club members."

River felt his eyes widen. "She told your entire book club?" He'd heard about this book club, which happened at Tess's shop. It was the justification that the guys at the tavern used for their Thursday-night get-togethers. If the women could have a social hour, so could they. River always held his tongue. They were all adults. They could have social hours when and where they wanted. No need for justification or excuses. Most of the guys were either dating or married to the women of the book club though. All but Gil Ryan and him.

Tess looked at him. Her black hair was down today, framing her face with tight curls. "Della just told me, Trisha, Lucy, and Moira. The book club is small."

River let that sink in. "Well, as long as Reva Dawson isn't part of your group. I don't really want to be known as the guy everyone goes to when they think their significant other is cheating on them. For one, no untrustworthy man would let their guard down around me again."

Tess sipped her coffee, silent for a moment. "For the record, I don't think Jared was cheating on me," she said, a bit defensively. Then she looked down. "It's a two-hour drive from here though. He said he was out of town for work, but that was a lie." She looked up and her brown eyes searched River's. "Now you're telling me this Ashley woman lives there. That's the first thing I've ever found that ties Jared to that town." Tess's ballerina poise was falling away right in front of River's eyes, and he could hardly stand to watch it.

He resisted reaching for her hand. "He and Ashley were good friends."

"And you as well?" Tess asked.

River frowned. "I wasn't exactly friends with Ashley. Just Jared."

"Did Jared remain close to Ashley after leaving the Marines?" she asked.

River hesitated. "You know that Jared and I weren't on speaking terms when he died. I don't know if he kept up with Ashley."

"But that's one of the things you're trying to find out?" Tess asked.

River nodded. "Yeah."

Tess straightened, looking once more like a well-poised ballerina. She lifted her chin just a touch. "Well, he was my husband. I deserve to know the truth as much as anyone. More so, don't you think?"

River had always believed that Tess deserved the truth. That's why he'd barged into her wedding in the first place, fully prepared to tell her what he knew. He hadn't though. Instead, he'd opened the floor for Jared to confess. That hadn't happened either. Tess hadn't gotten the truth that day, and River had always felt somewhat responsible. Especially now because, if Jared had indeed been keeping a mistress, then he hadn't changed his ways like he'd promised River he would. Instead, Jared had lied. To everyone.

Chapter Four

Tess couldn't believe she was sitting here on River's deck, sharing a coffee with him in any kind of civilized way.

River shifted and groaned in pain.

She whipped her head to look at him. "What's wrong? Are you hurting?"

River clutched a hand to his side and shook his head. "No. I'm just sore. It'll pass," he said through tempered breaths.

"You're a stubborn man, you know that?" she asked, almost annoyed that he'd made her feel any kind of concern.

"So I've been told." He sat up in his chair and slowly removed his hand from his side.

Her gaze lingered on him a little longer to make sure he was being honest about his injury and that he didn't need her to rush him to the hospital. She half expected to see a pool of blood on his T-shirt when he lifted his hand. Thankfully, she didn't.

"I have other jobs right now that I'm working on," River said. "Allowing you to hire me would be a conflict of interest. Jared was my best friend."

"Not for several years before he died. Need I remind you why?" Tess asked.

River still wasn't looking at her.

Tess watched him as he seemed to focus on the creek beyond them. "You barged into my wedding. On some level, you ruined what was supposed to be the happiest day of my life. Instead of talking about how wonderful an event it was, all anyone was talking about was you."

River looked over, his gaze holding hers. "I'm sorry that I hurt you."

She pondered that statement. River was a man who chose his words carefully. She didn't think he was one to say things he didn't mean. "But you're not sorry that you did what you did?"

River didn't answer that question. "Tess, forget about what you saw in my house. I'm sorry you even had to go there. I was looking into Ashley and the town of Morrisville for my own information. If I loop you in on whatever I discover, there's no going back."

"You're making assumptions that Jared was doing something he shouldn't have," she said, narrowing her eyes. "I don't believe that."

River's gaze was steady. "Well, he was doing something that he felt the need to hide from you."

Tess swallowed past a tight throat. Her instinct was to defend her late husband. Jared was a good man. She wouldn't have been with him if he wasn't. If he'd pulled the wool over her eyes so easily, what did that say about her? "Maybe he was planning a surprise for me," she said. "I don't know. All I know is that he was my husband. You might choose to believe the worst about him, but I can't."

"Tess, I've seen the truth haunt people. I've seen it do more harm than good."

"That's only if the truth is something one doesn't want to hear," she protested. "That's not the case here."

"I hope not," River said.

Tess swallowed. "So you're saying you'll let me hire you then?"

"No. I'm saying, go home, think about this—*really* think about it. If you still want to go forward with this investigation next week, then we will."

Tess exhaled. "Good. I'll be in touch on Monday."

At a quarter until closing, two women walked into Tess's bookstore.

Tess looked up from the book she was reading. "Hi, Eleanor and Nancy!" The two were good friends of Tess's aunt Sheila and used to be a part of their own little book club when Sheila had owned Lakeside Books. The women quit coming once Tess took over, even though Tess had extended an invitation to the weekly book club she ran with her close-knit group of friends. Eleanor and Nancy had politely excused themselves, saying they didn't read romance novels. The way their noses had wrinkled when they'd said so let Tess know they didn't exactly approve of books with kissing and happy endings. No hard feelings though. At least not where Tess was concerned. If they didn't want to read books with strong women and happy endings, they didn't belong in Tess's book club anyway.

"Oh, Tess. It's so nice to see you. We know you're about to close up for the night," Nancy said. "So we won't stay long."

"Take your time," Tess told them. "Can I help you ladies find something?"

Eleanor was looking around the store, her expression one of obvious disapproval. "You've really increased the number of books you carry, haven't you? It's hard to even turn around in here."

Tess took a breath. That was by no means true. The aisles were still plenty spacious. Tess had even made sure her store was handicap accessible for one of her customers who used a wheelchair. "Well, I wanted to make sure I had books that represented what everyone in town wanted to read. I found myself having to order books for folks because we didn't carry them. I think the only bookstore in town should have a wide variety for customers to choose from, don't you?" Tess admired her aunt but, for a woman of color, Sheila hadn't carried many books by authors of color. That was one of the changes that Tess was most proud of. Her book selection was diverse because she wanted everyone who walked in to find themselves in the pages of the books sold here.

"Good for you," Nancy said, sounding a touch condescending to Tess's ears. "Sheila kept a simpler store than this, but to each their own." Nancy's smile was firmly pinned in place. "I guess that's why Sheila never needed to hire extra staff."

Tess was glad that Lara had left early today. Lara had already witnessed Tess's less than welcoming response to River earlier in the week. Tess was going to do her best to be friendly to her aunt's friends right now, but she also intended to stand up for herself. "Aunt Sheila hired me," Tess reminded Nancy. "I was my aunt's staff."

Nancy turned to look around the store. "Yes, that's very

true. What would you recommend?" she asked, moving on to the next subject.

Tess thought her book recommendations might all get discarded with a sour expression. She doubted she shared the same taste in books as these women. "How about a journal? I just got some beautiful ones in stock."

"A journal? That's not a book," Eleanor said on a humorless laugh. "Sheila never carried gift items here."

"Well, it's not exactly a gift item," Tess explained. "One of my favorite self-help books recommends that everyone take up journaling. For self-discovery."

Eleanor and Nancy looked at Tess like she had two heads.

"I don't read that self-help stuff." Nancy didn't bother to hide her frown now. She shook her head, and then she looked at her watch. "Oh, we shouldn't hold you up. It's time to turn that sign on the front door to CLOSED. We'll just have to come back another time to shop," she said politely.

Tess tried not to take offense. She could tell her aunt's friends disapproved of the little changes she'd made to Lakeside Books. But this was Tess's store now. Aunt Sheila had insisted that Tess make it her own in any way she saw fit. Romance novels, self-help books, and journals were some of those ways. Tess was also finally adding author signings to the store's event calendar, which was something Sheila had never been interested in doing. "Thanks for stopping in, ladies. It was so nice to see you."

"You as well," both Eleanor and Nancy chimed as they turned to head out of the store, walking through the aisles with more than ample room, in Tess's humble opinion.

Tess followed behind them to flip the OPEN sign to

CLOSED. She didn't lock up though. For the last few years, Thursday had meant the gathering of her closest friends here in Somerset Lake for book club. It was Tess's idea, and because not all her friends were avid readers, they read only a couple of chapters a week. This made each book take forever to get through, but that wasn't the point of Tess's book club. The point for this one was friendship, food, and fiction. The best three f-words in the dictionary, if you asked Tess.

The book club that Tess ran was small by design. If it got too big, then the women wouldn't feel as comfortable sharing all the inner workings of their lives—and that was the best part. Even so, Tess wasn't sure if she would be sharing her personal business tonight. She firmly believed that Jared was innocent and anything River dug up would prove that. Therefore, there was no reason for Tess to open the floor for others to doubt him. Tess was his widow after all, and she'd done her best to honor him since his death.

A knock on the front door got Tess's attention. She looked up and waved her friend Lucy Hannigan inside.

Lucy breezed into the room, her auburn hair blowing behind her. "Happy Thursday!"

"TGIT. I wasn't sure you'd make it. Weren't you going to have guests at the B and B tonight?" Tess asked. Lucy had turned the large pink home she'd inherited into a bed and breakfast this year, catering to her midwife clients who were looking for a babymoon experience before their little bundles of joy arrived.

"Well, the baby was born earlier than expected, and the babymoon was postponed. We're going to do a B and B experience with the newborn next month. It'll be fun," Lucy said. "I'll watch the baby at night and give the parents a chance to sleep. Sweetie's Bake Shop will cater all the meals. It'll be fantastic."

"Sounds like it," Tess agreed. "Word about the Babymoon B and B is going to spread all over. Before you know it, you'll have a waiting list."

Lucy plopped down on the leather sofa in the back of the bookstore and placed her bag beside her. "Well, babies only book their reservations nine months in advance, so my waiting list can only be so long," she pointed out.

Tess laughed. "True enough."

They both turned as Moira and Trisha walked into the store. Della Rose followed right behind them. Della was looking extra cheery these days, thanks to her new love interest, Roman Everson.

Who'd have thought Della would ever be in love again after her ex cheated on her? That's what Della had hired River to find out. But look at Della now. She was practically glowing from the inside out. Her boys were with her tonight, as always. They broke off and went over to the kids' section along with Trisha's young son, Petey.

Tess took her usual place on the oversize armchair that sat catty-corner to the couch that Lucy and now Moira were seated on. Trisha sat on another armchair and Della on a third. Wordlessly, they all pulled their copy of the book club's pick out of their bags and placed it in front of them, almost like a prop. Then the discussion of everyone's love life began.

First, there was Trisha and Jake's. Then Lucy and Miles's. And Della and Roman's. Tess caught Moira's eye, and they shared a look. Was it pity or pride that they'd escaped the chains that romance put on one's heart? Tess was sure that Moira's look was prideful. She was happily single, and by all accounts, she had no desire to be half of a couple anytime soon.

Neither did Tess. That's what her mind said at least. Her heart too, most days. Other days, her heart was lonely. She missed going home to someone and having someone pour her a glass of wine. She missed bingeing a show with someone. She missed being a part of something at home, instead of being alone with a book.

"Earth to Tess!" Moira said.

Tess blinked and realized all the women were watching her with raised brows.

"What's up?" Lucy pointed a finger at Tess. "You have something weighing on your mind. What is it?"

"Is it the River Harrison thing?" Moira asked with a small grimace. "I wasn't the dispatcher when Lara called nine-one-one, but I heard all about it. He collapsed right here in your store, right?"

Della gasped as she pressed a hand to her chest. "What? I didn't hear about that."

Lucy snickered. "Well, neither did Reva Dawson apparently or else we all would have known. Is he okay?" Lucy looked a little guilty about asking.

Tess rolled her eyes. "I don't wish the man any harm. It's all right for you to want him not to die," she told her friend.

Lucy's mouth fell open. "Really? He was near death?"

Was River near death? Tess didn't think so, but he'd been bleeding an awful lot. She shook her head, mouth suddenly parched. Leaning forward, she poured herself a cup of lemonade. Book club always had lemonade and some sort of delicious treat to snack on. Tess took a sip before speaking. "River is fine. He was in the hospital overnight. I watched his dog for him."

The women all had that shocked look about them again. All except Trisha Langly-Fletcher, who was new to Somerset Lake and hadn't been around during the days of Tess and Jared. Trisha didn't seem all that surprised that Tess would take care of an injured man's dog while he was in the hospital, but she hadn't been present when River interrupted her vows.

Moira recoiled. Her black, cropped hair was down tonight, framing her freckled cheeks perfectly. "You watched his dog for him?"

Tess shrugged. "He didn't have anyone else to ask. His dog isn't very social with other dogs."

"Kind of like his owner," Moira retorted.

Tess felt the need to defend him, which was weird and unlike her. She was fiercely protective of her family and friends, but River was neither. She wasn't sure what he was to her these days. Not quite the enemy she'd considered him prior to the incident in her bookstore the other day, but far from friends. "My mom is getting on me about putting myself back out there in the dating world," Tess said, changing the subject. "She texted me a picture of a single guy at her church she thinks I should give a chance to."

Della leaned forward and reached for Tess's hand. "Maybe your mom is right, hon. Maybe it is time."

Moira made a gimme gesture, wriggling her fingers at Tess. "Let's see the picture of him."

Tess dug out her phone and brought up her text messages. She had a new message from River that made her heart rocket into her throat. She wanted to open it, but the women were watching, so she'd have to wait. Instead, she tapped on her thread of messages from her mother, where the photograph of the man was front and center.

He was a white man, tall and wiry, with thinning gray hair and a black goatee. His face was round, and there was something nice about his eyes. There was no mysterious jagged scar below his right eye though. No angled cheeks. No intense stare that rivaled River's looking back at her in this photo.

Tess blinked. Why was she comparing this guy's photograph to River Harrison? She turned the screen out toward Moira first.

Moira grabbed it and inspected the man's image. "You know, I think I've seen him before."

"Well, this is a small town," Della said.

"I think he goes into Mom's bakery," Moira added with an eyebrow waggle. "I can introduce you if you want."

Tess shook her head. "No thanks. He's not exactly my type."

"Do you have a type?" Della asked.

Tess considered that question. She'd gotten serious with only one man in her life, and she'd married that man. Jared was white, but Tess could also see herself with a man from any race. Being a Marine, Jared had been physically fit. He had dressed stylishly and held an affinity for shoes that rivaled most of the women here. That was Jared though, and he had never exactly been what Tess would consider her type. If she went by the movie stars she fancied, her type was the strong, silent, and mysterious kind. Denzel. Keanu. Daniel Craig... *River Harrison.*

Tess nearly rolled her eyes at herself. Why did she keep thinking of River?

She scanned the group, finding Lucy watching her closely.

"Why would your mom's matchmaking attempts be weighing on you?" Lucy asked, a note of suspicion in her tone.

Tess shrugged. "I don't know. Maybe because I'm not living up to peoples' expectations."

"If you don't want to date anyone, don't," Lucy said, as if that solution was obvious. "Who cares about peoples' expectations? They're just trying to make sure you're happy, that's all."

"And a man is not required for that," Moira said, just in case the rest of them weren't clear on her viewpoint.

"Do what's best for you," Lucy stressed. "We will support you in whatever you decide." She reached for Tess's cell phone and looked at the photograph. "He looks like a nice guy, though."

Tess retrieved her phone. She held on to it until the conversation switched to Trisha and Jake's adventures in getting pregnant, which Tess was fully interested in. Even so, she casually glanced down at her phone, brought up her thread with River, and checked the message he'd left for her.

> **River:** Buddy wants to know if you've chewed any good books lately?

Tess burst out laughing. When she realized what she was doing, she looked up at her friends, who were all staring at her.

"Something funny on your phone?" Moira's eyebrows raised suspiciously.

Tess shook her head quickly and dropped her cell into her bag before Moira snatched it straight from her hand. "I saw a funny meme. About dogs chewing books." It was almost true.

"Dogs chewing books doesn't sound like something you'd find funny," Lucy said.

Tess waved a hand. "Well, it wasn't one of the books we like to read. It didn't have a happy ending."

Moira frowned. "You got that from a meme?"

Tess hated lying. She wasn't any good at it. Not even tiny, little fibs. How did people do it on larger scales? Like, oh say, the kind of scale where you lie to your wife about working and go somewhere else for a week at a time?

She'd known Jared wasn't perfect, but she would never have thought him a liar. She still didn't buy that he was disloyal to her though. He would never hurt her like that. She'd never be with a man who could.

"Yep, from a meme," Tess said. "So, speaking of books. Should we actually discuss this week's chapters now?"

Technically, River was still supposed to be in the hospital, so he figured he better stay home tonight instead of joining the guys at the tavern.

He carried his laptop outside to his back deck and sat facing Mallard Creek. Moving here last year was one of the best decisions he'd ever made. It was serene, peaceful, and rife with nature. Buddy snorted at River's feet, laying his head atop River's shoe. He liked it here too. River could tell.

River opened his laptop, brought up his email, and clicked on a message from Ella Peters. He'd just wrapped up her case this week. Turns out, Ella's real mom and dad had been living in Magnolia Falls, the next town over, all this time.

The email loaded with a brief paragraph.

Mr. Harrison,

I just want to thank you for your assistance in helping me locate my birth family. I feel like a void has finally been filled in my life. We spent yesterday together, talking, crying, and picnicking at the park. I can never thank you enough.

Sincerely,
Ella Peters

Attached was a photograph of Ella with an older gentleman and woman whom he recognized from his investigative search. They were all three smiling from a red-checked picnic blanket spread out on the ground in a park. Not all his jobs were as rewarding as this one. In fact, investigating someone's cheating spouse wasn't much fun at all. Neither was tracking down which employee at a company was skimming money off the bottom line.

River looked at the photograph, satisfaction gathering inside him. There was another feeling too. One he couldn't quite place. Regret?

During his twenties, River had gotten a tip and followed a trail to locate his birth mother. By the time he'd found her contact information, however, he'd learned that she'd recently passed away. She had no other living relatives. It was just her. River hadn't had any information on his birth father.

The disappointment had cut through River like a jagged knife back then. That's when he'd decided to stop searching. He'd let his desire to locate blood relatives sizzle out like a fire's ember instead of catching wind. He hoped the same was true for Tess's desire to investigate Jared's past. As soon as he had the thought, his cell phone lit up. He reached for it, seeing Tess's name on his screen.

Tess: Tell Buddy I don't chew books.

Tess: Tell his owner that I haven't changed my mind.

Tess: I'm just waiting until next week, as he requested.

Chapter Five

River had never been what anyone would call a popular guy. Not in grade school, high school, or beyond. But for some reason, he was well liked at Weeping Willows Assisted Living Facility.

Douglass was every bit the proud dad. As soon as he'd moved into the facility last year, he'd started bragging about his son, the former Marine, who'd been all over the world, completing missions for his country. Douglass had told them all about River's interest in survival skills, and the residents all seemed to flock to River as soon as he walked onto the property. River wasn't convinced that Douglass didn't put out some sort of announcement when he knew River was coming.

"Hey, River," Cal Cunningham said, leaning heavily on his cane as he hurried to greet him on his way toward Douglass's apartment. "If you're looking for your dad, he's at the community building."

River turned and waited for Cal to catch up. "Oh?"

"Yeah. There are a few of us over there, eager to see you. We heard you were injured over the weekend. We want to hear all about it."

River suppressed a smile. These guys loved to share stories about their medical issues. "All right." River changed direction and began walking toward the large brick community building that sat in the middle of the property. "I'll even show you guys the scar."

"You have a scar?" Cal's eyes lit up.

"Twelve stitches," River confirmed.

"Nice." Cal was pushing eighty years old and had a head full of white, fluffy hair that lifted on the summer breeze as they walked. River suspected that, once upon a time, when Cal hadn't needed to slump over his cane, he'd been at least five inches taller. Cal was ex-military as well and had served with the Marines at Camp Lejeune, just like River. And Jared and Ashley. "We got a mountain of ropes too," Cal went on. "We thought you might show us those rope ties again. We've been practicing some days when you're not here."

River had taught them a series of rope ties one stormy summer evening a few weeks ago, and one would have thought he was the most entertaining guy in town. "I'm surprised you never learned those ties in the Corps."

"Nah. I can clean and shoot any gun, but I don't know how to tie knots. That's more of a Navy thing, if you ask me."

When they reached the community building, River held the door for Cal and let him walk through. Then he entered the building and looked around for his dad. People were always surprised when River called Douglass his dad, until they realized that River meant adoptive father.

Douglass smiled as River headed in his direction. "You okay?" he asked when River sat beside him.

"Yeah. It was just a superficial wound," River said, understating his injuries from earlier in the week.

"They don't put you in the hospital for superficial wounds." Douglass gave him a knowing look. River had been all-boy growing up, breaking bones, getting stitches, and bruising his shins until they were an entirely different color. He was sure he was responsible for at least half of the silver hair on Douglass's head these days.

"It got a little bit infected. It's fine now," River said.

Douglass shook his head. "A son is not supposed to die before his father. You bury me, not the other way," he said, not for the first time.

River held up two fingers. "Boy Scout's honor."

"Good." Douglass looked around at his friends from the assisted living facility and back at River. "All right. Lift up your shirt."

"What?" River laughed nervously.

"We all want to see the scar." Douglass mimicked lifting his own shirt.

River rolled his eyes, but he wasn't surprised in the least. He dutifully lifted his shirt and showed the guys his wound, telling them all the gory details, much to their obvious delight. After leaving the facility, he checked his phone and saw a message from Tess waiting for him. He was expecting to hear from her this morning. He'd told her to contact him on Monday if she still wanted to hire him. Tess was headstrong and determined. Knowing her, there was nothing that would change her mind once it was decided.

Tess: Meet me at Sweetie's Bake Shop?

He tapped back a quick reply.

> **River:**   I can be there in 10 minutes.
> **Tess:**   Perfect. I'll let Lara run the bookshop and walk over.

A few minutes later, River walked into Sweetie's Bake Shop for a coffee from his favorite bakery owner and thanked her for the blueberry muffin she'd sent through Tess the other day.

"You're welcome. I heard you were injured. I just wanted to send my well wishes for you. Looks like it worked. You're up and moving around just fine this morning, aren't you?" Darla asked.

River nodded and looked around. "I am. I'm actually meeting Tess here. Have you seen her yet?"

Darla started to shake her head but stopped. "Well, there she is now. Perfect timing."

River turned to see Tess push through the front entrance. She was wearing a pair of white cropped pants and a flowy blouse with a bright floral pattern. She offered up a wave when she saw him. That was more than River usually got from her. So, overall, his little weekend injury was working in his favor.

"Hey, Tess," Darla said in a cheerful tone. "Moira was in here earlier. She'll be sad she missed you."

Tess smiled back at Darla, her brown eyes dancing the way they did. "I'll have to meet up with her another day this week." She slid River a look as if to say her business was with him, and he knew exactly what she wanted to discuss. He just wasn't clear if it was to call off last week's request or to confirm it.

"I'll grab a table," he said.

She walked past him toward the front counter. "I'll grab coffee and breakfast."

"I know what you like. I'll bring it to you." Darla leaned toward them and lowered her voice. "Warning, Reva is here. If she sees you two having breakfast together, who knows what her blog will read tomorrow."

River glanced over at the older woman with her laptop open in front of her. "It's a business meeting. What could Reva possibly write about us having breakfast together?"

Darla snorted out a laugh. "That's all she needs to write for the town to make ado over it. Come on, River. You know how it works."

He sighed. "Unfortunately, I do." Although, for the most part, he'd managed to escape Reva's blog and her gossipy bullet points. He gestured at the table farthest from Reva's. "We'll be at that one," he told Darla. "Talking about business."

"Which means books or PI stuff?" she asked with raised eyebrows.

He gave her a look. "Not you too, Darla."

Tess pulled out a chair and sat down across from River. "So, are you going to let me in on this investigation or not?" she asked, cutting to the chase.

He gave her a steady look. "You don't waste any time, do you?"

"Well, I asked you last week, so there's lost time already."

They stopped talking long enough for Darla to set their coffees down in front of them along with a sesame seed bagel and a container of cream cheese for Tess and a piece of banana bread for River.

Tess reached for her cup of coffee. "Thank you, Darla."

"You're very welcome, sweetie. Anything else?" the shop owner asked.

Tess and River both shook their heads.

"All right then. Enjoy."

Once Darla was gone, Tess looked at River. "You said you would agree on Monday if I still wanted you to investigate the reason Jared was in Morrisville. It's Monday, and I still want you to. I haven't changed my mind."

River reached for his coffee and took a sip.

"Oh, come on. Don't tell me you're following some sort of male code of honor. You think he was up to no good and you're trying to protect him?"

"It's not that," River said. "It's you I'm thinking about. I don't want you to get hurt."

Tess took a breath. That statement implied that River thought she would. "Look, I need to know why Jared was in some town we'd never discussed. Why did he lie to me about where he was? I need answers."

River unwrapped his piece of banana bread without saying anything at first. She watched his hands work, steady and sure. She'd always had a thing for a man's hands, but having any kind of thing for River was not ideal or acceptable.

"I'll say yes at the end of breakfast. How's that sound?" he finally asked.

Tess furrowed her brow. "What?"

"Well, I usually eat alone. It might be nice to have someone sitting across from me for once." He looked up at her, and it almost felt like he was teasing her.

"What if I don't finish my breakfast here with you right now?" she asked, teasing him right back.

"Then you won't hear me say yes." He grinned as he bit into his slice of bread.

"You are one frustrating man, aren't you? I don't know what Jared ever saw in you," she said without thinking.

"I always knew what he saw in you," River said.

Tess looked up from her bagel. "You said that in my bookshop the other day too. Right before you fell over."

River chuckled quietly. "It's true."

She picked a piece off her bagel. "Then why would you barge into my wedding and tell Jared he was making a mistake in marrying me?"

River frowned. "I never said *you* were the mistake, Tess."

"Yeah, pretty much." She resisted the urge to continue down that path about her wedding. It was a sore spot between them, and she didn't want to argue. What she wanted was to put her differences with River aside and for him to say yes to her request. "So what kind of breakfast conversation does one have with River Harrison?" she asked, trying to keep the mood light.

"Douglass is about the only one who'd know." River took another bite of his bread, chewing and swallowing before saying anything more. "And I don't think you'd want to talk about the same things Douglass and I discuss."

Tess gave him a questioning look. "What would that be?"

"Well, Douglass can talk about the weather for at least fifteen minutes," River said, making Tess laugh. "It's true. The man will go on and on about the day's forecast and how it's going to affect his entire schedule."

"And what do you talk about?" she asked, sincerely wanting to know.

"I'm more of a listener."

Tess nodded. "I can see that about you. Jared was a talker, so he probably appreciated the fact that you listened to him."

River looked away, his gaze reaching to the people sitting around them. "Do we have to talk about Jared right now?"

So much for keeping the mood light. "You were his best friend. I was his wife. What are we supposed to talk about when we're together?"

"You like books, right? Tell me about the book you're reading."

Tess shook her head. "You wouldn't want to hear about it. It's a romance."

River reached for his coffee and chuckled before taking a sip. "You don't think a guy can like romance?"

"Well, considering that my aunt Sheila's friends don't attend book club anymore because they dislike romance, I highly doubt an ex-Marine, such as yourself, would enjoy books about kissing. You don't even date, from what I've seen."

"That's accurate," he agreed.

"Why not?" she asked, genuinely interested. River was a mystery to her.

He looked at her over his cup of coffee. There was a teasing quality to his expression. "You just veered the conversation from books to my dating life. Don't think I didn't notice."

She mirrored him by reaching for her coffee and taking a sip as well. Who would have thought she'd be enjoying this conversation as much as she was? Certainly not her.

"I guess I find that most women don't share my same interests," he finally said.

"Which are?"

"I like spending long weekends in the woods, where there are no bathrooms, showers, or Netflix. You can bring books though," he said.

Tess felt her cheeks grow warm at the implications. "I don't mind the woods."

"Well, if you ever decide to be adventurous, let me know."

Tess straightened. "You don't think I can be adventurous?" she asked, remembering Jared's comment about River thinking she and Jared were a bad match. The outdoorsman and the bookworm. "I can be adventurous."

"I'm sure you can."

Tess lifted a brow. "You're humoring me right now. I'll have you know that I'm more than a booklover."

River looked perplexed. "Of course you are."

"I've actually gotten into hiking in the last year or so," she told him, wondering about how defensive she suddenly felt. "As a matter of fact, I go on several hikes a week."

He popped the last bite of his bread into his mouth and chewed before washing it down with coffee. "That's great, Tess."

"I could probably hold my own if you and I were out there together," she added. "Booklover or not."

River grinned as he leaned back in his chair and watched her. "Well, it just so happens that I need a camping partner this coming weekend. Why don't we find out?"

Tess drew back. "What?"

He shrugged. "Last time I went camping on my own, I nearly died. You saw me. I need a partner."

"You hardly need a partner," she said, halfway rolling her eyes.

"Maybe I just want someone to keep me company then."

Tess shook her head. "Look, if I've given you the wrong impression, River, I'm sorry. I'm not looking for anything romantic."

"With me?" He laughed softly. "Of course not. You barely tolerate me. And I'm not looking for anything either. There's just something I want to show you."

"What is it?" she asked.

"A place that Jared and I liked to hike. I think you'd enjoy it too. Come with me."

There was yet another thing she didn't know about her late husband. "This weekend?" she asked. "Nothing romantic?"

"Nothing at all," he told her.

"What about the investigation? Will you find out why Jared was really in Morrisville? Because he wasn't there for an affair. I won't believe that." She couldn't. Jared was her husband. He'd made promises to her that he would never go back on.

River seemed to hesitate as he looked at her. "I told you I would agree to your request if you still wanted me to today. I'm a man of my word."

"Good. And you'll tell me everything?" Tess pressed. "No holding back?"

River offered his hand for her to shake. She stared at it before taking it. Then she met his steady gaze. "I've never been much on secrets anyway," he said.

Chapter Six

River looked at the picture of Ashley Hansley on her Facebook profile. She was beautiful, with long brown hair and green eyes—the kind of woman that River's best friend Jared would have flirted with back in the day. Jared had a type, and Ashley Hansley was it.

River scrolled through Ashley's Facebook profile. She posted infrequently, and it was mostly made up of funny memes. Her feed suggested that she liked cat memes the best. There were no online albums full of home and family for him to peruse. That would make his investigation easier. In her bio, it simply said that Ashley was single and had attended North Chase High School. She was a veteran, which River already knew. He also knew that Ashley had mercilessly flirted with Jared back in the day, and Jared had shamelessly flirted right back. And that Jared had a one-night stand with Ashley prior to his wedding to Tess.

Buddy nudged a muddy tennis ball into River's hand, waiting for River to wrap his fingers around it.

"That's gross, Bud."

Buddy looked up at him with doelike eyes. It was Buddy's favorite pastime since moving out here on Mallard Creek.

River lifted his arm high, and Buddy sat at attention. Then River propelled the ball toward the creek. Buddy took off after it, ears flying behind him in the wind as he raced to retrieve the ball before it was swept away. Chasing a ball was the only time Buddy showed any energy at all. Otherwise, he was about the chillest old dog there ever was.

River wiped the muddy residue from his hand against the thigh of his jeans and returned to his web search of Ashley Hansley. Most people in her age group had a bigger online footprint. Ashley barely had anything.

Buddy raced back toward River with a wet tennis ball lodged between his canines, pride dancing in his hound eyes. River retrieved the ball from Buddy and tossed it again, wiping his hand once more on his jeans before returning to his laptop to search Jared's last online footprint.

River moved to Jared's Facebook page, which was rife with photographs of Tess and their life together. They looked happy and in love. In these pictures, Tess wore her hair pulled back in a ponytail at her nape, which worked to accentuate her high cheekbones. Her eyes were the same golden brown but also different. There was an ease about her in these photos that was missing these days. River guessed that was due to becoming a widow much too early.

He sat there studying the pictures, looking for some proof that Tess and Jared weren't the happy couple they'd projected, but there was nothing. As far as River was concerned, until Ashley's name had come up the other day, Jared had made good on his vows to Tess.

River had been livid when he'd caught his friend with Ashley leading up to Jared and Tess's wedding. Jared, on the other hand, had been casual about it, saying he was sowing the last of his wild oats. That it would never happen again. He'd told River to drop what he saw. To let it go. But River couldn't. There lay the crack in their friendship. River believed in loyalty and honor, not just in the military, but in everything. And Jared believed in loyalty and honor only when someone else was watching.

Jared had gotten new friends, and he'd dropped River like a bad habit. River had only watched Jared and Tess's marriage from the sidelines. By all appearances, though, they had been happy. River wanted to believe that Jared had never looked at another woman again after saying "I do." That his one-nighter was a solitary lapse in judgment that he hopefully regretted every single day.

River stared at the creek beyond his home, trying to think of another way to research Ashley's life. Then he returned his gaze to his laptop and pulled up a browser. In the search bar, he typed: Hansley. Morrisville, North Carolina.

The first result was for a Rebecca Hansley, who owned the Lovebird's Bed and Breakfast. River tapped on the related website for the B and B and scrolled through an online album of the business. It was small and quaint. Then he returned to Facebook and typed in Rebecca Hansley's name.

Bingo. Unlike Ashley, Rebecca was very active on social media. She posted several times a day. River clicked over to Rebecca's bio. She was a widow with three adult children. She was, in her words, "a cat mama."

River clicked on the online photo albums. Rebecca Hansley had a wealth of albums proudly displaying her family. River scrolled through, and after five or six photographs of gardens and a large orange cat, he found a picture of Rebecca with her three daughters, one of whom River recognized as Ashley Hansley. Even though it had been years, Ashley looked about the same as she had the last time River had seen her. Which was three nights before Tess and Jared's wedding.

River's cell phone rang beside him. River glanced at the caller ID and reached to pick it up. "Hey, Sheriff Ronnie."

"Hey, buddy. I heard about your accident. Just wanted to call and check on you."

River shifted uncomfortably in his seat. He and Ronnie had grown up together in this town. They were friends before going into their respective careers. "Thanks. I guess I got a little careless out there. I'm on the mend though."

"That's good. A knife wound always gets my attention."

River chuckled. "No foul play, Sheriff. Just sloppy camping."

"Well, accidents happen. How's business?" Ronnie asked. "Anything I need to put on my department's radar?"

Sometimes River's investigations overlapped with the local sheriff department's.

"Not right now. I am working a case though. Do you happen to know anything about the year leading up to Jared Lane's death?"

Ronnie cleared his throat. "You're investigating a deceased person?"

"It's complicated," River said. "I'm interested to know if Jared had any issues or problems with the law."

"Not to my knowledge, no. Jared Lane was a straight shooter. Well, I assumed he was. I do know that he hired a lawyer right before he died. Maybe about a month before. I remember, because it wasn't his family's lawyer. The guy is a friend of mine. That's how I found out about it. But you know, I didn't ask why Jared was hiring him. If you go to someone other than your family lawyer, it's often because you're in a bit of trouble that you're ashamed of. Or you're doing something that your family might not approve of. Does that help at all?" Ronnie asked.

"It does if you give me the lawyer's name."

Ronnie was quiet for a moment. "Peter Browning. With Jared being gone, I guess Pete won't mind talking to you. If you find out something that will hurt Jared's reputation or his family though, let's just let sleeping dogs lie, okay?" Ronnie asked. "Jared was a good friend of mine."

"He was my friend too," River said. "And I would never do anything to hurt Tess or the Lane family."

"Good. That's good. Well, I'm glad you're feeling better. Let me know if you need anything," Ronnie told him.

"Thanks, I will." River disconnected the call and then blew out a breath, needing a mental break from this case. He got up and headed inside with his laptop. His left side still ached, reminding him of his misstep on Saturday. That, in turn, reminded him that he had offered to take Tess camping in the wild this upcoming weekend. What was that about? He went out into the woods solo. He hadn't had a partner out there since Jared. That had been one of the things they'd enjoyed doing together. And when Jared dropped River as a friend, Jared found other men to camp with while River had decided he preferred to camp alone with his dog.

Yet, River had all but insisted that Tess come out with him.

River opened his fridge and grabbed a bottled water. He twisted off the cap and drained half the contents in one large gulp. One rationale was that River could see that Tess needed something right now, and he always thought the woods offered whatever the soul needed, no matter how big or small.

Another motivation that River refused to entertain was that he still had a tiny thing for Tess Lane, from long ago, and he wanted to show her a side of himself that she hadn't seen. River wanted her to see the man with a love for a good view and fresh air, for peace and quiet. Instead of the man she loved to loathe. The one who'd single-handedly ruined her wedding day.

Tess walked out of the bookshop to meet her best friend, Moira, for breakfast at Sweetie's Bake Shop down the street. Now that she had regular help at the store, she was making a habit of leaving during work hours. That was the point though. The bookshop had become a second skin to her since Jared's death. Staying confined in its space was a way of concealing herself while also appearing like she was doing just fine. Fine was being out in the world and living her life outside of the bookshop though.

Tess walked through the bakery's entrance and breathed in the delicious swirl of aromas in the air. Her stomach protested the fact that she'd skipped dinner last night in lieu of getting in bed with her book earlier.

"Good morning, Tess," Darla said from behind the counter. "Moira just stepped into the restroom. She'll be right out. What'll you have this morning?"

"A coffee with cream and two sugars. Can I also get a plain bagel with cream cheese?"

"Of course you can," Darla said with a thick Southern drawl.

After paying and collecting her breakfast, Tess found herself a seat along the wall.

"Hey, you." Moira plopped down into the chair opposite Tess. She had cropped black hair, hazel eyes, and fair skin spattered with freckles along the upper edge of her cheeks. Moira was a striking woman who could undoubtedly draw a lot of attention from guys if she wanted to. "I'm so glad you hired someone for your store so that we can do this more often."

Tess had done this occasionally anyway. She used to have to close the bookshop and leave a sign on the door stating that she'd return soon. It wasn't the most professional thing, closing during store hours, but such was what a business owner without help did. "Lara is working out wonderfully."

"That's great."

Darla stepped over and laid their breakfasts in front of them along with two cups of steaming coffee.

"I love you, Mom," Moira said.

"Just because I come bearing caffeine and sugar?" Darla asked.

"Not just for that reason, but that does get you extra mom points."

"Aww. You've been eating too many of my sugary treats. The sweetness is rubbing off on you." Darla bent and kissed Moira's temple. "Let me know if you ladies need something else," she said as she straightened.

"Thank you, Darla." Tess looked at Moira. "How was the dispatch last night?"

Moira worked as a 911 operator out of her home during the hours when most folks were asleep. "Quiet. There was only one call, and it was for a dog that refused to come inside from the woods after being let out to pee."

"Seriously?" Tess asked on a small laugh.

Moira bit into her muffin. "I kid you not." She held a hand over her mouth to keep from showing a mouthful of food. "I dispatched the call to the sheriff's department and let them decide if it was worth sending a deputy out for."

Tess picked a piece of her bagel off and popped it into her mouth, chewing thoughtfully. "I had never called nine-one-one in my life until I asked Lara to call for River the other day in the bookshop. That was a true emergency."

Moira frowned. "I might have hesitated to dial just because of who it was."

Tess avoided Moira's gaze. Moira was her very protective friend, loyal to the core. Of course she would hold the biggest grudge against River for what he did at Tess's wedding. Well, her and all of Tess's family. And the Lane family too. "There's something I need to tell you," Tess said.

Moira lifted both brows in question. "What is it?"

"Well, when I watched River's dog for him, I had to go into his house for a few supplies. While I was there, I saw a picture of Jared that I had never seen before. He was with a woman named Ashley Hansley."

Moira took another bite of her breakfast as she listened. "Who's that?"

"Apparently, she was a Marine with Jared and River. She lives in Morrisville."

Moira's eyes rounded over the top of her muffin. "What?" she asked as she swallowed her bite of food down. "Is that the reason Jared was in that town when he had the accident?"

"I don't know." Tess picked another piece of bagel off but didn't pop it into her mouth just yet. "River is investigating that."

"What?" Moira practically yelled.

Tess looked around to see other customers glancing in their direction. Darla was also looking over at them with a concerned look on her face. Tess met Moira's gaze again. "Lower your voice, okay? This is just for your ears, no one else's."

Moira blew out a breath. "You're investigating your late husband? Do you think he was cheating on you or something? Because the guy I knew loved you. Jared would never do such a thing."

Tess believed that was true. But who was this Ashley woman? "I know that. River might be setting out to prove that Jared was having an affair, but there'll be another explanation for why Jared was in Morrisville. I'm sure of it. And I need to know what that explanation is. It's been three long years of wondering. River might not be my favorite person, but he's a good investigator. He'll find the answers for me."

Moira looked skeptical. "Since when do you put your confidence in River Harrison?"

Tess shrugged a shoulder and reached for her coffee. "I don't know. He almost died in my bookshop the other day. There's something about a near-death experience, I guess. We kind of came to a little truce. Nothing major, but we can at least be civil to each other now."

"Well, since you seem to have lost your mind, I can be skeptical enough for both of us," Moira said.

Tess nibbled at her bottom lip. She might as well tell Moira the rest of her involvement with River. "Also, I kind of agreed to go camping with him this weekend."

"You did what?" Moira nearly shouted.

"Shh." Tess ducked her head. She loved Moira to death, but while her friend was fully composed during other people's emergency situations, she was emotional in her real life. "He wants to show me one of his and Jared's favorite hiking spots. I should know about that, shouldn't I? Sometimes I feel like I didn't know my husband as well as I thought I did."

"So River is taking you hiking?" Moira asked.

Tess nodded. "That's right."

"Alone in the woods? Just the two of you?" Moira asked.

Chills rode over Tess's body. When her friend put it that way, it sounded like something totally different than it was. "Yes. And it'll be fine. I'll be fine."

"Like I said, I'll be skeptical enough for both of us." Moira took another bite of her muffin and chewed. The door to the bakery dinged behind her as another customer walked in.

Tess nearly choked on the bite of bagel that she'd finally popped into her mouth. It was Mayor Gil Ryan, who Tess had always adored. Moira, on the other hand, avoided him whenever and wherever possible. Gil had an obvious crush on Moira, and for some reason, that made Tess's friend skittish to a level that Tess had rarely ever seen.

"You okay?" Moira asked, looking at Tess as she cleared her throat and washed the bagel down with coffee.

Tess would have warned Moira, but it was too late. Gil was standing at their table.

"Morning, Tess. Moira." His gaze stuck longer on Moira. Not in a creepy way. Tess thought that Gil was maybe the nicest guy in Somerset Lake. Frankly, she wondered why he liked Moira so much. Moira had attitude. She was tough. She wasn't exactly sweet, especially toward Gil.

Moira frowned up at him. "Hi."

Gil smiled back. "Don't worry. I'm not intruding on your friends' breakfast. I'm just here for your mom's coffee, the best in town if you ask me." He said it loud enough for Darla to overhear.

Darla laughed from behind the counter. "I'm already making it the way you like it, Mayor."

He looked back at Tess and Moira. "I'm getting my breakfast to go. I'm meeting with the events committee for the Somerset Summer Festival this morning. We're going to finalize the plan."

"It's just a couple weeks away, isn't it?" Tess asked.

The Somerset Summer Festival was Mayor Gil's own creation. When he'd become mayor, he'd started the festival himself to bring in more tourists and to shine a light on the community.

"That's right," Gil said. "I hope you'll both attend."

"We wouldn't miss it," Tess said, nudging Moira under the table with her foot.

"Great. Good to see you both," Gil told them. "Have a nice day, ladies."

"We will," Tess said, while Moira said nothing. This time Tess swung her foot at Moira and gave her a playful kick. "I will never understand you," she whispered across the table to Moira.

Moira looked up, meeting her gaze. "Then I guess we're even because I will never understand you either."

Chapter Seven

The following afternoon, River hesitated in front of the office door of Peter Browning. Some secrets were meant to stay buried, but that wasn't River's nature or his job. He was a private investigator, which meant he needed to uncover every fact he could.

Maybe this would lead him nowhere. Or maybe this lawyer whom Jared had contacted before his death held a missing piece of the puzzle.

River lifted his hand and knocked before he could second-guess any longer. He'd called earlier and made an appointment. Peter knew that River was coming and that he wanted to discuss Jared Lane.

An older gentleman with dark brown skin and a neatly trimmed beard answered. "Hello there. You must be River Harrison."

"Yes. Thank you for meeting with me."

"Certainly. Come on in." The lawyer led River to a chair in front of his desk. It was fancier than Mayor Gil's desk, with designs carved into the cherrywood. Peter sat on the other side in an expensive leather chair. He folded his hands in front of him. "I hope I can be of service, although I'm afraid I don't have much information to offer. Jared was only a client of mine briefly. He died before our business was finished."

River hesitated. "Can I ask what that business was?"

"I'm a divorce lawyer, Mr. Harrison. That's my specialty. Folks who come to see me are usually seeking to end their marriages."

River had done his research online and already knew this. He was hoping there was some other explanation though. "I see. Is that what Jared Lane was here for?"

"My client was looking into leaving his wife, yes. Obviously, he didn't get that far in the process, and my judgment told me it was best not to inform his widow that her husband was planning to divorce her."

River swallowed. Tess would be devastated by this information for sure. "Did he tell you why he was divorcing Tess?"

Peter leaned back in his chair and bounced the fingertips of his hands together. "In my experience, there are a handful of reasons men leave. If the woman has been unfaithful, he'll leave. A man who has been unfaithful, however, doesn't usually leave. If he's fallen for another woman, that's different. Love is every bit as powerful a motivator as money, which is a third reason that couples divorce."

"You're being very vague, yet straightforward."

"It's the best I can do while honoring my commitment to my late client," the lawyer said. "I'm afraid that's all I can share with you."

"I appreciate it." And it was helpful information, albeit disappointing. River stood. "Thank you for your time, Mr. Browning."

"You're very welcome. For what it's worth, I do recall that Mr. Lane was heartbroken. More so than my typical client coming to me for these reasons. Mr. Lane was very concerned about making sure Tess was well cared for in the divorce settlement. He wanted her to have half of everything. Usually my clients are focused on keeping as much as they can. But not Mr. Lane. I respected that about him."

"Thanks for letting me know." River shook Peter's hand and left the lawyer's office. Some part of him wondered if he'd done the right thing in coming here, because now that he knew this truth, he was obligated to tell Tess, wasn't he? She'd insisted that he tell her everything he learned in this investigation. This new detail would be devastating though. Tess was so firm in her belief that Jared would never intentionally hurt her, but he was planning to divorce her.

Why? Did Jared feel guilt over a premarital affair? Had he had more affairs? Was he in love with his mistress? Perhaps River could wait to tell Tess what he'd found out just a little while, until he had more information. There were too many questions right now, and Tess wasn't ready for the answers that might be coming. River guessed no one could ever be ready to hear that the person they thought they knew best wasn't who they thought they were at all.

"It's six p.m. Time to turn the sign around," Tess called to Lara from behind the register.

Lara headed down the aisle and flipped the sign from OPEN to CLOSED.

"Another day down. You've learned the ropes here quickly. Before long, I'll be able to go on a week-long vacation and leave you to mind the shop," Tess said.

Lara walked back toward Tess. "I wouldn't mind. I don't have much of a social life beyond work anyway. By choice."

Tess had a little nagging feeling deep in her conscience. Maybe she should invite Lara to join her and the other ladies tomorrow night. It wasn't a public book club. It was made up of Tess's closest friends. The only reason Trisha had gotten an invite was because Lucy had insisted on having a feeling about Trisha. Trisha had been new to town, and according to Lucy, she'd needed friends as badly as Somerset Lake needed a movie theater.

"I can be social when I want to be," Lara continued, "but I prefer to be home alone. I'm weird that way, I guess."

"I see. Well, if that's what you enjoy, who can blame you?"

"My mother, that's who," Lara said with an eye roll and simultaneous head shake. "She doesn't like it one bit."

Tess laughed. "Ha. I have one of those too, and she is very vocal about her opinions on how I spend my free time."

Speaking of which, Tess was having dinner with her mother right after she left here. Hopefully, her mom wouldn't be playing matchmaker again tonight. If so, Tess might feign a headache and leave early. Most of the men her mom recommended were single for a reason. Tess was single for good reason as well. She was a widow and could stay stuck in this stage of her grief forever if she wanted to.

What stage of grief was it where you asked a private investigator to look into your late husband? Was that somewhere on the spectrum?

"I'll close out the register. You go on home to your book," Tess told Lara. "Do you at least have a pet?"

"Does a betta fish count?" Lara asked.

Tess thought about that for a second. "If it doesn't satisfy my mom, it doesn't count."

Lara grabbed her purse from below the counter. "I don't want anything more than that. Too much responsibility. I'm content just caring for myself."

"I respect that," Tess said. "Good night."

"Night." Lara headed out, leaving Tess alone to finish closing the store.

Ten minutes later, Tess locked up the bookshop and walked to her car in the parking lot. Her parents lived close by, which was nice. She tried to have dinner with them at least once a week, although it usually happened only every other week these days.

When Tess arrived at her parents' house, there was a sporty red Mustang in the driveway. *Whose car is that?*

Tess studied the red sports car as she walked past it toward the wide front porch. She wasn't in the mood for socializing past her parents' company tonight. She hoped whoever it was didn't stay long. She climbed the porch steps and then knocked and opened the front door simultaneously.

"Tess, is that you?" her mother called from the kitchen.

"It's me, Mom!" Tess confirmed.

"I'm glad you made it. Guess who's coming to dinner?" her mom asked.

Wasn't that a game show somewhere?

Tess closed the front door behind her and headed toward the kitchen, stopping by her father's recliner as she passed by.

Her father was a white man, and her mother was Black. It wasn't the case anymore but for a long time, Tess's parents were the only interracial couple in Somerset Lake. When Tess was growing up, she'd been hyperaware of that fact. Being different in any way was hard during the middle and high school years. "Hey, Dad," she said, bending to give him a kiss on the cheek.

"Hey, sweetheart. How are you doing?"

"Good." Tess looked down at him in his favorite leather chair. Her father had yet to retire. He typically worked long days at the accounting firm that he owned and operated. "How are you?"

"Every day above the ground is a blessing," he said.

He'd been saying that since Tess was a kid. He'd stopped for a while after Jared's death, but time had passed, and now he was back to reciting those words without a second thought.

"I'm going into the kitchen. Need me to get you anything?" she asked.

"No, thanks. A visit and a kiss from my favorite daughter is all I need." He gave her a wink.

"Such a charmer." Tess patted her father's shoulder and headed into the kitchen to find out who the mystery dinner guest was. *Please don't be one of my mom's matchmaking attempts. Please, please, please don't be that.*

Tess came to stand in the entryway for the kitchen and stopped. There wasn't a strange man in the kitchen with her mother. No. Instead, it was a woman with long brown curls and blue-gray eyes that reminded Tess too much of her late husband.

"Heather. What are you doing here?"

"Hello, my favorite sister-in-law. Well, I knew you were working, so I thought I'd come see your folks first." Heather broke into a large smile that also favored Jared's. Heather was Jared's little sister. As soon as Tess and Jared had gotten engaged, Heather had decided that she and Tess were sisters and that Tess's mother was her second mother by default.

"It's great to see you. How long are you in town for?" Tess asked, immediately thinking about the investigation. Having Jared's sister underfoot while Tess worked with River might be tricky. Going away for the weekend might also stir up questions.

"Just a few weeks. I'm between filming, so I thought I'd come home." Heather was an actress. She'd had one speaking role on her "big break," and then she'd been written into a coma, in which she'd spent an entire season of the show she was on. "You always said I could stay with you when I'm here in Somerset Lake…" Heather said, trailing off.

Right. Tess had said that. Life had the most inconvenient timing, didn't it?

Tess's mom looked between them. Her mother didn't have Tess's signature curls. Instead her mother's hair was more sleek and straight. Most days, she wore it down, cut neatly a few inches above her shoulders. When Tess didn't immediately respond to Heather inviting herself to sleep over, her mother took the liberty. "Of course you can stay with Tess. She's all alone in that spacious house of hers. She doesn't even have a dating life going on, despite my best efforts." Tess's mom gave Tess an exasperated look before returning her attention to Heather. "Maybe you can help me convince my daughter that it's time. Three years have passed. If she's not careful, one day she'll wake up and she'll be old and all alone."

Heather shared a look with Tess. It was the look of sisters who conspired against their parents. A look that implied she understood things that family outsiders never would. "Maybe you only get one soul mate in life," Heather said. "Maybe looking for a second one is a waste of time."

"Nonsense." Tess's mother slipped an oven mitt onto her hand and prepared to pull dinner from the oven. She loved to cook large family meals whenever there was even a hint that Tess might be coming over. In her mom's eyes, family time always involved lots of home-cooked food, and no one cooked better than Tess's mom. Meals were never complete at this house without a pitcher of sweet tea—the sweeter the better—and corn bread that was made from scratch, never from the box. "Falling in love is like riding a bike," her mom said as she lowered the oven door and reached inside to pull out what looked to be a roast of some sort. "A heart can do it over and over again, if its person is willing." She slid the dish on the oven top and glanced over her shoulder to give Tess a pointed look.

Tess swallowed, feeling the familiar throb at her temple. Maybe she wouldn't have to feign that headache after all. Maybe the pain would be real. "Mom, dinner looks and smells delicious. What is it?" she asked, changing the subject.

It was late when Tess got into her car and led Heather's sporty red Mustang back to her home. A couple of weeks in Heather time could easily be two days or one month. Tess wouldn't typically mind, much, if not for her new arrangement with

River. If Moira was anti-River because of his betrayal of Jared, Heather would be ten times as adverse to the idea of Tess having any relationship with him, especially one that was for the sole purpose of determining if her brother had skeletons in his closet.

Tess would just have to keep her business with River a secret from her sister-in-law. Shouldn't be too hard, since Heather was younger, and in the past, she hadn't wanted to hang out much with Tess or Jared when she was in town. Heather was a nightlife person. She liked lights, action, and theatrics.

"You know where the guest bedroom is," Tess said, opening the front door and leading Heather inside her home. She was pretty sure Heather's filming break would be brief. The land of movies and television moved fast, right? "Do you need anything else?"

Heather turned to look at her, her eyes watering. "I need to tell you the real reason I'm in Somerset Lake. I'm not actually on a break," Heather said, dissolving into tears. "I was fired on the set."

Chapter Eight

River rolled over and picked up his phone from the nightstand, blinking it into focus.

> **Tess:** You can't tell anyone about us.

He blinked again. Maybe he was dreaming. He tapped his thumbs against his screen to reply.

> **River:** Please clarify.
> **Tess:** Our arrangement.
> **River:** We already discussed that this would be a private matter.

For a solid minute, the phone was silent. There were no bouncing dots on his screen indicating that Tess was writing anything back to him. Then the dots appeared.

> **Tess:** Or the camping trip. Heather arrived in town tonight.

River let his head fall back against his pillow and suppressed a groan. Heather Lane wasn't on his list of favorite people. On an exhale, he lifted his head once more and looked at his screen, where another text was waiting.

> **Tess:**   She's staying with me a while.
> **Tess:**   She wouldn't understand if she knew I was involved with you in any way.
> **River:**   Understatement of the year.

Heather was what a guy might call a ball buster. Okay, Jared himself had called his sister by that name. Heather's MO was to kick a guy between the legs first and ask questions later. She was beautiful and tough, and headstrong, and she held a grudge as vehemently as her big brother had.

> **River:**   How will you explain going away this weekend?
> **Tess:**   ...
> **Tess:**   ...
> **Tess:**   ...

Judging by all the dots and the minutes that passed, River thought he knew what was coming next. It was probably for the best anyway. Spending time in the great outdoors overnight with his buddy's widow, who admittedly he was attracted to, was undoubtedly a bad idea.

> **Tess:**   River, I'm sorry, but can I have a raincheck on that camping trip?

River: Of course. I understand.

Tess: Thank you.

River: I understand if you want to step back from the other arrangement too.

Because that would make Heather's coming to town a good thing. River didn't want to find answers that would cause Tess any more grief than she'd already been dealt.

Tess: No. I want to continue with that. Just on the DL.

Tess: Down low.

River laughed out loud into the darkness.

River: You didn't think I knew what DL meant? You had to clarify?

Tess: You're not exactly the kind of guy I imagine texting people throughout the day.

Tess: I'm sure you know Morse code, but maybe not text abbreviations.

River: I know what DL means.

Tess: Great. TTYL!

River stared at the screen. TTYL? What did TTYL mean? After a prolonged moment, Tess texted with a question.

Tess: Need me to interpret?

She followed that text with a laughing face emoji.

River was surprised that he found text banter fun. Or maybe it was just Tess, because River hadn't been interested in bantering or flirting in a while now. He brought up a browser on his phone and did a quick search for the meaning of TTYL. Then he tapped out a reply to Tess.

> **River:** Talk to you later.
> **Tess:** It doesn't take a PI to know you totally just googled that.

She followed that message with a winking face emoji.

River set his phone back on the nightstand. He was disappointed about this weekend's camping trip, but also a little relieved. He hadn't thought things completely through when he'd made the invitation. His heart had been in the right place. But being alone overnight with Tess was probably a bad idea of epic proportions. He could control his body, of course. He was a man of steel will. His mind, however, sometimes got away from him. His heart too.

River always woke before the sun came up. It was a habit from his days as a Marine. Keeping a normal sleep routine was for civilians, not a guy with his training. He got up and moved through the darkness of his home as if he were wearing night vision goggles. He kept things in their place, always, and knew the floor plan like the back of his hand.

Even still, he tripped over the bone in front of him because

Buddy wasn't former military, and despite River's efforts, Buddy didn't think his chew things should have a place. River didn't mind—much. He made it to his coffee maker and flipped it on, listening to the familiar rumble as his thoughts jumped from various topics, as fleeting as rocks skipping across the water.

He reached for a mug from his cabinet and contemplated next steps for his investigation. He supposed he'd have to spend more time digging into Ashley Hansley before driving down to Morrisville next week. Ashley had been only an acquaintance when they served in the Marines together. River hadn't known her the way that Jared had. River planned to find her address and where she worked and just go see her. Yeah, she could lie to his face, but what reason would she have?

River's mind hummed with a dozen possibilities and questions. After next week's trip to Morrisville, he would likely have his answers. This wouldn't be a long, drawn-out case. Most of the ones he worked weren't.

The coffee maker rumbled to a stop. He reached for the pot and poured a full cup of brew. Then he carried his cup of coffee out onto his porch to watch the sun rise over the mountainous backdrop. The sky was lit up with vibrant oranges and pinks and a few birds were spreading their wings and celebrating another day.

River lifted his cup and took a sip, his mind moving back to Tess. She'd told him not to reveal to Heather that they were working together, but he hadn't promised to stay away from her altogether. Jared had been very close to his sister. They shared secrets. Would Jared have shared anything with her?

Heather had always had a crush on River. He guessed it was the whole big brother's best friend appeal. River had never reciprocated. For one, Jared would have killed him with his bare hands if he had. And while Heather had pretended to hate River's guts after he'd attempted to stop Tess and Jared's wedding, she'd made a pass at him at the tavern the following week. When River rejected her, she'd apparently decided to return to hating him.

If River had to guess, Heather would be down at the tavern tonight, which was convenient, because it was Thursday and he'd be there with his buddies. River would never flirt with a woman to get information, but he'd never had to flirt with Heather to catch her eye.

Buddy barked.

"Right," River said. "I've had my coffee. Now you need your walk."

He put on his tennis shoes, tied the laces, and headed out into the dark morning with Buddy tugging excitedly toward the sounds of birds. Buddy was a hound dog, technically, but, aside from a muddy tennis ball, he'd never caught anything in his life. He was old and mostly all bark, very little bite.

A simple walk to let Buddy use the bathroom turned into about a mile's hike down to the creek and back. Then River showered and decided to have his second cup of coffee away from home. Sweetie's Bake Shop was calling his name, and it had nothing, or very little, to do with the fact that it was just a few stores down from his newest client at Lakeside Books.

∞

It felt like Christmas in June in the bookshop right now. There were three brown boxes, heavy with various books to add to the shelves in the coming days. Tess didn't usually make such a big order, but she'd found holes in her selections recently that needed correcting. Every time a customer came in asking for a certain type of book, she made a note if she didn't have anything similar. She didn't want anyone in the community to feel like this bookstore didn't serve their reading needs. No matter what Eleanor and Nancy thought about it.

That was one reason she was so excited about the prospect of Jaliya Cruise coming for a book signing. Somerset Lake was an older town. There were plenty of widows and widowers who could benefit from Jaliya's wisdom. And everyone had lost someone they loved, even if it wasn't a spouse.

Tess left the three brown boxes on the floor and returned to the counter, where her laptop sat, resolve building within her with each step. Lara was somewhere in the store returning books to their proper place. Tess could have this private moment to check her in-box.

She opened her laptop, took a breath, and pulled up Facebook. A circle in the address bar began to spin because the internet reception was spotty sometimes here in the bookshop. As she waited, the bell jingled above the entrance door.

"Welcome to Lakeside Books," she heard Lara say in greeting, followed by, "Oh."

Tess moved to see who it was, stopping short of River, who was standing in the middle of the store holding a coffee carrier and three coffees.

"Hi," he said. "One of these is for you. And one is for Lara. For saving my life last week."

Tess's lips parted. "You didn't have to do that."

"I did. Also, I kind of need to use your public restroom. Am I still the last man on earth you'd let use it?"

Tess laughed unexpectedly. "Who knew you had a sense of humor?"

River lifted a cup of coffee off the tray and handed it to her. "I did," he said, his eyes connecting with hers. Then he reached for another coffee and handed it to Lara. "Darla wasn't sure how you drank your beverages, so I brought extra creamers and sugar packets. Darla sends her love."

"Thank you," Lara said, accepting the coffee.

"I'll set the cream and sugar on the counter." River headed in that direction. "I'm not staying," he called behind him. "I'm working a job today."

"Oh?" Tess asked, wondering if he was talking about her job.

"Yep." River turned to look at her, a conspiratorial look in his eyes. "But I can't talk about it. The woman who hired me asked that we keep it on the DL."

Tess suppressed a smile. "I see."

"That means down low," River said with a serious expression.

Tess cleared her throat, trying not to laugh again. "Yes, I know."

Tess could feel Lara watching them. She no doubt thought that River was still the least favorite person of Tess's. He'd grown on Tess though. She hadn't known he could be funny. She'd always thought he was so serious. What other things didn't she know about him?

"Well, good luck with the case you're working. Thank you for the coffee. I could actually use it this morning."

"You're welcome. As you can see, I got myself one as well." He held up his own cup.

"Let me guess. You drink yours black," she said, already knowing that was true.

River turned his cup around to see Darla's writing on the cup's side: *Grande Black.* "Your PI skills are good." He set the coffee carrier on the counter and gestured. "The bathroom?"

"Go right ahead." Tess ignored the fluttery sensation blooming inside her chest. Maybe she was tolerating River more these days, but attraction was absolutely unacceptable. The feeling was almost gone when River stepped back into the room. Then the flutters returned in full force.

"Do you need a book while you're here?" Tess asked.

"From the last man you'd let use your restroom to offering to sell me a book, huh?" He sipped his coffee. "I guess almost dying did me a favor with you." He looked around. "What's your favorite?"

Tess swallowed. Her favorite book felt so personal. "It's called *A Woman's Journey to Joy* by Jaliya Cruise. I somehow doubt you'd connect with that one." She winked at him when he looked at her.

River took another sip of his coffee, his gaze trained on hers. "I might surprise you. I'll buy a copy."

"What?"

River shrugged. "I have female clients. I already know all about the male experience. Why not learn about the female one?"

Panic gripped Tess. She really didn't think River would take her suggestion. The book was all about grief and being a widow, the road back to being whole after losing the other half of yourself.

She took a breath. She'd recommended a million books

to Jared when he was alive and had given him dozens. Jared never read even the first page of one. River would likely buy this book and it would be a paperweight somewhere in his house.

She grabbed a pair of scissors and ran the blade through one of the brown cardboard boxes that had arrived earlier, freeing the flaps. Then she removed one of Jaliya's books. She held it in her hand. It was hardcover and substantial in weight and size. It would make a nice paperweight, but it carried so much more weight inside its pages for its readers.

Tess carried it to the register and rang it up for River, placing it in a brown paper bag marked with the Lakeside Books logo. "Have a nice day," she said, like she would to any other customer.

"CYT," he shot back with a teasing glint in his blue eyes. Then he leaned in across the counter, too close for comfort. So close she could smell the woodsy scent of his aftershave.

Tess held her breath, perplexed by the heat that scorched through her chest and cheeks.

"In case you're wondering," he said in a low voice, "that means *See you tomorrow*."

Chapter Nine

Rule #1 of book club was that no one came without an invitation. And yet, Heather was sitting cross-legged on the worn leather couch among Tess's closest friends as if she belonged exactly there.

Tess held her tongue. She loved her sister-in-law, she did, but only because she had to. Heather had shown up at the bookshop at five minutes to close, knowing full well that tonight was Tess's book club night. Tess had told her she'd be home late for that very reason. But she hadn't extended an invitation.

"I've seen you on that TV show," Della Rose said to Heather, making small talk as if this wasn't a breach of book club etiquette. "How does it feel to be a big star?"

Heather usually loved to discuss her fame, but she looked oddly uncomfortable right now. Tess watched her sister-in-law closely. Heather's right eyelid was twitching. Her lower lip quivered. Was she about to start crying in the middle of book club?

"It feels amazing when I'm on set and when everything is going my way. But…" She struggled to catch her breath. "But…"

Oh no.

Tess tried not to be irritated that Heather was completely hijacking her book club with her usual drama.

"I just got fired from set," Heather told the ladies, her voice cracking.

She'd mentioned this to Tess the other night, but she hadn't given more detail because she'd been too upset to talk. Heather had retreated to the guest room, and Tess hadn't pressed her on the subject since. Tess had decided that Heather would tell her if and when she felt ready. But not at book club of all places.

"What did you do to get fired?" Moira asked, eyebrows lifted high in interest.

Heather hugged her arms around her body, making her appear even smaller than she naturally was. "What makes you think I did anything wrong?" she asked. "Maybe I'm innocent."

Tess doubted it. "Are you?"

Heather looked down at her crossed arms. "No. I mean, I didn't commit any crimes. I just, well, I had an affair with the director." She sniffled softly, continuing to keep her gaze lowered. "He didn't tell me he was married. I guess he got worried that I'd ruin his twenty-year marriage so he fired me to get me out of the picture—literally." Heather looked up with red-rimmed eyes now. "It wasn't my fault. I didn't know."

"That's despicable," Lucy said.

Tess was more skeptical. "How could you not know he was married? Didn't he have a ring?"

"He wasn't wearing one." Heather shrugged. "He came on to me, and I just assumed he was single. He was handsome and ambitious, so I thought why not?" Heather let her face drop into the palms of her hands. "And now I've ruined my career."

Della reached out and rubbed Heather's back. "Now, now, sweetie. You haven't ruined anything. You'll just head back out there to LA and land another gig with a director who knows how to keep his hands to himself and act professionally."

Della was the mama hen of the group. She wasn't much older, but she was nurturing, whereas Tess wanted to shake some sense into Heather and tell her about how she should have known better. Mixing business and pleasure was never a good idea, whether he was married or not.

"This is why they say not to have intimate relationships with coworkers," Tess lectured. "It can lead to problems like this. Now you're out of work. Can you even pay your bills for the month?"

Heather looked taken aback by the new line of questions. "Just this month. After that, I'm up the creek without a paddle. I was hoping to help out at the bookshop while I was here." She nibbled her lip sheepishly.

"I just hired Lara," Tess said as gently as possible, tempering her frustration. "I didn't know you'd be needing work."

"You can help me at the Babymoon B and B," Lucy offered. "I could use some overnight help."

"And you could assist me at the Somerset Cottages during the days," Trisha said. "There's some upkeep tasks that need taking care of that I'm sure you can help out with. The residents would love having a TV star in their presence."

Heather looked at Tess. "Wow. You're lucky to have such great friends."

Tess didn't need reminding of that. Her friends were the main reason she'd survived the last three years since Jared's death. That and Jaliya's book. She guessed her friends would be how she'd survive any revelations she might learn from River's investigation too. Friends were the backbone of any survival plan.

Della Rose reached for the treats Moira had brought in from Choco-Lovers. "I love Jana's chocolate-covered lemon squares," she said.

"Pass one over," Moira said. "I slept through lunch."

"When are you ever getting off the nightshift?" Tess asked.

"Next month." Moira picked up a lemon square and inspected it before taking a bite. "Starting in July, it'll be day-time emergencies only for me." Moira bounced her eyebrows. "That should be interesting. Not that anything of interest ever happens in Somerset Lake. River passing out in your bookshop was the most exciting thing here lately."

Heather paused as she reached for a lemon square as well. "*The* River Harrison? He passed out in your bookshop?" She looked at Tess.

Didn't they just discuss this at the last book club meeting? It was time to move on from that. "Um, yes. The very one you're thinking of," Tess confirmed.

"Why didn't you tell me?" Heather asked.

Tess shrugged. "It didn't come up. And why does it matter?"

Heather made an exaggerated expression, eyebrows stretching high on her forehead as her jaw dropped. "Because it does. Who does he think he is coming anywhere near you? What was he doing in your bookstore?"

"Bleeding out," Tess said. "Lara called nine-one-one."

Heather closed her open mouth and pinched her lips tightly as she listened. "The nerve of that man."

"Yes, the nerve of him nearly dying in my store," Tess agreed sarcastically.

"Well, let's just hope I don't run into him while I'm in Somerset Lake, because I might make him bleed out for real."

The women all stared at Heather. Tess knew that Heather had come on to River. It wasn't just the director on set that Heather had gotten tangled up with. Tess also knew that River had turned Heather down, and Tess suspected that accounted for part of Heather's resentment.

"Okay, who read this week's chapters?" Lucy asked, holding up her copy of *Love on the Rocks*.

Everyone had except for Heather, who didn't even own a copy of the book. Because she hadn't been invited. And she ate half the lemon squares and drank half the pink lemonade. When it was time to leave, Heather drove behind Tess and followed her inside Tess's home.

"Good night," Heather called as she retreated immediately to the guest room at the end of the hall.

Tess was thankful. She was all talked out for the night. She went about her nighttime routine, changing into her PJs and washing her face. Then she climbed into bed and placed her laptop on her thighs. She'd waited all day to check her Facebook messages. She needed to see if Jaliya had officially confirmed the twenty-third. According to the schedule that Jaliya had attached, she was signing in Charlotte the day before. It would be only a few hours' drive to Somerset Lake.

Tess's fingers tapped along her keyboard, pulling up a browser. She typed Facebook's address into the top bar and waited. A message from Jaliya Cruise was waiting for her when the page finally loaded. Tess sucked in a breath and held it as she read.

Hi Tess,

Good to hear from you again. June 23rd at 2 p.m., it is! It's on my calendar. I'm looking forward to meeting you in person and having a signing at your charming little bookshop. Thanks again for the invitation.

Sincerely,
Jaliya

Tess squealed quietly to herself. This was the best news. She'd been wanting to start having events at the store, and now it was officially happening. She loved the store that her aunt Sheila had handed over to her, but Tess was slowly making the place her own.

After his falling out with Jared, River had decided Buddy was all he needed. Buddy was as loyal as they came, but River enjoyed these nights at the tavern with the guys too.

He finished off his one and only beer and slid his plate of finished chicken wings away, looking around the tavern. He would have guessed Heather would be here tonight. He'd wanted to ask her a few probing questions about Jared. But maybe it was best to leave that rock unturned. Heather could be a loose cannon when she wanted to be. She was impulsive and unpredictable, two qualities that made River nervous when interacting with others.

Jake Fletcher pushed back from the table. "All right, guys. Trisha just texted me that book club is over. I've got to head home."

All the men started howling with laughter.

"You are so whipped," Miles said, scooting back in his chair as well.

Jake looked at him. "And where are you going? Let me guess. Home to Lucy?"

Miles gave a sheepish grin as he stood. "Guilty." He raised both hands. "I've been wrapped around her finger since high school, and I admit it."

River enjoyed listening to these guys. They'd all been friends with Jared, so it surprised him that they'd roped River into their weekly meetups knowing that he had betrayed Jared the way he had.

Gil Ryan glanced over at River. "I've got my dog to get home to. You?" he asked River.

River chuckled. "Buddy doesn't like it if I'm running late."

Gil nodded with a serious expression. "Same. Same. Goldie starts scratching the door."

"Oh, that's sad," Jake said. "You better go home to Goldie. Maybe one of these days you'll have an actual woman to rush back to."

River listened quietly, hoping the teasing didn't come his way. He knew it probably wouldn't. Gil was one of those guys, mayor or not, who got teased in a fun-loving manner. River guessed the scar running below his eye didn't contribute to his own fun-loving vibe. If anything, he had a don't-mess-with-me aura, which suited him well most days.

"Gil is holding out for Moira," Miles said. "So he might be stuck with Goldie for the rest of his days."

"Why is that? Moira isn't interested?" River didn't usually get involved in gossip, but he knew if he didn't include himself in this conversation, the guys would find a way to pry into his life before they left the tavern.

"Moira is like that well-guarded jewel that a thief is best to avoid because there are too many alarms and locks to get at it," Miles said.

The guys looked at him with bewildered expressions.

"I'm a deputy sheriff. That's the best analogy I have."

"So what you're saying is she's unavailable?" River asked.

Gil nodded. "That's right. And I stopped trying with her a long time ago." He opened his wallet and placed a twenty-dollar bill on the table where the check was. The other guys did the same.

River laid some cash down too. It'd been fun, but he wasn't kidding about being ready to get home to Buddy. He also had a book he planned on reading in bed. When Tess had sold it to him, River could tell she didn't think he would read it. But a good private investigator didn't just investigate the person of interest. A good PI also researched his client. It was always a good idea to know who you were working for.

River knew Tess well enough, but he wanted to go deeper. He wanted to know what made that book her favorite. What pushed her emotional buttons and left her turning the pages all the way until the end. He wanted to know more than he probably needed to for a reason he didn't want to investigate further.

By the time he got home, Buddy was ready to go outside. River let him out the back door and waited on the porch. His cell phone buzzed in his pocket. He reached for it and felt a jolt through his heart at the sight of Tess's name on his screen.

Tess: How's the investigation going?

Instead of texting back, River pressed CALL.

Tess answered after two rings. "Hey." Her voice was quiet, and River remembered that Heather was staying with her.

"Can you talk?" he asked.

"Not so much. I have company, and my walls are thin."

He liked the way her voice sounded in a hushed whisper. "Wanna meet tomorrow morning for breakfast?"

Tess cleared her throat. "River, we need to keep our arrangement quiet, remember? Being seen together—"

"My place then. I'll cook. Buddy misses you."

"Oh." There was a long pause. "Do you normally cook breakfast for your clients?" she asked.

"No." And he didn't read his clients' favorite books either. Or invite them on a camping trip. Or text flirty banter.

Another long pause stretched between them. "Are you a decent cook?" she finally asked.

"I am a man of many talents."

She cleared her throat again. "All right. The bookshop opens at nine, so I'll be at your place at seven thirty. Is that too early?"

"That's perfect. See you then."

"See you then." She disconnected the call.

River blew out a breath, wondering at the skip in his heart as he watched Buddy race back up the porch steps. He opened the door to let his dog in and followed behind, where a book waited with clues about the inner workings of the woman coming for breakfast tomorrow morning.

Chapter Ten

River had stayed up late reading the book he'd bought from Tess's store. Then he'd woken at five a.m. He didn't require much sleep to function. His days of being a Marine had trained him to be primed on a good five hours. After waking, he'd walked Buddy and spit-shined his place for Tess. She could eat off his floor if she wanted to. It was probably the cleanest in Somerset Lake.

Now his kitchen smelled of delicious foods: bacon, eggs, toast, and coffee. He had jam and butter on the table too.

He surveyed it all, and well, it was obvious that he was trying too hard. He briefly considered letting Buddy run out into the creek and walk around the kitchen with muddy paws to make it look less clean and orderly. The doorbell rang before he could follow up on that idea, though, which was probably a bad one anyway. Tess was a clever woman. She'd probably understand that whatever he did was on purpose, including reading her favorite book.

River walked to the front door and opened it, his breath snagging in his chest when he saw her standing on his stoop in a sundress and sandals, a jean jacket pulled on to complete the look. Buddy bumped past River to greet their guest.

"Hey, you." Tess ran her hand through Buddy's fur, scratching gently behind his ears the way he loved. "I've missed you, my friend." She looked up at River. "Maybe you need to pay another visit to the hospital so I can take him for a couple of days."

"Ha. I think you probably have your hands full right now with Heather." River closed the door behind Tess and led her toward the kitchen.

"Mm. It smells like heaven in here," she said on a sigh.

River breathed in the smells in the kitchen again. Add a new aroma to the earlier ones, something floral and fresh, something wholly Tess, and it just might be heaven in River's kitchen.

Tess pulled out a barstool and sat down.

"Nu-uh. No sitting on the job," River teased. "You have to earn your portions here."

Tess straightened. "Oh. I'm sorry. I guess I was in guest mode. What do you need me to do?"

He pointed at the cabinet. "The food is about to hit the plates. Can you pour us both a coffee? Unless you'd rather have orange juice, which is in the fridge."

"A man with orange juice in his fridge. I love it. But coffee is calling my name." She moved toward the cabinets and grabbed two mugs. River glanced over just in time to see her dress rise on her thighs as she reached toward his middle shelf.

Tess caught him watching. "Good thing I'm tall," she said. "Otherwise, I'd have given you a mini-show of leg before breakfast."

River lowered his gaze back to the task. "Full disclosure, I was just silently reprimanding myself for not putting the mugs on the top shelf for that very reason," he said as he arranged the plates beside the frying pan, preparing to fork the bacon onto them.

Tess burst into a laugh. "Are you always this honest?"

"I try to be." After divvying up the bacon, he added mounds of eggs to both plates. In his peripheral vision, he saw Tess carry the mugs of coffee to the table. River added toast to the meal and carried it over as well.

"Can I get the milk from your fridge?" Tess asked. "For my coffee."

"Of course. And I'll get you some sweetener."

A couple of minutes later, they finally sat down.

"Wow, I feel pretty special with this huge meal. No one has ever made me breakfast like this before."

"That's hard to believe," River said.

"Well, it's true. Dinner, yes. Breakfast, no." There was something shaky about her smile, and River knew instinctively that she was thinking about Jared. She was making a small comparison between her late husband and River right now, which felt...wrong.

River looked down at his plate. There were other things that felt wrong about this whole scene, but he ignored them and concentrated on what felt right. "I started reading *A Woman's Journey to Joy* last night."

Tess coughed and began to choke on a bite of bacon. She beat a hand against her chest until the food went down while River got up and prepared her a glass of water.

"Here. It's hard to gulp hot coffee when you're choking."

She drank a few swallows and looked at him. "You're not really reading that book."

"I am. I'm on page fifty-four."

Her eyes rounded. "Seriously?"

He sat back down. "It's great. I think I'm going to buy myself a journal like the author suggests."

She eyed him suspiciously as if he might be mocking her. But she didn't think he was. "I sell them in the store. I started selling them after I read the book the first time."

"The first time?" River asked, swiping butter on his toast. "How many times have you read it?"

"Six and counting. It helps somehow."

"Six, wow. You must have it memorized by now."

"Some parts," she agreed.

"Well, I can see how it would be helpful." The book was all about moving past grief and loss and creating a spark of hope to hold on to. "I'm a guy, and we're not supposed to be in tune with our emotions." He gave her a look as he chewed and then swallowed a bite of toast. "But the book helped me tune into a few of those anyway."

Tess grinned. "You're so serious. Who knew you had emotions?"

He shrugged. Talking about Jared in any personal way was a bad idea right now, but he'd lost Jared too. Even if Jared hadn't claimed him as a best friend for years before his death, River still cared about Jared. He had still felt the void when Jared died, maybe more so than others because of their fractured relationship. He'd always assumed that they'd have a talk, man to man. That Jared would agree that he was a jerk for what he'd done to Tess and that he and River would mend their differences.

"Are you going to read the whole book?" Tess asked.

"I'm a slow reader. I'll probably finish it next week," he confirmed. "I'm not sure I'll read it six times like you. But I'm an elephant." He tapped his head. "I'll have it memorized and stored up here."

Tess grinned again. It was addictive, making her smile. His heart kicked, his blood rushed, and his brain demanded a repeat. More, more, more.

"I've invited the author to have a signing at the bookstore. She responded last night and agreed to come next month. On June twenty-third." Tess seemed to glow from the inside out.

"Yeah? That's amazing."

"If you've read her book and you're a fan, you should be there. I'm sure she'd love to have a guy in her line."

"I'll be the only man, won't I?"

Tess nibbled her lower lip. "If you love the book, maybe you could recommend it to Miles, Jake, and Gil. Then you could drag them to the signing with you."

River let out a soft laugh. "I think they'd probably boot me from our Thursday-night meetups."

Tess reached for her coffee. "I'll get Lucy and Trisha on the case for Miles and Jake. They've already read the book so they have copies."

The conversation lulled momentarily, and River knew this was where Tess was about to bring up the topic at hand.

"What have you found out about Ashley Hansley's involvement with Jared?"

He noticed that her hands were suddenly shaking. River watched as she set her silverware down. Then he reached over and laid a hand on hers. She met his gaze and seemed to take in a steadying breath.

"I want to shoot straight with you. No secrets. That's what you asked from me," he said.

Tess nodded. "That's what I want," she said, but something in her expression told him she wasn't quite sure. That's why the timing was off for telling her everything he'd learned so far. Tess wasn't in a place to hear that Jared had wanted a divorce.

"Well, I researched Ashley's social media."

Tess stiffened beneath his touch. "Oh? And what did you find out?"

River shook his head, going with his gut on what to tell, or not tell, Tess right now. "Not a whole lot. Ashley has the online footprint of a person who's been living in a cave for the last decade. Kind of like me, I guess."

Tess laughed unexpectedly. Once again, she was surprised that River was the one who provoked it. "I really always thought you were so serious."

"I am," he agreed, showing her a grim expression to prove it. "Jared's online footprint is even less. He doesn't have anything."

Tess nodded. "His work made him paranoid. He always said social media made it too easy for people to snoop into your business."

River stabbed at a chunk of eggs. "That's why I don't keep social media profiles too."

She lifted her fork and tasted her eggs. "You're a good chef."

"Thanks. Breakfast is my specialty."

And she never expected to be having breakfast with River Harrison. Tess breathed out a quiet chuckle.

"What's funny?"

"Well, my mom would be over the moon to know I'm having breakfast with a man right now. Breakfast implies that maybe I..." She trailed off. "Well, you know. But as much as she wants me to start dating again, I think she'd lose her mind if she saw me eating breakfast with you."

"What's so bad about me?" he asked.

She thought maybe he was teasing until she saw the seriousness on his face. It wasn't a mock expression this time; it was real. "Nothing. You're actually not so bad. I villainized you after the wedding. So did Jared." Now she saw pain flash in River's eyes. "My mom too, because she wanted that day to be perfect for me and, well...it wasn't."

River looked down at his plate of food.

"Heather says she doesn't like you because of that, but I know the truth."

River looked up from his plate. "And what's that?"

"Heather made a pass at you, and you turned her down."

A smile flickered on his mouth. "You would make a great PI yourself."

"Before I started reading romance novels, I devoured mysteries and whodunits," Tess told him. "What I can't figure out is why you would turn her down. She's gorgeous."

"She's not my type," River said quietly, his gaze holding Tess's. It was hard to take in a full breath as she looked at him, her instincts telling her that River's type was more aligned to someone like her. In some alternate reality, would they be having breakfast together for a whole different reason? Would she ever find herself in River's arms?

"So, what you're telling me is that your entire family dislikes me?"

"Not all of us." She broke off a piece of her toast, crumbling it between her fingers. "So what's next in the investigation?"

"Well, I'm going into the woods this weekend, as planned. Even though you're not coming. Assuming I come out, I'm heading to Morrisville on Monday."

"You're going to see her?" Tess straightened, sitting up tall in her chair.

He nodded. "I might stay for a couple days."

"Stakeouts of her home and workplace?" she asked.

River frowned. "You weren't kidding about those mystery novels, were you? No, that's more in line with stalking. But I am going to find out where she lives and works. I might check the local library for newspaper mentions. The main thing I'll do is make contact and ask for a meeting."

"Just like that?" Tess asked.

"Just like that."

Tess nibbled her lower lip. "I guess I thought we'd be more secretive."

"I don't think that's necessary. I know her, remember? We weren't friends, but she'll remember me. Hopefully she'll be open to talking to me too."

"Okay." Tess nodded. "I think you're right. Being upfront is for the best." Her breakfast felt heavy in her stomach as she made quick plans. "I can tell Heather that I'm going on a business trip."

River furrowed his brow. "What?"

"I mean, bookshop owners don't really need to go on business trips too often, but Heather has never really cared about what I do," Tess explained. "I don't think she'd even question me on it. Lara can watch the shop for me."

"What are you talking about?"

"Come on, River. You're a PI. You know exactly what I'm saying. I'm going with you."

He watched her for a long moment. "You don't need to. I've already promised to relay anything I find out."

Tess folded her arms over her chest. "I want to hear every detail straight from this Ashley woman's mouth. I can help you with the investigation," she said. "I'll be your Watson."

"This Sherlock doesn't have a Watson."

"This one time, he might." She wanted him to agree, even though she hadn't exactly thought this through. They really would be staying overnight together in this scenario. Although for a completely platonic reason. And in separate rooms, of course. The only thing they'd be sharing was a truck ride.

River sipped his coffee, seemingly in deep thought about this prospect. Finally, he set his mug down. "If you want to come, it's fine by me. I know that Buddy would be happy."

Tess exhaled. She hadn't even realized she'd been holding her breath, waiting for his answer. "Great. Then it's settled. We leave for Morrisville on Monday."

Chapter Eleven

River's bag was packed. On his survival weekend trips, he packed only one, which strapped to his back. A lighter load made it easier for him to navigate through the thick brush and rugged terrain, and the whole point of honing his survival skills was to not have every modern convenience at his disposal.

One change of clothes in case he fell into water. One emergency kit with bandages, sewing materials, etc. One beef jerky because he'd catch the rest of his protein in the river.

He was just about to set off on Friday evening when his cell phone buzzed at his side. The name of Weeping Willows Assisted Living Facility got his attention. He answered quickly.

"What's wrong?" he asked, because the facility didn't give courtesy calls on Fridays at six p.m.

"Hello, Mr. Harrison. This is Alice Ingram. I wanted to let you know that Douglass was having pain in his right side. It might be his appendix, but we don't have confirmation of that yet. The ambulance just came and took him to Magnolia Medical," the facility's director said.

River dropped the camping bag from his back, leaving it on the floor at his feet. Normally he would take the time to unpack and put everything back where it belonged, but he didn't want to waste time before going to the hospital. "I'm heading over there now."

"I thought you would. Please keep me informed on how he's doing," Alice said.

"I will."

They disconnected the call, and River immediately grabbed his keys and headed out to his truck, leaving Buddy in the house.

There wasn't a hospital in Somerset Lake, so all the patients who couldn't be treated by the local urgent care had to drive to Magnolia Medical in the next town over. For the entire drive, River's stomach twisted on itself. Losing his adoptive father would leave River a true orphan in this world. Douglass was still young at seventy-five. He moved around fine and did what he wanted. River was expecting the old man to hang around until at least his nineties.

River loosened his grip on the steering wheel as he drove. He hadn't realized he was squeezing so hard. Alice had said maybe it was Douglass's appendix. That was serious, but not a death sentence. Right? River needed to calm down and not automatically assume the worst. Everything would be fine.

The trip took twenty-two minutes because River broke the speed limit where he could. He always thought that age-old question—if a tree fell in the woods but no one was around to hear it, did it make a noise?—applied to pretty much everything, including speeding. If a man drove five miles over the speed limit, but there was no law enforcement to mark it, did he really speed?

He turned into the parking lot of the hospital, parked, and stared at the five-story building. He hadn't realized there were tears burning his eyes until he blinked and one slid down his cheek. He quickly swiped it away, the back of his hand gliding across the roughness of the scar under his right eye.

If a man cries alone and no one is there to see him, does he still have tears in his eyes?

River blew out a breath. He had been here for himself just last week. For a guy who avoided hospitals, he was here more often than he'd like these days. He knew the way to the emergency room. He walked down a long corridor and stopped behind a desk in the emergency waiting room. A middle-aged man read off Douglass's room number from the computer screen and pointed the way.

Douglass looked up when River walked into his room.

"Hey, Dad. How are you feeling?"

"Like someone got hold of a voodoo doll and jabbed a toothpick in its right side."

River lifted his eyebrows as he sat in the bedside chair. "That's pretty specific."

Douglass pointed a finger at River. "You jinxed us. We've stayed out of the hospital for years, and now look at us. First the son and then the father." He grinned widely, no sign of pain in his expression.

"I'm just glad you were in a place where other people were around to assist you. If you were still living alone, you may have never made it to the hospital."

"Maybe so," Douglass agreed.

River leaned back in his chair, bending one leg over his opposite knee. "What do the doctors say?"

"Appendicitis. They'll admit me and put me on some medicine," Douglass told him. "Hopefully no surgery will be required."

River nodded. "That's good."

"And don't even think about canceling any of your plans

for me," Douglass said. "I'm not going anywhere. No need for you to hang around and be miserable."

River shook his head. "I just got here, and you're already trying to kick me out?"

Douglass chuckled. His skin was ashen, but he looked good overall. River guessed they'd already given him pain relievers to ease the discomfort.

"I'm just glad you're okay, Dad," River said.

Douglass reached for his hand. "I'm okay." It wasn't often that Douglass frowned, but his lips formed a barely perceptible downward tilt. "I'm your last relative, and I'm not even blood."

"You know that doesn't matter to me."

Douglass squeezed his hand. "One day, this trip to the hospital won't be such a relief. I want you to have people in your life. You should find your blood family."

River had never mentioned to Douglass that he'd already done that in his early twenties. The sting of discovering that his birth mother was already gone had deterred River from ever trying to locate any more blood relatives that might be out there. "Dad..."

Douglass waved a hand. "I'm not asking just for you, but for me too. I need to thank them for giving me the best thing that ever came into my life. You."

River resisted the tears that pricked behind his eyes. He wasn't alone this time, and he didn't cry in front of others.

"You're a PI. It would be easy for you to find them, wouldn't it?" Douglass asked.

"If I wanted to," River said.

"It wouldn't change the fact that I'm your dad and you're my son," Douglass said.

River met his gaze and shook his head. "Nothing could change that."

"So you'll do it?"

River exhaled a heavy breath. "I'll think on it, okay? But right now, you're in the hospital. The focus should be on you and what you need to get well again."

Douglass sighed. "Since you're not leaving, I need good company. I thought I'd watch TV until they admit me upstairs. They say I'll probably be staying for a couple days, for observation."

River despised TV, especially the shows that Douglass enjoyed. Douglass was a sucker for old sitcoms, the cheesier the better. But for Douglass, River would suffer through a couple of episodes of anything. He owed this man so much. Who knows where River would be without his adoptive parents? They'd stepped up when, for whatever reason, River's birth parents couldn't be there for him. Maybe that reason mattered more than he realized.

If two parents gave up their child, when no one was watching—and the child just appeared on the steps of the fire station—did the birth parents ever exist at all?

River guessed he'd find out—one day. Not this one.

When River got home, he took out his phone and texted Tess.

> **River:** I can't leave for that trip on Monday after all. Douglass is in the hospital.
> **Tess:** What?! Why?

River: The doctors suspect his appendix.

River: I want to stay in town and be sure he's okay.

Tess: Of course. Whenever you're ready to go to Morrisville, just let me know.

Tess: I'm still going with you.

River chuckled to himself.

River: I would expect nothing less.

River: How does next Friday sound?

River: Douglass should be out of the hospital and hopefully recovering at home by that time.

Tess: Next Friday is perfect for me.

Tess: Maybe Heather will have gone back to LA by then too. One can hope.

Tess awoke well before her alarm clock the following Friday morning. On the day of a big trip, her nerves never let her sleep. She wasn't taking a train or plane today. She wasn't going anywhere special, not really. But this trip was huge in so many ways.

The thing she was most nervous about as she lay in her queen-size bed wasn't what she'd learn from Ashley Hansley. It was spending time with River, strange as that sounded.

She shuffled down the hall toward her fridge, opened it, and grabbed a carton of orange juice. Then she poured herself a cup, which she drank while she waited for her coffee to brew. Jared used to poke fun of this routine, saying the orange juice soured the mouth for coffee. How could coffee ever taste good after half a glass of orange juice? he'd asked. The way he'd said it though had been flirty and teasing. She smiled to herself even now every time she drank her cup of orange juice in the morning, remembering him and his mock dismay at what he'd called her disgusting habit.

The coffee maker spit out its last drop, the motor sputtering to a stop. Tess grabbed a mug from the cabinet and headed over to pour herself a serving. She added cream and sugar and sat at the kitchen table in the quiet morning. The thing about being a widow was that one became intimate with silence. It left too much room for thoughts and memories, and for regrets. That was one of the purposes of the journal that Jaliya had recommended in her book. To release those thoughts, memories, and regrets to paper.

Over the years, Tess had learned to live loudly. She had a guest in her home right now though, sleeping right down the hall. Tess didn't want to wake Heather because, as much as she didn't exactly enjoy sitting in silence, sitting with her sister-in-law first thing this early in the morning didn't appeal to her either.

After drinking her coffee, she showered, dressed, and grabbed her bags on the way out the door. She'd told River that she'd meet him at his place to avoid the risk of Heather seeing him pick her up. For good measure, Tess parked her car around the back of River's home so no one would ask questions.

"I feel like we're sneaking around," she told River as she stepped out of her vehicle where he was waiting for her.

"We kind of are."

"Well, for good reason," Tess said. "Imagine if Reva Dawson saw my car parked in your driveway for several days. What would her town blog read?"

River shook his head. "I don't read her blog, so I would never know or care."

"I read it," Tess said. "I'd know. My mom reads it. She'd care."

"Right. Because your entire family has marked me as enemy number one." He turned and led her toward his truck. Buddy looked at Tess as if to say, *Are you coming?* Tess had never known an animal to have such readable expressions.

Tess walked around the passenger side and loaded her belongings in the cab before climbing in. "How is Douglass doing?" she asked.

"He's feeling much better now. The doctors and nurses took good care of him."

Tess exhaled softly. She didn't know Douglass very well, but she did know, because of Jared, how much Douglass meant to River. "Do we need to postpone this trip a little longer?"

"Nah. Douglass was adamant that I not cancel my plans. He even wanted me to go camping last weekend, but I won that fight. I don't get reception out in the woods. In Morrisville, however, I should be fine. If anything happens, we can head back at a moment's notice."

"Of course." Tess asked a few more questions about Douglass, and then she looked around, noticing that River had driven them down Hannigan Street and parked right in front of Sweetie's Bake Shop. "What are you doing?"

"Getting us a coffee for the road."

She felt her eyes widen. "River, you would be horrible at hiding a relationship."

"That's the thing. I would never hide a relationship." His gaze was steadfast.

Neither would Jared, she wanted to say, because she was pretty sure that River was implying otherwise. But after this weekend, she'd prove him wrong.

"You don't have to go in. I'll get yours and bring it out," River offered.

Tess nodded. "Thanks. Cream and four sugar packets please."

"And what do you want to eat?" he asked.

"A slice of banana bread."

River pushed his door open and turned back to look at her. "Do me a favor while I'm gone. Take care of my dog, will you?"

Tess glanced at Buddy in the back. "I can do that."

Ten minutes later, River was back on the driver's side with two coffees, a slice of banana bread, and an apple.

Morrisville was a two-hour drive, which Tess fully expected to utilize reading. She had a new book, one with a happily ever after, thank you very much. She knew River wasn't much of a talker, and she didn't mind. Except, for some reason, he was a Chatty Chad this morning.

"You said you're having the author of the book you sold me sign at your store next month?"

"Jaliya. That's right. I'm amazed that she agreed." Tess crossed her legs, angling her body toward River's in the driver's seat. "She lives somewhere in the state."

"North Carolina? Small world."

"It really is."

"I made it to chapter twelve last night," River said. "I

like her thoughts on grief and how she worked through it by traveling around the world. Most people just climb into their little holes. I guess I disappear into the woods with stuff like that."

Tess watched him as he drove, fascinated by what he was telling her. She was also intrigued that he was talking about her favorite book as if he'd actually read it. Was he truly reading it? "Grief over losing your mom?" she asked.

River looked over. "Yeah. Losing Julie was a difficult time. I went into the woods frequently after she passed. I went in after Jared died too."

Tess should be surprised, but she wasn't. She was beginning to realize that, even though Jared had given up on River, River had never given up on him. River was a loyal kind of guy. He stuck when the going got tough or when the other person let go. "I'm glad you're enjoying the book. I honestly didn't think you would read it."

"Just a few chapters a night. I'm looking forward to going to the signing and meeting her next month."

Tess side-eyed him. "You know she's remarried, right?"

"Good for her," River said.

Tess shrugged and unwrapped her piece of banana bread. "Just checking your motivations."

"If I wanted to find a date, there are easier ways than reading a *New York Times* bestselling author's book and tracking her down at a signing," he said, navigating the truck away from Hannigan Street and the eyes of nosy town folk.

The rest of the ride was more of the same easy discussion, all the way to Morrisville. The conversation didn't let up, and when River's truck passed a sign that read WELCOME TO

MORRISVILLE, NORTH CAROLINA, Tess felt a little sad that the road trip was coming to an end. She'd enjoyed being boxed up with River. For the rest of their time here, they'd be in separate rooms somewhere, minding their own business. Good thing she'd brought a book to read.

Tess turned to look out at the scenic little town as River slowed and turned his truck into the parking lot for a quaint bed and breakfast. He cut the motor. "What's going on? Why are we here?" she asked.

River tipped his head forward. "This is where we're staying."

Tess shook her head. "A bed and breakfast? I think a hotel would be better, don't you?"

"A lady named Rebecca Hansley owns this place," River said. "According to my research, she's Ashley's mother. Might be a good source of information while also providing a roof over our heads."

Tess looked at the place again. It was a one-story log cabin that had beautiful stained glass windows with quilt-inspired designs. The place was a lot more romantic than the cheap motel setting that Tess was envisioning for her and River, where they'd get neighboring rooms with thick walls between them. There'd still be walls here though. That's all she really needed.

"Shall we?" River asked.

Tess gave him a serious look. "Okay, but I'm not sharing a room, and I'm not pretending to be your girlfriend."

He laughed a deep belly laugh. "That's a plot straight out of a romance novel. Why would we pretend to be romantic?" he asked, as if the idea were absurd.

Tess furrowed her brow. "Because we're undercover and staying at a B and B." It made perfect sense to her.

"I told you, I would never hide a relationship. I'm an open book. In fact, I plan to walk in there and tell Mrs. Rebecca Hansley exactly why I'm here."

Tess blinked the surprise out of her eyes. "Oh. And what reason are you giving her?"

"That I served with Ashley in the Marine Corps and I want to talk to her about another Marine we served with."

"Jared. I guess that makes sense." Tess looked at the cozy little B and B in front of them. "Okay. Let's go inside and get a room then." Her gaze quickly cut to River's. "Two rooms," she clarified. "Let's go get two rooms."

Chapter Twelve

River held the door open for Tess as she entered ahead of him. He heard her subtle intake of breath as she took in the front room. It had low lighting and lots of amber-colored glass. The aroma of an essential oil flowed through the air, something fragrant and calming. In a chair against the wall, a large orange cat stared at them with wide, bored eyes.

"Well, hello there." Tess turned back to River. "This might not bode well for staying here with Buddy."

"Is Buddy your dog?" a petite woman asked, walking into the front room to greet them. She had cropped brown hair and wore a pair of oversize glasses.

River recognized her from the website that he'd already looked at for this place. He also noted the resemblance between her and her daughter. "Yes, ma'am." He knew from the website that Buddy would be accommodated.

"I can put Nora away for houseguests with dogs. It's not a problem. Just give me a minute."

River thanked her and watched as Mrs. Hansley scooped up the large cat. The cat seemed to overflow from her arms as she held on to it. It looked at River and Tess as if it knew they were the reason it was being bothered.

A few minutes later, the woman returned to the front desk. "One room for the happy couple."

"Two," Tess said quickly. "Please."

River nodded. "Yes. Two rooms would be great."

The woman furrowed her brow. "Oh. You're not... together?" She bounced her pointer finger in the air between them.

"No." Tess shook her head quickly. "We came together, but we're not a couple. We'll need two rooms."

"Well, I'm afraid this is a very small bed and breakfast. I have only one room to host one couple at a time." She looked between them. "It has a king-size bed and a sofa though. And it's spacious."

River had researched well, but he hadn't noticed that little detail, which seemed huge right now. "You don't have a guest room where I could sleep?" he asked.

Mrs. Hansley smiled politely. "The guest room is the B and B room."

Tess deflated beside him. She looked over. "We can't stay here, River."

"There's only one hotel in town, but it doesn't allow dogs," Mrs. Hansley said. "I'm afraid this is the only bed and breakfast."

Morrisville was in fact a tiny town. It was smaller than even Somerset Lake.

River looked at Tess. "I can take the couch, and you can have the bed. Will that work for you? Otherwise, I'll sleep in the truck."

"I'm not letting you and Buddy sleep in the truck," Tess said. "The couch and the bed will work. We're adults. It'll be like camping, right?"

Staying in a bed-and-breakfast room would be nothing like camping, although staying overnight with Tess might test River's survival skills for a number of reasons.

"How many nights?" the woman asked.

"Two," River said. He'd thought the night he'd spent in war conditions, waiting for daylight to strip his enemies of the cover of darkness, was the longest night of his life. Or the one that Tess and Jared had wed—*that* had been a long night.

These two nights with Tess might prove to be longer though.

River paid, went out to the truck, and retrieved Buddy and the bags. Then Mrs. Hansley led Tess and him down the hall to the one available room at the very end of the hall. It was the primary bedroom of the home, which River guessed was never meant to serve as a bed and breakfast. The bed dominated the room with its large four-poster frame that reached toward the vaulted ceiling. The couch was more of a loveseat resting below a bay window that overlooked a quaint garden outside, abloom with brightly colored flowers. Those same flowers—gladioli maybe—were cut and placed in a vase on the bedside table in the room.

"Will this work?" Mrs. Hansley asked.

River wanted to shake his head no. Sleeping outside would be more comfortable than trying to get shut-eye on a loveseat. His legs would be hanging off or he'd have to sleep curled into a fetal position. How was that going to work? He wasn't one to complain, but this promised to be a rough setup. "It should be fine," he said anyway. "What about breakfast?"

"In the dining room tomorrow morning. What time do you want to wake up?"

"Seven thirty?" River looked at Tess.

Her wide eyes told him she'd been hoping to sleep in, but he doubted he'd get any sleep at all. "Sounds good."

"Great. Well, I'll leave you two lovebirds alone." Mrs. Hansley clapped a hand over her mouth. "Sorry. Force of habit. I've never had a couple stay in this room who wasn't actually a couple." She furrowed a brow. "This is strange indeed. Can I ask what business brings you to Morrisville?"

River looked at Mrs. Hansley. "We're here to talk to your daughter."

Mrs. Hansley frowned. "Shay?"

Tess shook her head. "No."

"Miranda then?" Mrs. Hansley asked.

Tess shared a glance with River. "Not Miranda."

"Ashley?" Mrs. Hansley finally guessed.

"Yes, Ashley," River said. "I served with her in the Marine Corps. Tess and I are in town to talk to her."

Mrs. Hansley wrung her hands at her midsection. "I am so sorry. That's just like Ashley to overbook herself."

"Oh, she didn't. We don't have a meeting set up. She didn't even know we were coming to town," Tess said.

"Well, that's a relief, because she's not here," Mrs. Hansley said. "She'll be back sometime tonight, but who knows when?"

River was taking mental notes. "Do you know where she went?"

Mrs. Hansley finally thought to look skeptical. "You said you served with my daughter? That was a very long time ago. What business do you have with her now?"

Tess lifted a hand. "It's my business with her actually. She knew my husband. My late husband," Tess amended. "I just want to ask her a couple questions."

Mrs. Hansley's expression softened. "You poor thing. I'm a widow too. Ten years now. It gets easier."

"That's what I've found as well," Tess said.

River wondered if that was true. If so, why hadn't it gotten easier for him? He didn't feel any less salt in his wounds than on the day that Jared had died.

"Have you read *A Woman's Journey to Joy?*" Tess asked. "By Jaliya Cruise."

Mrs. Hansley shook her head. "No, I've never heard of that title. It's a book?"

"It is. I have a copy in my bag. I'll give it to you, if you'd like. It's about being a widow, but it's also about living beyond loss. I think you'd love it."

River smiled to himself as he listened. It wasn't enough that Tess had a bookshop full of books, she also carried them in her purse and handed them out to strangers.

Mrs. Hansley's face lit up. "Well, thank you. I'd love to read that book." She looked at River. "Ashley will probably be in tonight or tomorrow morning by breakfast. She has an event this weekend so catching her might prove spotty."

"An event?" River asked.

"You really haven't kept in touch, have you?" the B and B owner asked.

"I'm afraid not," River said.

"Well, after Ashley left the Marines, she did a complete one-eighty. She's a wedding planner now. Tonight is the rehearsal dinner, and tomorrow is the big day. My daughter has always been fascinated by love stories." Mrs. Hansley said this with a chuckle. "Do you want me to let her know you're looking for her?" Mrs. Hansley asked.

"No." River shook his head. "Maybe we'll surprise her and pop over to see her right before the rehearsal dinner."

"Oh, how nice," Mrs. Hansley said.

"Do you know where the rehearsal will be held tonight?" River asked.

"Oh yes. It's over at Dooley's Dungeon." Mrs. Hansley offered a bright smile.

"Dooley's Dungeon?" both River and Tess repeated in unison, their tones thick with disbelief.

"We're very relaxed here in Morrisville. There's a nice outdoor area for weddings. A good rehearsal dinner is beer and wings. Plus, it's tradition to ride Dooley's mechanical bull the night before your wedding. Half the time, the groom gets kicked off, but there usually aren't any serious injuries. Just that one time."

River cleared his throat. "One time?"

"Nasty concussion," Mrs. Hansley said with a sour expression. "He got his memory back eventually, but not before the honeymoon."

River shared a glance with Tess. "Sounds like a wedding to remember."

"Oh, indeed. Ashley always plans a great wedding event," Mrs. Hansley said. "Anyway, if you want to catch her early, she'll probably be down there by five thirty setting up."

"Thanks for the tip." River looked at the time on his cell phone. It was only midday. That left plenty of time to settle in here and explore the town a little bit.

∞

"What do we do now?" Tess asked once they had lugged their bags into their room. She was on the bed and River sat back on the loveseat.

"When in Rome…" he trailed off.

"Except this is Morrisville," she said. "And it's midday. We can't meet with Ashley for a few more hours."

"Why don't we take Buddy for a walk and see what we can learn?"

"About Ashley?" Tess asked.

River shrugged. "A person's hometown tells you a lot about them."

She gave him a skeptical look. "I think you just don't want to be pent up in this room alone with me all day."

"And you'd be right about that." He stood. "You don't have to come along. You can stay back and read."

Tess shook her head. "No. I'm your Watson, remember?"

River chuckled. They left the B and B and headed down Main Street on foot.

"Okay, I'm curious. What is Morrisville telling you about Ashley so far?" Tess asked thirty minutes into their exploration of the town.

"Well, this town is small, cozy. They like dogs because everyone seems to have one, and half the people here seem to be without a job because they're all out walking or dining in the middle of a weekday. So (a) they're either independently wealthy or (b) this is a town full of teachers who get the summers off."

"All good observations."

River nodded. "So a fair assumption is that Ashley must love dogs too."

"Who doesn't?" Tess asked in jest.

"And…" River tapped his chin thoughtfully as he held on to Buddy's leash. "She probably likes to eat at Delphine's Café. Which apparently has world famous cheese fries over there." He pointed at a sign in the café's window.

"Delphine's Café?" Tess searched the shops in front of her until she spotted what River was seeing. Her feet froze in place.

"What's the matter?" he asked.

"After Jared died, I was given a box of his belongings that were taken from his car." Tess reached into her bag. She'd brought a few of the items with her on a hunch that she might figure out what they meant while she was here. She pulled out a matchbook and showed it to River. "It's from Delphine's Café. I didn't know where it came from."

River took the matchbook and looked at it. "It's definitely from this place." He handed it back. "We should sit down and have some of Delphine's famous fries. What do you say?"

Tess dropped the matchbook back into her purse. "I feel like I'm retracing Jared's last steps before he died."

"We can always stop. Let secrets lie," River said. "If there are any secrets."

She side-eyed him. "You mean *I* can stop. I have a feeling that you wouldn't."

River didn't argue that point. "Fries then?"

"Yes. I'd love some. As research."

"You read my mind, Watson."

They stepped inside the little café and sat down at a small table with a pale blue cloth draped over it. When the waitress stepped over to them, River asked her if Delphine was working today.

The young woman shook her head. "She's not in yet. She goes to the market to get fresh flowers before the dinner crowd that'll come in this evening. She'll be here any minute, I'm sure."

"Great. We'd love to speak to her when she arrives. If that's okay," River said.

The waitress nodded politely. "Of course. I'll let her know. Would you like something to eat while you wait?"

"How about one order of cheesy fries for me and my friend to share?" River asked.

"Coming right up."

Sharing a ride. Sharing fries. And tonight they'd be sharing a room. This was a man Tess had once loathed. She wouldn't have shared anything with him. It felt like she'd entered some alternate universe where having food with an old enemy was completely normal.

A few minutes later, the waitress set an order of fries in front of them. "Enjoy."

River and Tess reached at the same time and momentarily played tug-of-war with a cheesy fry that they'd both picked up.

He looked up and let it go. "You can have it."

"I can see why Delphine is famous for them," Tess said, after biting into it.

"People can be famous in a good way or a bad one."

Tess eyed River. "Her cheese fries are delicious. She's famous in a good way." Tess's gaze lowered to River's scar as she popped the fry into her mouth. She didn't mean to. Her eyes just seemed to gravitate to the smooth pink skin below his right eye. When she looked back up, he was watching her.

"I guess I'm famous in a less than positive way," he said, gesturing at his face. "People are afraid to ask me what happened."

Tess looked down at the table. "I'm sorry if I made you uncomfortable."

"You didn't. I don't mind talking about it, actually."

Tess looked at him again. If it was her scar, she'd mind. She probably would have had cosmetic surgery to soften its appearance by now. Maybe that made her shallow or superficial, but it was an impressive scar. It wasn't ugly. In some ways, it was beautiful. "How did you get it?" She imagined that he got it while in the military, doing something noble and heroic.

River reached for another fry. "I got it from a bobcat attack. Saving my dog."

Tess paused with her fry midway to her mouth. "You risked your life for your dog?"

River looked at her strangely now, as if the answer to that question was obvious. "Buddy would have risked his life for me. He's family. Maybe the closest thing I have to a brother."

"Your dog?" Tess tried to keep her tone of voice normal, because she could tell that River was being serious. She'd heard of people considering their dogs to be like children but not like brothers.

"I grew up as an only child. And I begged Julie and Douglass to get me a dog for a long time, but they wouldn't. Then when I joined the military, I didn't have a dog for a long time because I was on the go too much. Buddy is my first dog. He's loyal to me, and I'm loyal to him."

"Loyalty seems to mean a lot to you," Tess said.

"Good observation, Watson."

A tall, thin woman with sandy blond hair stepped up to their table. "Hello," she said in a thick French accent. "I'm Delphine. Did you want to see me?"

River looked at her. "Yes. Hi, there." He offered his hand to the woman to shake. "I'm River." He gestured at Tess. "This is Tess. We had just a couple questions we were hoping to ask you, if that's okay."

Delphine pulled out a chair to sit at their table. "Yes, of course." She looked between them expectantly. "What can I help you with?"

"We're in town to talk with a friend of mine. Her name is Ashley Hansley. Do you know her?"

"Yes, of course I do. Ashley planned the party for my parents' fiftieth wedding anniversary. It was beautiful."

"That's wonderful. She and I served in the Corps together once upon a time," River said.

"I had no idea she was a veteran," Delphine told them. "She's a woman of many talents. She comes in here frequently."

"Does she come in alone or with someone?" River asked.

Delphine frowned. "She's usually alone. Sometimes she comes in with one of her sisters."

River flashed a picture of Jared. "What about this man? Have you ever seen him in here before?"

Delphine squinted at the picture. She lowered the glasses from the crown of her head and placed them over her eyes to get a better look. "Yes. He used to come in with Ashley. It's been quite some time since he's been here though."

River swallowed. "When he and Ashley came together, what was your impression of them? Friends? More?"

Tess flashed River a warning look.

"Friendly for sure." Delphine smiled. "I always wondered what they were to each other, but I didn't want to come off as nosy. He was very nice."

"You said he used to come in? More than one time?" River asked.

Delphine nodded definitively. "Several times over a period of months."

River looked at Tess. There was an emptiness in her gaze. He wanted to slide in next to her and put his arm around her. He wanted to shield her from whatever they would learn this weekend.

"Thank you for answering our questions," River told Delphine. "You've been very helpful."

She pushed back from the table and stood. "You're very welcome. Tell Ashley I said hello."

"We will," River promised. He waited until Delphine was gone before looking at Tess. "Are you okay?"

She shook her head as her eyes filled with tears. "Not really."

"What can I do for you?"

She rolled her lips together. "Just take me back to the B and B. I need some time to decompress before we meet this Ashley woman. Otherwise, I might be tempted to get into a girl fight."

"Let's try to avoid a girl fight at a place called Dooley's Dungeon." River pushed back from the table. He stood and held out a hand to Tess. "Back to the B and B we go. Maybe Mrs. Hansley can prepare you a cup of hot tea."

Tess nodded and took his hand. Once she was standing, she let go. River wished he could keep holding her hand.

She was a strong woman, but the revelations of this weekend might be enough to break her.

Tess had spent the last hour lying on the bed and pretending to read. River was sitting at the small desk in the room with his laptop open. He'd been quiet since they'd returned from Delphine's Café. Now they were passing time until they could go to Dooley's Dungeon to meet with Ashley.

Tess closed her book and sat up, her legs crossed in front of her. "I can't focus. I'm so nervous about tonight. This is it. I'm going to find out what this woman was to my husband." Tess heard her voice shake, and tears rushed to her eyes. "I'm glad I have a friend by my side."

"A friend, huh? I kind of thought you were just using me."

Tess tilted her head to the side. "I was. But I've actually started to like your company."

River offered a steady gaze across the room. "Are you sure you want to be friends with me? Because I take the business of friendship seriously." He pointed to the scar below his eye.

"What you're saying is that you'd fight a bobcat for me?" she asked, teasing him.

"If I had to, yes."

"You know what? I think I could use a friend like you," she said.

River stood and walked over to her, reaching out his hand for her to shake. Her breath caught as she took his hand for the second time today. "Whatever happens tonight, I'll be there beside you."

"I mean, what could possibly go wrong at a place called Dooley's Dungeon?"

River grinned. "Who gets married in a dungeon anyway?"

"And what kind of wedding planner sets that up?" Tess asked, spirits already lifting.

"I guess we're about to find out." River glanced at the time on his phone. "I just need to save what I was working on and change clothes."

Tess glanced at his laptop. "What were you working on anyway?"

He gave her a hesitant look. "Personal stuff."

"Sometimes focusing on someone else's problems helps," she said, her tone of voice rising with a hopeful note.

"Ah. Is that why Reva Dawson is in everyone's business in Somerset?"

Tess laughed. "Maybe so."

River seemed to consider whether he wanted to disclose his secrets to her. "In my twenties, I located my birth mother. I was too late in finding her though. She was already deceased."

"Oh, River. I'm so sorry," Tess whispered.

He nodded. "I don't know anything about my birth father. I'm thinking about trying to locate him."

Tess blinked. "Wow. That's huge."

"Yeah. I've helped a woman in town find her birth family recently, and I don't know, I guess I'm back to wondering who might be out there for me. When Douglass was in the hospital last week, he brought up the idea too. He doesn't want me to be all alone when he dies."

Tess gasped. "I thought you said he was doing better."

"He is. He'll live to be a hundred."

Tess tilted her head as she looked at him. "Well, when you find your birth family, I'll be by your side to fight off the bobcats. Because we're kind of becoming friends now, Sherlock."

"Thanks. I appreciate that, Watson."

She cast him a playful grin. "I guess I'll freshen up and change clothes. How does one dress to attend an event in a dungeon?"

Chapter Thirteen

River followed the GPS on his phone as it relayed directions to the venue. The place pretty much looked exactly how he imagined it would. It was a one-story brick building with darkened windows and bars on the outside. The place could have passed for an old jailhouse. It had a huge sign out front with a painted dragon breathing fire and the words DOOLEY'S DUNGEON.

"So romantic," Tess muttered sarcastically from the passenger seat.

River chuckled. "To each their own. Who knows? Maybe this is where the bride and groom met, in which case, it's very romantic."

"I met Jared in high school, and we didn't marry at the campus there. Although that would have been more romantic than a dungeon."

River pushed his driver's side door open. "Romance is subjective." He walked around, fully prepared to open Tess's door for her, but she was already out by the time he reached the other side of the truck. She looked nervous. "Relax. We'll just say hello and ask Ashley for a good time to sit down and talk to her tomorrow. That's it."

Tess nodded. "Okay. What if she wants to talk now though?"

"She won't. She'll be focused on her job, which is making sure the bride- and groom-to-be are happy."

"Right. You're right." Tess blew out an extended breath.

"Then you and I will head back out to this truck, and we'll grab something to eat somewhere."

"Okay. Sounds like a plan."

"Good." He led her toward Dooley's Dungeon. She was right. It didn't sound like a romantic place for a wedding at all, not that he was an expert. He was surprised that Ashley had gone into wedding planning as her post–Marine Corps career. It was an interesting choice for a single woman who'd slept with a man just days before his wedding to someone else. River wasn't clear if Ashley had known Jared was engaged at that time though. Maybe she hadn't.

He opened the entrance door for Tess, and she gave him a skeptical look before stepping inside.

"I know you're trying to be a gentleman, but I think the polite thing to do when it comes to dungeons is to step in ahead of the lady. Just in case there's actually a fire-breathing dragon in there."

River chuckled and then dutifully stepped in ahead of her, holding the door open from behind him. Tess walked in, and he let the door swing closed. It was dark, living up to its name, and the place smelled of beer and smoke. Not the usual scent a bride would want her gown to take on.

A balding man with a long black beard looked up from where he was shining glasses behind the bar. "You two need help?" he asked in a gruff voice.

River headed in the man's direction. "Yes, we're looking for Ashley Hansley. Her mother at the bed and breakfast where we're staying told us we'd find Ashley here ahead of the event she's planning."

The man's hard gaze bounced between River and Tess. "Are you friends of Ash's?"

"I served with her in the Marines," River said.

The man frowned and then called behind him. "Hey, Ash. There's two people here to see you." He turned back to River and Tess, his gaze clearly relaying that he didn't welcome strangers easily. This may be a small town, but it wasn't Somerset Lake, where everyone, even strangers, were greeted with handshakes or hugs.

A second later, Ashley appeared in the doorway where the man had called back. She walked in a hurried pace but skidded to a quick stop when she saw River.

"River Harrison? What are you doing here?" A friendly smile flickered on her lips.

"Hey, Ashley. I ran into Joey Mancuso last week. He mentioned that you lived in Morrisville now."

Ashley furrowed her brow. "So you came to my hometown just to catch up?"

"Not exactly," River said.

The man behind the bar cleared his throat. "Do you want me to ask these people to leave?" Judging by the sound of his voice, that's what he was voting for.

Ashley's gaze moved to Tess now and recognition seemed to flicker over her serious expression. "No. They can stay," she finally said, looking at River again. She gestured for them to follow her. "Let's talk outside."

Tess and River walked out into a small courtyard.

"I'm afraid I can't talk long. I'm working tonight," Ashley explained. Her tone was less friendly than it'd been before she'd recognized Tess.

River held up his hands. "Your mom told us."

"My mom?" Ashley crossed her arms over her chest.

"We're staying at the B and B," River told her.

Ashley grew visibly tense as she looked between them. "What is this about, River?"

Directness was key in any relationship. River had always believed that. "I want to talk to you about Jared Lane."

Ashley's lips parted. She seemed to take a breath before responding. "Jared is dead, as I'm sure you know. He died in a car accident three years ago."

"I know," River said quietly. "I want to talk to you about the time leading up to his accident, which happened in Morrisville. I'm sure you're aware."

Ashley's eyes widened. She wasn't looking at Tess, and River wondered if her avoidance was out of guilt or jealousy. "Not now, okay? I'll find you at the bed and breakfast tomorrow before the ceremony."

"Okay. Sure. We'll leave now and talk tomorrow."

Ashley folded her arms over her chest as she looked around the courtyard. "I'll meet you for breakfast."

"Sounds good." River gestured for Tess to follow him. They headed back inside, where other people in matching black leather and tees had started to arrive. Dooley's Dungeon appeared to be a biker's hotspot.

River waved at Dooley as they walked by. Dooley did not wave back.

"The polite thing to do in this situation is to let the lady leave first," Tess whispered, leaning in close.

River dutifully held the door for her. "After you," he said, letting Tess walk through. He followed behind. The sound of motorcycles revving grew louder as they stepped into the sudden brightness outside. It was a sharp contrast to the cave they'd just exited. River's senses heightened with the light and the sound of grinding motorcycle engines. He instinctively pulled Tess back to his side, assessing the parking lot, when a bike buzzed off the main road, barely slowing as it peeled in. A woman with long black hair and dressed in head-to-toe leather walked directly in the path of the motorcycle as she headed toward the door.

River let go of Tess and ran at the woman, swiping her out of the motorcycle's path and tossing her to the ground with force. River fell to the ground as well.

"Ow!" the woman cried out as he tumbled on top of her.

River lifted his head to look at her. "Are you okay?"

The woman was visibly trembling. She wasn't looking at him though. Instead, she was looking past him. River turned and looked up to where several bikers were standing and watching them.

"I, uh…" How was he going to explain knocking this woman to the ground? "I…"

"This man just saved my life!" the woman shrieked. "Can you believe this?" She pushed River off her and sat up. "I can't believe I almost died the night before my wedding." Mascara-stained tears streamed down her cheeks. "This man came out of nowhere and saved my life. He's my angel!"

River looked at her and then ran his gaze around the group

of bikers. Then he looked past them to Tess, who was still standing in the same spot, watching it all from a distance.

One of the bikers reached out a hand to River and helped him stand. "I'm marrying this woman tomorrow. I guess I could have been planning her funeral." He pulled River into a tight hug and then stepped back and looked River in the eyes, something warm there in the depths of his irises. "I don't even know my hero's name."

"River Harrison."

"The idiot who almost ran over my bride was supposed to be my best man. I'm firing him though. River Harrison, will you take his place by my side tomorrow?"

River hedged. The last time he'd been asked to be someone's best man, it hadn't worked out so well. "I don't even know your name," River said, searching for an excuse to politely decline.

"Deacon Malcoy. My sweetie here is Val Price."

River looked at the still-trembling bride. He didn't have a good excuse and perhaps he'd learn a little more about Ashley if he stuck around and attended the ceremony. "Sure. I'd be honored."

"Great." Deacon gave River an assessing gaze. "I think I have some leather pants that should fit you just right."

Later that evening, Tess came out of the bathroom, where she'd washed her face and changed into a pair of silk pajamas. She was waiting until the lights went out to put on her satin sleep cap. It kept the moisture in her curls while she slept, but in Tess's opinion, it wasn't the most attractive thing to be seen in. Not that she wanted to be attractive for River. She definitely didn't.

Tess passed River on the loveseat without looking in his direction or saying a word and headed toward the bed, where she would sleep comfortably tonight. She was tempted to feel guilty about that because River's legs didn't even fit on the loveseat and he would probably sleep miserably, but right now she was having a small temper tantrum and she was well aware of it.

"You don't have to go to the wedding tomorrow, okay?" he said once she turned the lamp off on the bedside table, making the room dark. "I'll tell them you don't feel well."

"Then I'll look rude, and they'll know that I'm probably lying." Tess blew out a huge sigh. "I'll go. I don't want to miss my chance to see you in leather pants anyway."

"You're sure?"

"Yeah. I'm just feeling nervous about everything. I want to know why Jared was in this town. There's nothing here except a biker's bar and Delphine's famous French fries. There's also the fact that I'm just not a huge fan of weddings."

"No thanks to me," River said quietly. "Did I really mess yours up so badly?"

She let out a humorless laugh. "Yes. You made a scene and left me thinking Jared's best friend thought I wasn't good enough for him."

River was quiet for a moment. "I never thought that for one second. If I had known that's what you thought…"

Tess shrugged, even though the room was dark and River probably couldn't see her. "No one ever thought anything

150

negative about Jared. Not that I was aware of, at least. Jared was Mr. Perfect. Perfect son. Perfect son-in-law. Perfect husband. I had no reason to think your beef was with him."

"No one is without fault, Tess," River said.

Tess knew that, of course. But Jared had seemed pretty close. Now that the room was dark, she pulled her sleep cap over her head, tucking her curls inside. Then she leaned up on her elbows and looked at River's shadowed figure on the loveseat, where his legs hung off in the air. "Heroes shouldn't have to sleep on an uncomfortable loveseat all night. This is a king-size bed. You can share it with me if you want." She watched his dark silhouette look up at her.

"What?" he asked.

"It'll be fine. As long as you stay on your side."

More silence stretched across the room. She was beginning to think his answer was no. Then he asked, "Are you sure?"

"We're both adults. I'm sure that I trust you. The hero type isn't really the type to take advantage of a woman."

"I would never," he said quickly.

She didn't doubt that. River was the very epitome of honor and loyalty. "Come on, before I change my mind."

"No, that's not how it works. If you're going to change your mind, go ahead and do it before I come over. I don't want to do anything that you're not comfortable with."

Tess groaned. "You're kind of annoying, you know that?"

She heard his low laugh. It moved closer as he got up and walked closer to the bed. Then she noticed his dark shadow standing on the other side of the mattress. He stood there as if waiting for her to send him right back to the loveseat.

"I'm not changing my mind, Sherlock."

"Okay." He slowly peeled back the corner of his side of the covers, and he got on the mattress. She felt the weight of his body shifting around. She was wide awake now, not at all tired, with a man six inches away from her in the dark. How long had it been since she'd been this close to a man?

Three years. And if she allowed her memory to be accurate, the years before Jared's death were as platonic as tonight promised to be. Jared had often claimed to be tired when he'd climbed into bed beside her. He would roll over to kiss her cheek, but his touch hadn't been like that of a lover. She'd assumed that's what happened after being married for a while. The flames died. The fire dulled to embers. They both had jobs and daily stressors. It didn't mean they were less in love. Right?

"Tess?"

"Hmm?" Her voice came out in a nervous squeak.

"You're sure this is okay?" River asked. "It sounds like you've stopped breathing over there. Do I need to perform CPR?"

Reflexively, the breath whooshed out of her. She did not need River to come closer or give her mouth-to-mouth. "No. That's okay…It's just, I'm not a woman who gets into bed with a man I barely know. I mean, I know we're not jumping into bed together, but this is more intimate than I'm used to. I wouldn't normally be in bed at this point in our relationship. Not that we're in a relationship." Yeah, she was nervous.

"I'll get up," River said, starting to rise from the mattress.

Tess reached out her arm across the bed and stopped him. Now they weren't only lying in the same bed together, she was touching him too. She slowly slid her arm back. "Let's just talk for a while."

"Pillow talk?" he asked, a touch of amusement evident in his voice.

"It'll help me sleep." She rolled onto her side and stared at the window, where slivers of light slanted through the blinds. "Tell me something that no one else knows about you."

"Wow. You want secrets."

"It doesn't have to be deep or dark," she said.

"Okay." River didn't say anything for a long moment.

She watched and listened to him breathing on the other side of the bed as she tried to relax. Then he began to talk in a quiet voice.

"It was a dark and stormy night," he began.

"I want a real story," Tess objected.

"This one is real. Just listen, okay?"

"Okay."

He began again. "It was a dark and stormy night. I had come home for the holidays, and it turned out my best friend in the Marines called it home too."

Tess realized he was talking about Jared.

"We hadn't gone to the same school or anything like that. My parents moved after I graduated high school. It was just a few miles from where I grew up, but it crossed the town line into Somerset Lake. The fact that my new buddy lived there too felt like fate handing me something great. We drove home together. He dropped me off at Julie and Douglass's place and told me he'd pick me up later to introduce me to his local friends later that weekend."

River paused, seeming to take a breath. "I took Douglass's truck out that night to explore the town on my own. Julie told me to stay in because the weather was a mess, but I promised

I wouldn't be gone long. I just wanted to maybe walk along the lake. I parked, got out, and did just that. I've always loved a good storm."

"Me too," Tess said. In fact, walking along the lake just before a storm was something she liked to do. Sometimes she got caught in it, but she never minded.

River rolled his body toward hers. "I met this girl on my walk that night. She was the most beautiful girl I'd ever seen. I wasn't even going to talk to her because she was that pretty. No way she'd even look at a guy like me. But as I got closer, I realized you were upset. So I stopped walking and asked if you were okay."

"I remember," Tess whispered, tears pricking behind her eyes. She remembered that night and meeting River by the lake. She was waiting for Jared, who was supposed to have met her there a half hour earlier. He hadn't shown though. He'd left her waiting, not for the first time. "I felt so silly for crying that I told you I lost a ring. I just made it up. I said it fell off during my walk, and I didn't know where it was."

"You made that up?" River asked.

Tess laughed softly. "I thought you were an investigator. I wasn't crying over a silly ring."

"Hmm. Well, I guess that's why we never found it."

Silence settled between them.

"Why did you tell me that story?" Tess asked.

"You asked me to talk to you. That's the first thing I thought of. It's the night we first met."

"Jared was supposed to meet me that night. He didn't show up. That's why I was really crying," she said. "Did you know that?"

"If I did, I wouldn't have gotten you a ring the next day to replace the one you lost."

"You did that?" she asked, surprised.

"Yeah."

"Why didn't you give it to me then?"

"Because the next time I saw you, Jared introduced you as his girlfriend. You don't give another guy's girl a ring."

"I'm sorry that I lied to you."

"Sorry he wasn't there that night."

"I'm glad you were though," she whispered. A thought came to her mind that surprised her. "I can't believe you bought me a ring. That's sweet, River."

He cleared his throat. "Yeah, well, I felt bad that I couldn't find the one you lost."

"You have such a hero complex," she teased in the darkness. "Do you still have the ring?" she asked.

"Somewhere, I think."

"You never gave it to anyone else?"

"No. It was meant for you," he said quietly. "It was your ring."

Tess found River to be such an interesting guy. So loyal. So devoted. So true. "I like that story."

"Except for the part where Jared didn't show up. Did you find out where he was?" River asked.

"He said his new friend needed help with something and that time got away from him. He forgot to show up for me."

Silence swam once more between them.

"I didn't realize at the time, of course, that I had spent the night with his new friend walking around the lake," she said. "And when I did, I didn't really feel like I could call Jared out on his lie because, well, then I'd have to explain why I was with you."

"But we didn't do anything wrong."

"Maybe not. But if you feel the need to hide something, you're doing something slightly south of right, aren't you?" She was asking for herself and for Jared. What was Jared hiding that night? Who was he really with? Why hadn't she pressed him harder for answers back then? She still didn't want to believe Jared had been cheating on her, but she couldn't stop the doubts from coming.

"I never told Jared that I met you at the lake before he introduced us. That ring felt like it was burning a hole in my pocket the night he took me to Sunset Over Somerset." Sunset Over Somerset was something that happened every Friday down at the town green during the summer season. There was live music, and people brought picnic blankets and packed their own food to enjoy conversation with town folk. "That was the first crack in our friendship, I guess."

"So I came between you two?" Tess asked, talking about River and Jared.

River was quiet again. He got that way a lot. He wasn't one to answer quickly when the question was important. "I would say that Jared came between you and me."

Chapter Fourteen

How does one go to sleep after confessing their feelings for a woman?

River rolled onto his other side and pretended, but he didn't sleep a wink until sunlight streamed into the room through the open curtains. He could hear the rattle of pots and pans down the hall and knew that Mrs. Hansley was preparing the gourmet meal she'd promised them. The one that Ashley would also be attending this morning.

River blinked a few times to restore moisture to his eyes. He'd kept them shut, and he'd rested, but his mind had been too wired to drift off. What was he thinking telling Tess in no uncertain words that he had feelings for her? It was the whole darkness thing that had gotten to him. It made the situation feel dreamlike and unreal, like his words weren't going to be heard or understood or remembered.

Tess shifted around beneath the covers and rolled toward him, watching him. Oh yeah, judging by the look in her eyes, she remembered what he'd said last night.

"Hi," he said.

"Good morning. How'd you sleep?" she asked in a sleep-coated voice.

"I, uh…"

"Me too," she said, not waiting for him to offer up a white lie, which he wasn't great at anyway.

"Sorry. I guess that's my fault," River said.

She smiled. "I never sleep well in a new place, even one as nice as this. At least we'll get a delicious breakfast in just a little bit."

"Might be hard for me to fit into a pair of tight leather pants after eating a huge meal," River quipped, making Tess laugh. That eased the tension that rolled between them.

"Thank goodness I don't have to wear leather. I get to wear a flowy sundress."

"Lucky you." River watched her from across the bed.

"I'm sure you could also wear a sundress if you wanted." She winked and then got up, sitting with her back to him. "I'm nervous about meeting with Ashley this morning," she said, all business.

"I'll be there with you the entire time." River sat up and let his legs hang off the other side of the bed. Buddy jogged over and pressed his nose into River's palm. "Yeah, Buddy. I'll take you out in a minute." He'd slept in his clothes last night, for Tess's sake, so all he needed to do was slip his shoes on and head down the hall. "Ashley will fill in the gaps on our mystery today, and then we'll know the truth." He stood and gestured for Buddy to follow. "I'll be right back. I need to take this fella out to do his business."

"And I need to freshen up and shower before breakfast."

River didn't want to be in the room one door away from Tess showering, so maybe he and Buddy would take an extended walk around the premises.

As if reading his mind, Tess said, "I'll be quick so you can have your turn. Give me ten minutes?"

"You got it." He attached Buddy's leash and headed out. He used the entire ten minutes walking around the garden and mentally kicking himself over what he'd told Tess in the night.

I would say that Jared came between you and me.

It had been dark, but Tess's eyes had gone wide. He must look like some kind of fool. Or a stalker. An idiot at the very least.

He sat down on a cement bench in the garden and checked his cell phone for messages. He had an email waiting for him from Mayor Gil Ryan. He clicked on it and read. Gil wanted to set up a meeting about a potential job as soon as possible. River tapped out a reply that he'd be back in town by Sunday and would reach out to set up a time. Then he scrolled through his timeline on social media while giving Tess enough time and space to shower in private.

The first ad that popped up in his Facebook feed was 23andMe. He'd used the company a couple of times recently to help clients, including Ella Peters, locate relatives. Maybe he'd bite the bullet when he got back to Somerset Lake and do a search with his own DNA. Sending off his sample didn't mean he had to connect with whoever showed up as a match for his bloodline.

River kept scrolling on his timeline and then headed through the back entrance of the B and B. The aromas of food were thick in the air now.

"Breakfast is almost prepared," Mrs. Hansley called to him.

"We'll be out in just a few minutes." He hurried down

the hall toward his and Tess's room. All he needed was a quick shower. He opened the door and closed it behind him, making long strides toward his packed bags and running right into Tess.

She let out a small squeak and nearly dropped the towel she was clutching to herself. River cleared his throat, realizing how close he'd been to accidentally seeing more of Tess than he ever should.

He whirled to face the wall, putting his back to her. "I'm sorry. I didn't realize you would be out here, uh, without, uh…"

"I accidentally left my fresh clothes in the room," she explained. "But I'm not naked. I have underclothes on."

River shook his head. "Stop talking, Tess." Because he didn't need any mental images.

She laughed behind him, the sound musical in a way. "I'll just grab my clothes for the day, get dressed, and then the shower will be all yours."

"Thanks. Mrs. Hansley told me that breakfast is ready. We need to hurry."

"I won't take long." That was good, for the sake of a warm breakfast and for River's sanity.

Tess could barely taste the food even though she was certain it was probably the best she had ever put into her mouth.

Ashley was seated across from her and River. "You could have just called me to ask your questions, instead of showing up at one of my jobs," Ashley told River, her tone thick with defensiveness. She still wouldn't look at Tess. "I would have told you what you wanted to know."

"Okay." River reached for his mug of coffee. "Why was Jared in Morrisville? Was it to see you?"

Ashley's gaze flicked toward Tess and then she looked down at her plate. "Yes," she finally said. "But it was completely innocent. I asked Jared to come here as a favor to me. I had just started my wedding planning business, and I was working on a wedding for a couple who was worried about security. I knew Jared worked in security, and I thought he might be able to help out without running up the total cost of the wedding."

Tess blinked and felt herself exhale. "That's it?" she blurted out.

Ashley looked at her. "What else were you expecting me to tell you?" Her eyebrows dove toward her hazel-colored eyes.

Tess shook her head, looking for the right response. She'd been adamant that Jared was innocent, but on some level, she had still been expecting bad news. After hearing Delphine's story about Jared and Ashley appearing close, her confidence in Jared had begun to waver.

"Jared owed me a favor from our time in the service. I called him, and he was happy to come work the wedding for me." Ashley shrugged as if it were no big deal.

"Why wouldn't he tell Tess what he was doing then?" River asked. He placed his mug of coffee down on the table and reached for his fork. "That's not something you hide from your spouse."

Ashley shrugged and shook her head. "How should I know? Maybe he didn't want his wife to jump to conclusions like his best friend did." She cocked her head to one side and lifted a brow.

River seemed to consider that answer. "So Jared worked security for this wedding you were planning and then he left? And on his way out of town, he got into an accident?"

Ashley looked down at her plate again. "Look, I feel bad about that. Horrible." She looked at Tess now. "I am so sorry for your loss. I feel like what happened to Jared is in some way my fault."

"Then why didn't you reach out to Tess?" River asked, gruffly.

Tess looked over at him. He almost looked irritated at Ashley. Did he think Ashley was lying? Because her story made complete sense to Tess. "Cut her a break, River," Tess said quietly.

Either River didn't hear her or he was ignoring her.

"I guess I didn't reach out because I felt guilty. Jared was here because of me. Maybe if he hadn't come here, on my request, he would still be alive." Ashley's eyes grew shiny as she looked between River and Tess.

Tess reached out and touched the woman's hand. "It's not your fault, Ashley," she said gently. "I'm just glad to finally know why my husband was here in Morrisville. I've always wondered and now I have the answers I needed."

"I'm sorry I didn't contact you," Ashley said.

Relief poured through Tess. Jared had been faithful. She regretted that she'd ever doubted him. She picked up her fork and started to stab at her eggs, suddenly starving. From her peripheral vision, she saw River poking at his food.

"Wedding planning is an interesting choice," he finally said. "What made you choose this field, Ashley?" he asked.

Ashley reached for her glass of juice. "I guess I've always loved weddings. I don't really think I'll ever have one of my own, so I thought it would be nice to organize them for other happy couples."

"Why wouldn't you believe you'd have a wedding yourself?" River asked.

Tess could feel that he was doubting Ashley. He was still trying to figure out the answers to questions that Ashley had already explained. He was still trying to prove Jared's guilt.

"It's just not in the cards for me," Ashley said quietly. She kept her head low as she looked at her food.

"Well, I think it's a great profession," Tess said. "Running your own business is a huge job."

"You own a bookstore, right?" Ashley looked up.

Tess hesitated before answering. How had Ashley known that? Tess hadn't owned the bookstore when Jared was alive. Her aunt Sheila hadn't given it to her until afterward. "That's correct."

"Mom told me you gave her a book," Ashley explained.

"Oh. Yes. It's one of my favorites."

"Following your passion is admirable. To answer your question, I guess that's why I plan weddings," Ashley told River.

He chewed and swallowed the bite of food in his mouth. "Because you love weddings, but you don't believe you'll ever have one of your own," he repeated.

Ashley looked down at her plate again. Tess wondered if Ashley had been in love once. If that was why she thought her chance of marriage had passed. Tess felt bad for the young woman if that was true. Just as long as the man Ashley had once loved wasn't Jared.

Tess slipped on the yellow sundress she'd packed in her suitcase for today. Thankfully, it could be casual or dressed up enough for a wedding. At least one where the groom and groomsmen were wearing leather pants. She stepped out of the bathroom and posed in front of River, who was sitting on the bed. "How do I look?"

He looked up, his serious expression melting into something softer. "Beautiful as always."

She smiled back at him. "Are you still thinking about Ashley?"

He didn't answer, which meant that he was.

"She gave a perfectly reasonable explanation. It made sense."

"You think so?" River asked.

Tess crossed her arms. "You know what I think? I think you're upset that the answer wasn't something more nefarious. I think you were hoping Jared had cheated on me so that you could be off the hook for busting in on our wedding."

River gave her a long look. "I want to believe Ashley. I wish I did, but my gut says she's not telling the truth."

"Maybe your gut is just jealous," Tess blurted. Why couldn't River just let this go? She'd felt nothing but relief since breakfast with Ashley. If not for River's mood, she'd be walking on air right now. Her husband hadn't been a cheater. He had been the good and loyal guy she'd always assumed he was. She hadn't been played for a fool.

"Jealous of what?" River looked up at her.

"Well, last night, you told me something. You said that I came between you and Jared. What you meant was your feelings came between you two. One might conclude you were jealous of him."

River frowned. "Yeah, of course I was. But I would never do anything to hurt him. To hurt you."

"If you valued Jared's friendship so much, why are you intent on believing the worst about him? Am I missing something? Is there something you know that you're not telling me? Because you promised that I would know everything that you did. You gave me your word."

River looked away for a moment, and then back at her. He seemed to take a breath and then he spoke. "Do you want the truth? Because there's no going back once you know."

Tess held out her arms. "Yes. Please. If you have something to say, River, just say it already."

"Okay. Here it is. Don't say I didn't warn you." River cast her an apologetic look. "I walked in on Jared and Ashley three nights before your wedding."

Tess's heart dropped. "What? Walked in on what?" she asked.

River shook his head. "Kissing mostly, but some of their clothes were on the floor at their feet."

"What?" she said again. It felt like the wind had been knocked out of her chest. "No. You're lying. Why would you lie about something so horrible?"

River stood and stepped toward her. "I wouldn't. This is true, Tess. That's why I backed out of being Jared's best man. That's why I told him he was making a mistake. I wanted him to tell you the truth before you got married. He owed it to you to let you know what he'd done."

Tess shook her head and stepped back. "But I met Ashley today. She's nice. She and Jared were friends. Just friends."

"Maybe that was true after Jared married you. I don't know that it wasn't. All I know is what happened three days before your wedding."

Tess's head was spinning. She pressed her hands to both temples to make the sensation stop. "Jared wouldn't do that to me. I would have known if he was seeing someone else."

River reached for her, but she held up a hand to stop him. "I don't need your comfort. And I don't want it. You're wrong, River. Whatever you think you saw before my wedding, it was a misunderstanding. That's all."

River was silent, which was equally as frustrating as anything he might have said.

"Let's just go before we're late." Tess grabbed her purse and headed toward the bedroom door. "I really dislike weddings," she muttered to herself, loud enough for River to overhear. He also heard what she didn't say: *He* was to blame. For everything.

Chapter Fifteen

No good deed went unpunished. Of all the days to wear black leather pants, it was the hottest one of the summer.

River glanced over at Tess with the women's side of the wedding party. She'd been avoiding him since they arrived. She was upset, but he owed her the truth. He didn't believe Ashley's story at breakfast this morning. Maybe Jared had worked security for one of her weddings, but River guessed that more had happened on that trip.

"There's my best man," Deacon said, heading over. He was wearing a short-sleeved white button-down shirt, black tie, and black leather pants. He didn't seem to mind sweating off his second layer of skin out here the way River did.

"About that," River said. "A best man should be someone you've known longer than a day, don't you think? Someone you'll know for the rest of your life. I'm honored that you asked me, but I wish you'd reconsider the original person you asked to fill that role."

Deacon's expression pinched. "After he almost hit my fiancé on his bike?"

"Not on purpose," River reminded him. "Sure, the guy

was probably careless. Reckless, maybe. But he was willing to stand beside you on one of the most important days of your life. That's gotta count for something, right?" River asked.

Deacon ran a hand through his overgrown blond hair. "Yeah, I guess so. He's been a good friend since we were kids. He's had my back more times than I can remember."

"All the more reason he should have your back this time. Not me." River hoped Deacon was hearing him.

Deacon gave him an assessing look. "You're not only a hero you're also a wise man. You're right. I still want you up there with us though. You saved Val's life. You're important."

River was hoping to get out of wearing the leather pants. He had a soft pair of jeans waiting for him in his truck. "Sure. I'd be happy to."

Deacon slapped a hand along River's back, nearly knocking him forward. "All right. I'm going to see if my buddy will be my best man again. Thanks for the advice."

"Anytime."

River watched Deacon head toward his former best man. At least he'd done something right today. Repairing the relationship between a groom and best man felt like a full circle moment. Kind of. River couldn't repair what had happened with Jared, but mending this situation was some conciliation.

River's gaze stretched across the courtyard to where Tess was standing. She met his eyes and quickly looked away. Still upset. And he hadn't even told her all the things he knew. There were still the divorce papers that Jared was planning to file before his death. Finding out about that would absolutely crush Tess. River was firmly in favor of the truth, but maybe it was better to believe the lie in this case. Maybe, for Tess's sake, he could tuck that one little piece of information away and pretend he'd never met Mr. Peter Browning.

The sun was now on its descent, the wedding nuptials were exchanged, and River had a pair of jeans in the truck that he planned to change into for the reception. If they stayed. That would depend on Tess.

River walked over to where she was standing on her own. She looked lost in her thoughts. She'd appeared that way since their argument before the wedding. "We don't have to stay. We can leave now if you want."

She stared at him. "I was in the wedding party too. The bride wants pictures, and there'll be the bouquet toss. Can't miss that," she said sarcastically.

"Hmm." River leaned against the outside railing that bordered a river running through the town. It cut behind the courtyard of Dooley's Dungeon. "If my memory serves me, you caught the bouquet at Trisha and Jake's wedding on New Year's."

This brought a soft smile to Tess's face. It felt good to see it. Maybe she was warming back up to him. "By accident. I didn't even have my hands up. It was catch it or let it hit me in the face. I will be standing nowhere in the vicinity of the bouquet toss this time. Some other hopeful can have that bouquet."

"Well, if we're staying a bit, I need to peel these pants off," River said.

Tess leaned in to keep their conversation private, but it

felt intimate somehow. Something inside River longed to tug her to him. To wrap his arms around her waist. "You'll need to pose for those wedding party pictures first, I'm afraid. You don't want to disappoint the groom." She puckered her bottom lip as if she regretted what she was telling him, but he thought the opposite was true.

"I think you're enjoying that fact too much."

"Oh, I am," she agreed.

He chuckled. "Save me a dance? Once I get my jeans on."

The humor left her face, along with a little bit of color. "If I can fight the ladies off you. You're a hot commodity in those pants."

Tess had tried, but she couldn't stay mad at River. His heart was in the right place. She believed that. He honestly thought that Jared was being disloyal to her, and in a way, she guessed River was trying to protect her. That was noble, even if misplaced.

She watched him walk around the building and guessed he was probably going to his truck to get a change of clothes. It was a shame because, mad or not, she'd noticed how hot he was in those tight leather pants.

"Hi," a small voice said.

Tess looked down at a little girl with long brown hair and big blue eyes. "Well, hello there." She recognized the child as being one of the flower girls in the wedding.

"I like your dress," the girl said. She was barely audible over the music. Tess guessed the child was around three years old. She was small. Where was her mother?

"I like yours too."

The girl looked down at her dress and then back up with a wide grin. "Want to dance?" she asked.

Tess looked around again for any sign of the girl's parents. "Sure." She took the little girl's hand in hers and walked out onto the dance floor. Tess was so tall that she had to bend over in order to hold the girl's tiny hands. The girl giggled as Tess spun her around and they swayed to the fast beat of the song. "What's your name?" Tess asked.

"Mia."

"That's a beautiful name. I'm Tess. Is your mommy or daddy here?"

The girl nodded. "My mommy is. I don't have a daddy."

"Oh, I see." Sadness swelled around Tess's heart. That was one thing she was thankful for, that she and Jared hadn't had children before he died. She didn't like the thought of a child of hers growing up without a father. "Where's your mom?"

The girl looked around to show her and then pointed as Ashley stepped up.

"There you are!" Ashley said to Mia. "I've been looking for you everywhere."

"Sorry, Mommy. Meet Tess," Mia said.

Tess met Ashley's gaze. There was something frightened and apologetic at the same time there. What was she sorry for? Tess looked down at Mia, and her heart sank a notch. "Mia is your child?" she asked Ashley as dread gathered in her gut.

"She is." Ashley took Mia's hand.

A child without a father. Where was he? Tess didn't like the suspicions she felt about her late husband. Mia didn't even look like Jared. *Did she?*

Tess looked at Ashley, remembering what River had told her. Tess wanted so badly to believe he was lying, but she'd never known him to tell her something that wasn't true. She had caught Jared in a lie before though. Several, in fact. "Just tell me one thing," Tess said to Ashley. "When you were with Jared, did you know about me?"

Ashley seemed to wilt under the question. She hesitated and then shook her head. "I didn't know about you until his funeral. I am so sorry."

Tess swallowed back the flood of tears rising through her. She nodded and rolled her lips together tightly. "Let's have breakfast again tomorrow. Can we?"

Ashley hugged Mia to her side and nodded. "Sure."

River had lost track of where Tess had gone. He'd seen her dancing with a little girl and then she'd disappeared on him. He was about to go looking for her when someone tapped a glass. The room went silent and all heads turned toward the event's planner.

"It's tradition for the best man to say something," Ashley said. "But the official best man is currently too inebriated to speak, so the backup best man will have to do." She eyed River. He suspected she was getting a little payback for him showing up yesterday without warning and grilling her over breakfast. "River, will you step up here and say something for the happy couple?" Ashley asked.

He was about to respectfully decline, but the bikers went wild, clapping and cheering. River didn't really have much choice, he guessed. He started toward Ashley and the microphone. He hated public speaking. He wasn't quick-witted or fast on his feet. Hopefully, he wouldn't say anything that would ruin the couple's big day.

River cleared his throat, which came out loud in the microphone that Ashley handed him. The room was silent with everyone watching him, including Tess in that yellow dress. She'd always been a bright star in the dark from the first night he'd met her. "Hello," River finally said. "My congratulations to the bride and groom, who I only met yesterday."

There was a flutter of nervous laughter in the audience. River guessed the alcohol at the reception was helping him out.

He cleared his throat again. "Time is relative. People can know each other a long time and not really know those people they're standing next to. Before the wedding, I asked Deacon a question. You see, I'm a private investigator in my day job. That means I probe into people's lives. I asked Deacon, 'How do you know Val is the one? The only one.' Deacon's answer came quick. That's one way I know he was shooting straight with me. He looked me in the eye and said, 'Because as soon as Val walked into my life, I felt complete. And if I ever lost her, I would be broken.' That sounds like true love to me," River said, looking around the audience.

He didn't intend for his gaze to land on Tess, but it did. He didn't want to make the comparison, but he'd felt complete the night he'd met her too. There was something in her eyes that felt familiar, like he knew her. It was a strange feeling. And he had indeed felt a little bit broken when he'd realized she was Jared's girlfriend later that weekend. Somewhere deep inside, he'd known he'd found the one and missed his chance.

River turned and lifted his glass to Val and Deacon. "So here's to true love, which I'm pretty sure you two found."

Applause broke out in the dungeon. River handed the mic back to Ashley. Then he began walking toward Tess. She noticed him when he was almost to her, and her eyes widened just a touch. When he was only a couple of feet away, he held out his hand. "Can I have that dance now?"

Tess hesitated before slipping her hand into River's. It was just a dance. Everyone was doing it. She met River's gaze, and something closed in around her heart. A feeling that she'd been steadily ignoring since he'd cooked her breakfast at his house the other day. She'd convinced herself that she hated this man for years. Turns out, he was only acting in her best interest. Some part of her wished she could still find it in her to hate him because that would be easier than allowing herself to explore this feeling that was currently flooding every cell of her body as he held her close.

"That was some speech you just made, Sherlock," she said, her throat suddenly dry as she wrapped her arms around his neck. She'd never been this close to River before. "I know you were just repeating what Deacon said, but do you believe it?"

"What?"

"That there's one person out there for everyone, and that when that person is gone, they leave you broken for anyone else." She swallowed, trying to moisten her throat, but she couldn't. Her emotions left her parched. Was that why

Ashley didn't believe she'd ever find love? Because her one person, Tess's husband, was gone?

River's hold seemed to tighten until she looked up at him. "You are not broken, Tess. I don't know if Jared was the one for you. Only you know that. I do know that, if you were the one for him, he wouldn't have left you crying on Somerset Lake the first night I met you. Where was he?"

Tess didn't know where Jared was that night. He just wasn't where he'd promised he'd be. He'd broken a lot of promises, and she'd excused them all, buying his reasons. Sometimes he'd even bring her flowers to make it easier for her to overlook the times he'd let her down.

"He wouldn't have seen Ashley the week of your wedding. He wouldn't have lied to you about where he was on the weekend of his death." River held her gaze as tightly as his arms held her body.

"Why are you recapping these things, River? You're telling me I'm not broken, but these things make me feel shattered inside." She broke eye contact and lowered her head, resting her forehead against his chest and taking in a shallow breath. Then she felt River's finger lift her chin, gently tipping her face to look up at him again.

"I'm telling you these things because I can't say if Jared was the one for you. I like to think that life gives you what you deserve though, and you deserved so much better than the way he treated you."

She blinked and felt a tear slip down her cheek as they danced. "I found out that Ashley has a child. A three-year-old without a father."

River offered a barely perceptible head shake. "I didn't know."

"Her name is Mia," Tess said. "And if what you believe is true..." She shook her head, her eyes shining under the lights. "If it's true, what if Mia is Jared's child?"

River's gaze was steady. "You are one of the strongest people I've ever known, Tess. You'll get through whatever comes."

"I don't feel strong though. I feel weak and tired."

River tightened his hold on her. "You don't have to go through anything alone. I'll help you get through this."

Tess searched his eyes. He'd told her he had feelings for her once. She suspected he still did. And she couldn't deny that she felt something for him too. More than she'd felt for anyone in a long time. She couldn't do this though. Not when her heart was hurting so badly. "I think I'm done with love, River. I don't think I can ever go through any of that pain again."

River was quiet for a moment. Then he said, "Not every man would put you through that. Not every guy would break your heart, Tess. I wouldn't."

Her arms dropped from around his neck.

"I'm sorry. I shouldn't have said that." He stammered and ran a hand through his hair.

Tess looked around at the crowd. All the guests were absorbed in their own fun tonight. Then she looked at River again. She was so conflicted about her feelings for him. She was hurting, but there was also that feeling that she'd been ignoring in her chest, blooming outward. What if she just stopped ignoring this magnetic pull between them? She was already broken, after all. She could break a little more or maybe piece herself back together at the same time.

With her swirling thoughts and the DJ's blaring music, she couldn't seem to think clearly. All she knew was that River was standing before her, and he looked a little broken himself. She also knew that his hands around her had felt incredible, and she wanted to feel them on her body again. She wanted to feel something other than the sting of Jared's betrayal.

She stepped toward him and wrapped her arms around his neck. Going up on her tiptoes, she held his gaze and brushed her lips to his before returning to flat feet.

"What was that for?" River asked.

Her heart was beating so fast. "For being you."

He wrapped his arms around her waist again, holding her close. Her arms returned around his neck under the pretense of a dance as the music switched. Then both of their mouths moved toward each other, simultaneously, wordlessly, hungrily, meeting in a kiss that was much more than a simple brush of the lips. It was everything that Tess hadn't felt in such a long time. If she was honest with herself, maybe she'd never felt exactly this. This feeling was raw and magnetic. It felt inevitable. Falling for her late husband's best friend was messy. But here they were, wrapped up in a kiss and at the beginning of what promised to be a beautiful mess.

Somewhere between kisses, Tess grabbed her cell phone and snapped a picture. She wanted to remember feeling so good because she was pretty sure, once she returned to Somerset Lake and the revelations of the weekend set in, she'd be devastated.

Tess dropped her cell phone back into the tiny purse looped over her shoulder. Then River took her hand and led her outside.

"I think we can leave now," he said.

"Where do we go?" Because the idea of going back to the

B and B after kissing like that sounded crazy. It was definitely a bad idea.

River seemed to read her mind. "You can have the room. I always have camping gear in my truck. I'll camp out."

"What? No. You don't know this area. That's silly." Her thoughts were racing. "We can just set boundaries. Because I don't think it's a good idea to, you know…" She trailed off.

"Tess, I don't want to do anything that you're not ready for. The kiss was enough for me." There was something warm in his eyes.

She loved that he would say so. "We shouldn't kiss when we get back to the room. I think that should be one of the boundaries we set. Because people can get carried away."

"Agreed. We should keep all of our kissing here." His gaze fell to her lips and stayed.

Heat flared through Tess's body, scorching every single cell from her mouth all the way down to her toes.

"Any other boundaries?" he asked.

"Yeah. Maybe we shouldn't sleep in the same bed tonight," she said. "I can take the loveseat if you want."

"You're not sleeping on the loveseat, Tess," River said, his eyes staying on her mouth. "I'll camp out on the floor."

"Okay."

"Anything else?" he asked.

"Just…River?"

"Yeah?"

She sucked in a nervous breath. "Did you mean what you said in there?"

"Which part?" he asked.

"When you said you wouldn't break my heart. Because…" She didn't complete that sentence. She didn't need to.

"I know," he said. "I meant it."

The breath she was holding came out like a shaky stop on a roller-coaster ride. "Okay. One more kiss before we head back to our room." She held up a finger. "Just one."

"Then we better make it count," he said, pressing his mouth to hers and making her forget all her reservations. Everything escaped her mind except him.

Chapter Sixteen

River tossed and turned restlessly as he lay on the floor later that night. It wasn't the fact that he was on a hard, uncomfortable surface keeping him awake. He could sleep anywhere. It was knowing that Tess was a mere few feet away from him on the bed. He'd kissed her tonight, several times, and she'd kissed him back.

The kiss had reached inside his heart and revived it as efficiently as a jolt of electricity. Now he felt every beat in the darkness. He could practically hear his heart, pulsing beneath the thin sheet that was draped over him. What next? He'd had a thing for Tess since he was nineteen. She'd imprinted the standard of the perfect woman on him that night on the lake, and if there was such a thing as love at first sight, he'd fallen for her the first time he'd laid eyes on her.

The question *What next?* was on his mind. He'd promised not to break her heart, and he took promises seriously. So did he pursue a relationship with her, knowing that he'd never really been in a relationship other than those he had with the Marines, his adoptive family, and his friendship with Jared? Or did he back off before they went any further? He couldn't break her heart if she hadn't yet given it to him. And he didn't think Tess was the kind of woman who offered up her whole heart after only a couple of kisses.

"River?" Tess's voice floated in the darkness, finding him.

"Hmm?"

"Are you up?" she asked.

"Yeah. I guess you are too."

"Your thoughts are so loud, they're keeping me awake," she teased. "Are you regretting kissing me?"

"No," he said honestly. "You?"

"No. I'm more regretting the boundaries we set," she said.

He groaned into the darkness. "Well, now I'll never sleep tonight, Tess. Thanks for that."

She laughed a little too loudly. Then he heard her clap a hand over her own mouth, no doubt not wanting to wake Mrs. Hansley down the hall. "Well, just stop thinking so hard. It was just a kiss, okay? We can do it again tomorrow."

He groaned again. "Not helping, Tess."

She laughed more quietly this time. Then he heard her roll onto her side. "Good night, River."

"Good night, Tess." He listened as her breaths grew steady, and he was lulled by the sound. Closing his eyes, he drifted off as well.

The next morning, River awoke to a woman leaning over him.

"Rise and shine, beautiful," she said, grinning down at him.

River draped an arm over his face. "How are you up before me?"

"I wondered the same thing." She lowered herself to the floor next to him. "You must have slept well."

"Or just fallen asleep an hour ago." Which was more in line with the truth. He looked at Tess.

"I should have let you share the bed."

"Trust me, that wouldn't have helped."

She cracked a beautiful smile. "I can smell breakfast cooking down the hall. Ashley is coming over again."

"You okay?" he asked.

"Yeah. I'm ready to hear the truth. Hopefully she's ready to tell it."

River reached for Tess's hand and squeezed it. "Right beside you, no matter what."

"I appreciate that. You should get the first shower this morning since I got the first one yesterday," Tess offered.

"I forfeit my right to first shower. I need to take Buddy for a walk. You go." River had an undeniable urge to lean in and press his lips to hers. They'd kissed last night. What was the rule now? Could they just kiss whenever they wanted to? He did try his best to be a gentleman, so he was letting Tess set the pace and show him what she wanted, *if* she wanted anything more.

"In that case…" She got up and collected her things before heading toward the bathroom. Then she turned back to River. "Thank you, River."

"For what?" he asked.

"For being such a good friend."

Friend. That word hit River with the force of any word he'd ever been called. Was Tess backing out of what they'd started last night? Did she regret kissing him? "Of course," he said.

She stepped inside the bathroom and closed the door behind her.

River stood, slid on a pair of shoes, and took Buddy for a walk around the garden just like the day before, pondering what Tess meant by using the *friend* word. Then he met her back in the room. Thankfully, she was already dressed versus wrapped in a towel this time. She didn't greet him with a kiss, so he guessed, after she'd had time to think about last night, she had regrets. Maybe she was just using him to forget her troubles. Not that he could blame her.

"I'll be out in just a second," he told Tess, disappearing into the bathroom. He quickly showered, and then they headed to breakfast where Ashley was now waiting for them.

Their food was already on the table.

River pulled out a chair for Tess and she sat. Then he took a seat as well. "Good morning, Ashley."

Ashley tucked a strand of hair behind her ear shyly. "Morning." She looked at Tess and back to River.

"Let's try this again," River said. "And this time, why don't you give us the true story. What was Jared doing here in Morrisville on the weekend of his death?"

Ashley's face was pale. She nervously chewed at her lower lip. "He was here to see me."

Tess wanted to cry right now. The fact that she wasn't meant she was doing pretty well. Jared had told Tess that he wasn't ready to start a family just yet. She'd wanted to. She'd been ready after one year of marriage, but he hadn't. Tess had pressed the issue after one year and then two, but Jared still wasn't there. Yet here was this single mother, sitting across from Tess. Was her daughter Jared's?

Tess picked up her fork and shakily moved her food from one side of the plate to the other. She willed herself to remain calm. *No tears.*

"I am so sorry," Ashley said. "I didn't know Jared was even married. He never wore a ring when he was with me. He said he was single. I knew he worked a lot." Ashley looked down at her plate. "We served together, and we were good friends. I trusted him. I didn't have any reason to doubt what he told me was true."

"You said Jared was busy working?" River asked, pulling out his little notepad.

"With the security firm," Ashley responded. "He was trying to help me get a job where he worked too."

River jotted down notes as he bit into a biscuit. He didn't seem to have any trouble eating, unlike Tess, who felt like she might throw up if she put any food in her stomach right now.

Ashley looked at River. "The night you caught me and Jared together...that was our first time. It just happened. He called me, and he seemed upset about something. He didn't tell me what. He just invited me to come meet him in Somerset Lake, where he was staying, and it kind of just happened." Ashley shrugged. "But then afterward, he ghosted me. I didn't hear from him again until a couple years later."

Tess looked at River, nausea rolling through her. River had already told her that story. She'd wanted so badly to believe he was lying, but somewhere in her gut, she'd known he wasn't. He couldn't.

River turned back to Ashley. "What happened a couple years later?"

Ashley chewed a bite of her biscuit and swallowed. She didn't seem to be having any trouble eating either. "I was on my way to an event that I had planned, but my car broke down on the side of Evans and Blue Bonnet Street. My phone was dead, and I was worried that I'd be late for my job. Then, out of nowhere, Jared showed up. He was like some kind of hero."

Tess felt her frown deepen as her heart sank lower into the pit of her empty stomach.

"It was a fiftieth wedding anniversary party, and the couple were also renewing their vows. Jared ended up coming with me as my guest, and we stayed up all night talking and laughing. We fell hard for each other." Ashley seemed to wilt when she remembered that she was talking to Jared's wife.

"When was this?" Tess asked.

Ashley looked flustered, her cheeks a dark shade of pink. "Mia is three, so it was about four years ago." Ashley seemed to have difficulty swallowing. "My daughter was conceived that night."

Tess pressed a hand to her chest, willing her heart to keep beating. So it was true. Ashley's daughter was Jared's. Tess wanted to scream. Cry. Instead, she just sat there wordlessly and listened.

Ashley looked between River and Tess. "Think what you will about me, but I didn't know he was married. Jared kept coming to see me after that weekend. As often as he could."

Tess looked at Ashley. "You said you didn't know about me until his funeral?"

"That's when I realized that you were Jared's grieving widow." Ashley looked at Tess guiltily. "I was so overwhelmed with shame and disappointment. You were rightfully upset, and I knew I couldn't bring more pain on you. So I sat in the back pew during the service and afterward I retreated home."

"To have Jared's child?" Tess asked quietly.

Ashley nodded. "Yes."

River cleared his throat. "We need to verify paternity before we proceed. We can use a strand of hair for DNA evidence."

"Is that really necessary?" Ashley asked. "I mean, I don't intend to put any claims on what Jared had. I don't plan to meet his family or introduce Mia to them."

"Why not?" Tess was doing her best to keep her composure right now. "If Mia is Jared's... If she's his, she deserves to meet her family. And they deserve that as well," Tess said.

"I doubt they would want to become family with Jared's mistress. I'll be an outcast. No." Ashley lowered her face.

Tess reached across the table until Ashley looked up. "Maybe that would be true at first. I can't promise that it wouldn't be. But knowing where you come from and having people who love you unconditionally, family, is so worthwhile. It's what Jared would have wanted." And regardless of what Jared had done, Tess still wanted to honor him. "If you ever cared about him at all, you'd consider it."

Ashley seemed to swallow hard. "I did care about Jared, quite a lot. I'll think about it," she said.

Tess brought her hand back to her side. "Good." She pushed back from the table and stood. "I need some air."

"Want me to go with you?" River asked.

"No. You two finish talking about next steps." Tess didn't

need to hear any more about her late husband's affair. She'd thought she'd wanted all the details, but she was done. She turned and headed outside to a garden area. Just like with the taste of the gourmet food, the pleasure of the sights and smells was lost on her.

She took a couple of steps and stopped to sit on a cement bench. It was hard to take in a full breath. So much for fresh air. She suddenly felt like she might hyperventilate. Her mind was fitting together pieces of a puzzle. Ashley and Jared had had a one-night stand a couple of years before they'd met here in Morrisville. Jared would have been with Tess at that time. They would have been engaged and then newly married. How could Jared have done this to her?

Tess blinked, and a tear dripped down her cheek. She leaned forward over her knees. All this time she'd only wondered at River's reasons for barging in on her ceremony. She wanted to be angry at him, but he'd tried to tell her. It was Jared she should be livid at. And she was. But more than anything, she felt crushed.

"Hi," a small voice said.

Tess looked up. "Hi, Mia." It was difficult to hold hard feelings against a child who'd done nothing wrong. And if she believed Ashley's story, which she did, Ashley had done nothing wrong either. They were all just victims of Jared's lies and deception. Even River.

Mia stepped closer and reached for Tess's hand, a wide grin spreading through her apple cheeks. "I remember you from last night. You're one of Mommy's friends."

Friends wasn't exactly the right word. "I remember you too. You're a good dancer."

"You too," Mia said with a giggle.

Mrs. Hansley's voice filled the garden, calling her grand-child back. "Mia!"

"I have to go. Bye!" Mia said, turning and sprinting off awkwardly, the way young children did.

Tess watched, thinking about her in-laws in Somerset Lake. Jared's mother would be thrilled to have a grandchild. Heather would be an aunt. Ashley would somehow push Tess out of her place as Jared's left-behind love. Things would get complicated, and weird, after this.

Tess stood and sucked in a huge breath, her gaze connecting with River's across the garden. He was Jared's former best friend, and two nights ago he'd confessed that he'd once harbored feelings for her. Something light fluttered around in her chest despite the revelations of the morning. Things were already getting complicated and weird.

Secrets weren't easy to keep. Tess had left her car behind River's home all weekend so that no one would know she was with him. When they'd returned to Somerset Lake, she'd climbed in and shared an awkward goodbye with River.

She'd thrown the *friend* word between them earlier that morning like a heavy stone, not because she regretted the kiss—not wholly—but because she'd had a restless night as well, worried that kissing River would somehow land her in a place where her heart would once again be broken. She didn't want to go back to lonely nights, crying tear after tear. Or go through days with a forced smile and lying that everything was fine. She wasn't sure she could do that again.

And when she'd thought about it last night, she didn't think River was a relationship-type guy anyway. Maybe he was a world-class kisser who made her toes curl, but there wasn't long-lasting potential there. From what she'd seen, River didn't make a habit out of dating, and she didn't either. So what was the point?

Tess turned the key in the lock of her front door and stepped inside, hoping she could ease in without having to make conversation with Heather, but no such luck. Heather was sprawled out on the couch in the living room watching TV with a bowl of popcorn against her midsection. She grabbed the remote, pointed it at the television, and clicked PAUSE.

"There you are," she said, looking at Tess.

"No need to pause your show on my account," Tess said, still hoping to disappear into her room. She continued in that direction. "I'm actually pretty tired and just want to shower and—"

"What? I've been lying here waiting for you. I was hoping we could catch up. Almost as soon as I get to town, you take off on some business trip. You're a bookstore owner. What kind of business trip do you even go on?" Heather's question wasn't serious. She sat up and started talking again as Tess searched her brain for an answer. "Not that I minded having your whole house to myself. It was kind of fun housesitting for you. You have some majorly hot neighbors, you know?"

Tess tried to think of who Heather meant and wondered if Heather had flirted with her neighbors.

"I helped out at the bookstore too with your new employee, Lara."

"I didn't ask you to help at the bookstore, and I'm pretty sure Lara didn't need any help."

"Oh, she appreciated it. We became fast friends." Heather stood and walked over to the kitchen. "I bought some wine. Want a glass?" she asked, ignoring Tess's earlier comment that she wanted to take a shower and disappear. She hadn't actually gotten to say that's what she wanted, but it was. She wanted to disappear into a hot bath and do her best not to think about River Harrison.

"It's too early for wine, don't you think?" Tess asked, leaving her bags and following Heather into her kitchen.

"I've been living in LA. There's no such thing as too early or too late for anything there." She grabbed two glasses despite the fact that Tess hadn't agreed.

"Maybe just one glass." Tess plopped down on one of her barstools. "It seems you've made yourself at home in Somerset Lake. You must be planning to stay awhile."

Heather poured a glass for both of them. "You know, you've got it made in a way."

Tess raised her brow while simultaneously lifting her glass of wine and sipping. "Oh yes. Small-town widow. My life is golden." Not to mention that her late husband had fathered a child with his mistress. Tess took a healthier gulp.

"I'm serious. In my line of work, it's all about appearances. Nothing else matters. Sometimes I want to disappear the way you do into your bookshop."

Tess was surprised by this comment. Heather had always loved attention. Life outside of the limelight would never satisfy her. "All the conflict going on in your life right now will blow over. The bookshop is my life. Your life is in front of the camera."

Heather sipped from her wineglass. "Maybe. I still plan to have a little small-town fun while I'm here though."

"Please don't have it with any of my neighbors, okay?" Tess asked, only half in jest. "I have to live with these people."

Heather grinned. "What about..." She seemed to hesitate. "I know you're not exactly his biggest fan, but I always kind of had sparks with Jared's former best friend. You know, the whole big brother's best friend trope."

Tess sipped more of her wine, trying to place who Heather was talking about. It didn't register at first, even though Tess had been thinking of nothing but River for the last twenty-four hours. "Who?"

"River Harrison." Heather's cheeks bloomed a dark pink color. "I always thought he was so handsome, and I think we had a connection once upon a time. I never acted on it because I knew how much you hated him. But I was thinking that, since so much time has passed, maybe you'd be okay with it now."

Tess blinked. Her heart was sinking and pounding at the same time. "River? You want to do what with him exactly?"

Heather giggled. "You know? I want to talk to him and see if there are more sparks. Maybe kiss again."

"Again?" Tess's heart dropped lower. "You've kissed River before?"

"Well, it wasn't just me kissing him," she said with exagger-ated sarcasm. "A kiss takes two."

"Right. Of course. When was that?" Tess tried to sound casual. Her mind was also trying to imagine a scenario where River and Heather made a good match. They didn't. He was serious and introverted, and Heather was an extrovert to the nth degree.

"It was right before your wedding. Before he went and

messed everything up by objecting to the whole thing. We ran into each other at the tavern, and he bought me a drink. I daresay he'd had quite a few already by that time."

Tess couldn't imagine that scenario either. River liked to keep his composure. He struck her as a one-and-done type drinker. Was he drinking because he was upset about catching Jared and Ashley together?

"I dragged him out on the dance floor. He protested a little, claiming that he didn't dance, but I proved him wrong. Then we kissed."

Tess swallowed. She and River had kissed at the end of a dance just yesterday. It'd felt special, but now she wondered if maybe that was his MO. Sweep a woman off her feet with a slow dance and then kiss her.

"Are you mad?" Heather asked, concern playing in her voice. "It's been a while since he ruined your wedding."

"He didn't ruin it," Tess said. "He just put a damper on it, that's all." She shook her head. "No, I'm not upset."

"Do you still hate him?" Heather asked.

Tess looked up, meeting her sister-in-law's blue-gray eyes. Were they the same color as Mia's? "No. He's a hard man to hate."

"A secret charmer, right?" Heather nibbled at her lower lip again. "So if I run into him and sparks fly…?"

Tess wasn't sure how to answer that question. She'd already decided that she and River probably wouldn't be crossing the friends line again, so she shouldn't prevent Heather from connecting with him if that should happen, right? "I don't mind," she said quietly, bringing her glass of wine back to her lips.

"Great. Because a little birdie told me that he likes to go to the tavern every Thursday night." She clucked her tongue. "I think I might just end up at the tavern this Thursday night as well." She winked at Tess, a conspiratorial grin curving her lips.

"If you and River run into one another and hit it off, who am I to ask you not to see each other?"

"You're my sister-in-law," Heather said. "You know I'd never hurt you."

As frustrating and annoying as Heather could be, Tess did know that about Jared's younger sister. "You have my blessing, not that you needed it." It would hinge on River and whether he decided to pursue Heather back. Why hadn't he mentioned that he and Heather had had a thing before?

Tess swallowed painfully and looked at her feet. She really just wanted to disappear into that hot bath now. "You know what? I'm tired, Heather. Can we catch up later? I think I'm going to retreat to my room."

"Oh yeah. Sure. We can chat later," Heather said. "How about I cook dinner tonight?"

Tess didn't even know what was in her fridge. "You went shopping?"

"Mm-hmm."

That was a sign that Heather was staying longer than Tess hoped. "Dinner sounds good." And maybe by then, Tess would be ready to talk about the possibility of seeing her sister-in-law make a play for the man she couldn't stop thinking about. Maybe she'd be ready to tell Heather about her maybe niece in Morrisville and the secret side of Jared that no one else knew. Or maybe Tess would find an excuse to skip dinner too.

Chapter Seventeen

River parked his truck and headed toward the Weeping Willows Assisted Living Facility. He'd been thinking about what Tess had said to Ashley all morning. Tess had told Ashley that having family was worthwhile, despite the costs. He'd gone down the rabbit hole looking for family once before and the cost had been great. Did he want to open himself up to that kind of disappointment again? Maybe there was still someone out there for him.

River opened the door to the community building and beelined toward his father, who was sitting alone at a table in the back corner. River was surprised Douglass didn't have a group of men surrounding him like he always seemed to.

Douglass looked up at him when he saw him walking in his direction. "My boy. How was your trip?"

That question conjured images of mostly Tess. Kissing her and resisting her. "It was good."

Douglass assessed River's face the way he always had when River used to come home at night after being out. "There was a girl involved?" He cleared his throat. "A lady friend," he corrected.

River pulled out a chair and sat down. "What makes you say that?"

"The shine on your skin. It's glowing." Douglass chuckled. "I'm your father. One of them, at least. Did you start your search for your birth parents, like I asked you to?"

River expelled a breath. "I researched a company I might use to check into things for me. I could send off my DNA and see if it matches anyone else in the system."

Douglass sat up straighter. "Perfect. What are you waiting for?"

"I'm not sure if I want to get any hits on blood relatives yet. No one can top you, so why would I go looking?" River said it in jest, but Douglass didn't laugh. Instead, he looked disappointed. He was about to say something when a couple of the other men from the facility spotted them and headed over.

"River! What are you teaching us today?" Cal Cunningham asked.

"I'm afraid I didn't bring anything with me." Much to River's regret.

"I'll tell the guys you're here," Cal said anyway.

River looked at Douglass, who still looked disappointed. "I'll think about it some more, okay?"

Douglass perked up just enough. "Good. That's good." He leaned forward and patted River's knee. "How about you give us more survival tips? We all like those. Jim Barron wandered off the other day. He could've gotten lost in the woods. You never know when you'll need survival tips."

River smiled at Douglass. "Okay, Dad."

∞

After recounting the main things to do in a survival situation and leaving Weeping Willows, River headed over to the town hall to meet with Mayor Gil Ryan about a PI job this coming weekend. The town's annual summer festival started Friday evening and ran through Sunday, and River's friend wanted help regarding a person who had evaded law enforcement for the last couple of years.

River stepped out of his truck and headed into the one-story brick building in front of him. Gil met him at the door, looking relaxed in a pair of jeans and a T-shirt.

"Hey, buddy. Thanks for meeting me today. Let's talk in my office." Gil led River down the hall and veered into a room off to the right. He took a seat behind the least pretentious desk a town's mayor could ask for. It was all pine and simply made without any of the intricate carvings of some desks that River had taken a seat opposite of.

River sat back in the chair across from Gil. "What do you need from me?" he asked.

"As you know, the Somerset Summer Festival is a passion project of mine. I started it the year I became mayor to bring in money for the community and to celebrate the people and traditions of the town."

"I think that's great," River said.

"Well, not everyone does. Every year, someone rigs something at the festival and causes quite a scene around here. It's pretty embarrassing, to tell you the truth." Gil sat back and propped his legs on his desk. "One year it was a set of sprinklers going off on the main stage during the town's talent show. Another year it was fishing worms on the pies."

"I've heard about the pranks," River said with a grimace.

Gil frowned. "They aren't harmless pranks. They make good fodder for Reva's town blog, yeah, but they're starting to scare some people off from the festival. People don't want to eat the food if there's a possibility there might be worms in it. They don't want to sign up for a talent show if they might get drenched in water in front of the whole town."

River nodded. "I see your point."

"And it's hard because law enforcement can only investigate the crime after the fact. Then they have to wait a whole year until the next festival. They don't know what the next prank will be. Everyone knows who the members of the sheriff's office are. Including whoever this joker is. But you..."

"Hiring me would be a long shot," River said honestly. "I can't be everywhere or see everything. The festival runs for two days. That's not a lot of time to locate the culprit."

"But maybe you'll see something," Gil said. "I'm desperate, buddy. It's just a weekend job, and I figure you'd be at the festival anyway, right?"

"I thought you knew me better than that." River avoided crowds when at all possible. "Do you happen to have any gut feelings about who the person might be?"

Gil offered a grim expression. "I've always wondered if it was the teenagers around here. A couple years ago is when I implemented the curfew for kids under eighteen. Right after that is when worms were found on the pies."

River chuckled. "Sounds like something a kid would do. I heard they were in the pies."

Gil sighed. "Just on top, but it still left them inedible."

"So I'm looking at teenagers?"

"Maybe." Gil shrugged. "I would guess so. Can you help me?"

River nodded. "I'll look into the situation for you."

Gil lowered his legs off the desk and leaned forward to shake River's hand. "Thank you. Do you need a date to go with you to the festival?"

"A date?" River asked. "Why would I need one of those?"

"So that you don't stand out. No offense, but you're kind of a loner type. A date might make you less suspicious to these wise guys or women."

"Woman? Perhaps Moira?" River teased.

Gil frowned. "She does seem to hate me."

River shook his head and responded to the earlier comment. "I don't need a date," he said, although he knew who he could ask if he wanted one. Not that Tess would say yes. She'd kissed him and then shut the door on anything more.

River sat with Gil in his office for a little while longer, discussing the past crimes at the festival and the festival's layout this year. He got the schedule of events to study for the weekend. It was an extrovert's fantasy. When the conversation was done, he stood and shook Gil's hand again.

"See you at the tavern on Thursday night?" Gil asked.

River nodded. "I'll be there."

Gil leaned in as if disclosing a secret. "Let's keep this arrangement between you and me, okay?"

River looked at him with interest. "Why is that? Do you also suspect one of the guys from the tavern?"

"No way." Gil shook his head. "But, even though I have my suspicion about the town's teens, at this point, I can't completely rule anyone out."

∞

Tess turned the sign on her store door to CLOSED and prepared for her book club friends to be here any minute. Lara was in the back collecting her things. She'd been a lifesaver these last couple of weeks, and Tess had really enjoyed her company here in the bookshop. They'd become friends, which was nice.

Lara came back through from the back room. "Have fun tonight."

Tess hedged. "You know what? Why don't you stay and join us?"

"What?" Lara's smile dropped a touch at the corners.

"We'd love to have you. I'm sure the other ladies would agree. We don't invite others too often, but you'd fit right in."

"I don't know." Lara shook her head. "I haven't read the book you guys are reading."

"It's okay. We're almost done with it anyway, and then we'll choose another. You can just sit and listen. We mostly talk about our personal lives anyway and eat sweets from Choco-Lovers down the street. Jana sends them through Moira every week without fail. It's a seventy percent discussion about our lives and thirty percent talk about the book kind of club."

Lara seemed to be thinking.

"No pressure of course. If you would rather go home, that's fine too. This isn't your boss asking you to join us. It's your friend."

Lara nodded slowly. "Okay." She shrugged. "Yeah. Thank you for the invitation. I'd love to stay if you're sure the other ladies won't mind."

"Oh, I'm sure. We're all so laid back. But just so you know, what's discussed in book club stays in book club. That's pretty much the only rule."

Lara laughed. "I can agree to that."

They both turned at a knock on the door. Trisha was standing on the other side and waved. Her son, Petey, was beside her. Then Della Rose and her two sons stepped up.

"There they are! The women of the book club are starting to arrive." By the time Tess opened the door, Lucy and Moira were standing there as well. And, as predicted, they all welcomed Lara with excited hugs.

"What did Jana send us tonight?" Trisha eyed the bag from Choco-Lovers that Moira had placed on the coffee table at the epicenter of the circle of comfy chairs and a sofa.

"Brownies and truffles," Moira said. "I extended another invitation that she politely declined, of course."

"Of course," Tess said. "Good thing Lara said yes." They all turned their attention to Lara and bombarded her with questions as Tess's mind drifted to the tavern, where Heather had told her she was planning on looking for River tonight and seeing if there were sparks.

Tess curled her legs to her body, hugging her arms around them as she listened to her friends laugh about something or other. Tess and River had texted back and forth a bit this week, mostly about the investigation. He'd needed Jared's DNA to test against Mia's. Hair or nail clippings. Saliva. Anything. But Jared had been dead for more than three years. There was nothing.

Tess had searched the house from top to bottom, going through all of Jared's old things. All she'd found were more clues that made her suspicious. Another matchbook, this one from a hotel she'd never been to. A pen with a logo for a restaurant where she'd never eaten. Had Jared been alone or had he been with someone?

The texts with River had been mostly business, aside from the few where he had asked how she was doing, to which she lied and told him she was fine. Everyone knew that *fine* was always a lie though. So if it was a known lie, then it was barely a lie, right?

"Earth to Tess." Moira raised an eyebrow.

All the women were looking at Tess.

"Hmm?" She looked around at the circle of women. "Did you ask me something?"

"How's life with your sister-in-law in the house?" Lucy asked, apparently for the second time. She took a bite of the brownie in her hand.

Tess blew out a breath. "Fine," she said. Once again, a tiny lie.

"That bad, huh?" Moira snickered.

"Well, she's at the tavern as we speak, probably making a move on River Harrison," Tess told them. Maybe that was disclosing too much because Moira's eyes seemed to narrow.

"And why would that bother you?" Moira asked.

"It doesn't." Tess reached for a brownie too, looking for some sort of distraction. "Heather can date whomever she wants."

"Except him?" Lucy asked.

Tess let her gaze ping-pong around the circle. "Of course she can date him, if he wants to date her too."

The women shared looks. At least Lara seemed oblivious to what they all seemed to be thinking.

"What?" Tess asked.

"Oh, come on. You can't honestly hate someone that much unless you secretly kind of like him," Moira said.

Tess's mouth dropped open. She closed it. Then she pointed a finger. "Mayor Gil Ryan."

Moira frowned. "No, I legitimately dislike him."

"You like him so much that it scares you to death," Tess accused.

They stared at each other.

Moira dropped her finger first. "Fine."

"Fine," Tess agreed.

"No, not fine with me," Lucy said. "If you like River, don't let Heather go after him. What he did at your wedding was a long time ago. You should forgive him."

"I have." Tess sucked in a breath. She didn't keep secrets from her friends. She didn't typically have secrets to keep. She looked at Della Rose, who'd been mostly quiet. "The truth is, I actually hired River to help with something."

Della's eyes widened. "Oh?"

Tess folded her hands in her lap. "Mm-hmm."

"He's a private investigator, right?" Trisha asked. "What is he helping you with?"

Tess swallowed as tears sprang to her eyes. Then she told her friends everything. The only detail she spared was the kiss she'd shared with River the other night. They didn't need to know about that.

"Do you really think Jared had a mistress?" Moira asked. "You think he would actually do that to you?"

"I don't want to believe that, but I met Ashley. That's where I was last weekend. I met her daughter Mia too." Tess pulled out her cell phone and tapped on her camera app. She brought up a picture of Mia that she'd taken at the wedding reception and held her camera out to show the women.

"Oh." Moira clapped a hand over her mouth.

Lucy leaned in and looked at the screen as well, gasping softly. "Oh my!"

"Let me see," Trisha said. Her lips parted as she looked over the others' shoulders.

Eventually everyone was staring at Tess's screen, their eyes lifting to look at Tess and lowering back to the screen.

"What? Do you think she looks like Jared?" Tess asked.

"I don't know about that," Moira said. "You're not showing us a picture of a little girl. You're showing us a selfie of you and River, and I am one-hundred-percent right. You like him."

Tess turned her screen back to look at what she'd just shown her friends. It wasn't Mia. It was the selfie she'd taken of her and River dancing. With her in a yellow dress, him in jeans and a T-shirt after he'd changed out of those awful leather pants. He was staring at her like a man in love. And she was laughing like a woman having the time of her life. That was before the kiss that made her feel giddy, a welcome distraction from Ashley and Mia.

Tess's cheeks burned. "Oh, sorry."

"So you spent last weekend with River?" Lucy clarified.

"Well, he's investigating this woman and her involvement with my husband. I went along with him to get the story firsthand," Tess explained. "Because I wanted to help prove his innocence."

"And you somehow ended up at a wedding, dancing together?" Trisha asked.

"It's a long story." Tess swiped her phone's screen and found the picture of Mia, flashing it outward to show the women. They leaned forward to look. Tess kept her focus on

Moira, because Moira's expression would tell her everything she needed to know.

Moira frowned, the crease between her hazel eyes deepening. "Wow," she finally said.

Tess lowered her phone. "Yeah. We're doing a paternity test. Only, there's no DNA for Jared left, so I'm going to have to use someone else's."

"Someone else's? Like whose?" Della asked.

"Like Jared's sister. Heather." Tess grimaced. "She's living with me for free so a hair sample is the least she can give me."

"She's okay with that?" Moira asked.

"I haven't exactly asked her yet. I'm going to. Tonight. Assuming she comes home and doesn't run off with River." Tess took a bite of her brownie.

Della tsked. "The way River is looking at you in that photo you just flashed us, he's not going to run anywhere with Heather. There are sparks in that picture. You have a very complicated situation going on."

"Investigating your late husband with the help of his former best friend who you have a shared attraction with. That's very complicated," Lucy agreed.

Tess chewed and swallowed her bite of brownie. She was done denying any attraction. Done saying she was fine. She looked at Lara. "See? I told you we talk about our personal lives more than the book."

Lara smiled warmly. "And I promised that what is said in book club would stay in book club."

"Thank you," Tess said on a sigh. "So does anyone have any advice?"

Trisha raised her hand. "I do."

They all looked at her.

"If you like him, you tell him. We're all adults now," Trisha said. "Crushes are for teenagers. There's no time for playing games. Otherwise, the guy of your dreams might get snatched up by your sister-in-law."

Tess frowned. "I already married the man of my dreams. Or I thought I did."

"You did." Della Rose reached for her arm. "No matter what River discovers for you, I know that Jared loved you."

"I know that too. Was he still in love with me the night he died though? Had he fallen out of love with me along the way?" There were so many unanswered questions.

"There's no rule that says you can't fall in love with two different men of your dreams. I'm living proof of that." Trisha had gone through a messy divorce from her son's father and fallen in love with Jake Fletcher last summer.

"I'm proof too," Della Rose agreed. She'd also gone through a messy divorce and had found love with Roman Everson last year.

Tess shook her head, feeling silly. "I never said anything about falling in love anyway."

"Exactly. You haven't been interested in anyone since Jared's been gone. If you're interested in River in the slightest, you should see where it leads," Lucy said.

"And if Jared did cheat on you," Moira added, "then the best kind of payback is dating his former best friend." She bounced her eyebrows, making Tess burst into laughter, which was better than the alternative of crying.

Chapter Eighteen

River was usually the people watcher, not the one being watched. But he felt Heather Lane's eyes on him from across the tavern, where she'd been sitting at the bar for an hour now while he sat at one of the tables with his buddies.

"I'm glad Douglass is doing better," Miles said to River, sitting on his left side.

River nodded. "He is. Thanks. The old man is too stubborn not to get better." This made the other guys laugh.

Miles leaned forward and lowered his voice. "Don't look now, but Heather Lane is walking over here, guys."

River inwardly groaned, suspecting she was heading his way.

Sure enough, she stopped behind his chair and laid a hand on his shoulder. "Hi, guys," she said, squeezing his shoulder muscles softly. River had to will himself not to pull away. One, because that was rude. Two, because he didn't want to embarrass Heather in front of the other guys.

They all greeted Heather politely.

"Want to have a seat with us?" Gil asked.

River would be sure to thank the good mayor for that later.

"Oh no. This looks like a guy's night if I've ever seen one. I was just hoping to steal away one of your men for a dance."

All the guys' eyes landed on River. *Tag*, he was it. Could River decline? Could he say no?

"We can part with River for one dance, I think," Gil said with a wide grin.

River offered his friend a steady gaze. There would be no Christmas present in the mayor's future.

"Uh, sure." River pushed away from the table as Heather stepped back. He stood and faced her. She was beautiful, no doubt about that. And any guy would be lucky to hold her in his arms. River had eyes for only one woman in Somerset Lake though, and she wasn't in this tavern tonight.

"Lead the way." River gestured toward the far corner, where there was a dance floor.

Heather waved at the guys. "Thanks for sparing him. I'll bring him back."

"Take your time with him," Miles called at their backs.

Maybe River couldn't trust his friends as much as he thought.

When Heather reached an empty space on the floor, she turned to River and stepped toward him, not hesitating to drape her arms around his neck. He did hesitate to put his arms around her though. He and Tess weren't even together, so why did this feel like a betrayal of some sort?

"How've you been, River?" Heather asked.

"I'm doing well. And you?"

She shrugged. "I'm having some rough spots in my career. That's why I'm hiding out in Somerset Lake for a little bit. It seems I like to attract drama as much as I like to create it."

He chuckled. "And as much as I like to avoid it."

This made her smile. "Except for that one time," she said, lifting her brows.

"That time we shouldn't mention," he agreed. He didn't want to get caught up in the details of Tess and Jared's wedding.

Heather shifted her arms and drew him closer. "So is there anyone special in your life right now, River?"

Tess came to mind. Her dancing brown eyes. Her touchable brown skin. "Actually, there is."

Heather's eyes widened, and her lips parted. "Oh? I didn't know."

River shrugged. "I'm not even sure she knows, to tell you the truth."

"I see. But she's special enough to keep you from getting involved with anyone else?" Heather asked, her words coming out slowly, hesitantly.

River nodded. "Yeah. She's that special."

"Wow. Must be some woman. Why don't you tell her how you feel?"

"It's complicated," he said.

"Matters of the heart always are, in my limited experience." Heather offered another smile that read *no hard feelings*. "You have always struck me as a loner, River Harrison, but never a man who was meant to be alone."

"There's a difference?" he asked.

"There's a big difference. If you like this woman, you should let her know. Simple is overrated. Drama-free is overrated," she added with a head tilt.

River laughed quietly. "I'll take your word on that one. Thanks for the advice, Heather."

"Thanks for the dance, River."

The song ended, and she dropped her arms from around his neck. "Go back to your men's night. I'm heading back to the bar."

"I'm leaving actually. And I'm guessing you've had a few too many drinks to drive. Do you need a ride home?" he asked.

"Such a gentleman." Heather winked. "I'll grab my purse. I'd love a ride back to Tess's."

Tess saw the headlights spill into her driveway. Oh, good. Heather was finally home. Her book club had convinced her of a few things tonight. One, that she needed to go for it with River. It was time to start dating again. The things she once held against River now felt irrelevant. Two, she needed to talk to Heather about Jared. She wasn't going to collect DNA from Heather without her permission. That felt invasive, even if it was just a piece of hair.

Tess walked to the window and peeked out the blinds to check on what was taking Heather so long, and her heart tumbled to her feet. Heather was getting out of River's truck, and she was laughing. She waved and started walking toward the front door.

Tess nearly tripped over her own feet as she hurried to the sofa. Why was Heather with River? Heather had gone to the tavern tonight to flirt with River and see if there were any sparks left. It appeared she'd found some.

The front door opened, and Heather walked in, her gaze immediately finding Tess. "Hey. Are you waiting up for me?"

"Oh, um, not really." Tess shook her head quickly. "I haven't been home long from book club."

Heather nodded. "How was book club?"

"Oh, you know. We talked books and personal lives." Tess shouldn't ask about Heather's mission to charm River. She didn't really want to know. She just needed to know. "How was your time at the tavern?"

"Amazing," Heather said without missing a beat. She headed over to the couch, where Tess was sitting.

"So you and River hit it off?" Tess felt like someone had punched her square in the solar plexus. She didn't have any claims on him though. They'd shared a couple of kisses, and then Tess had been the one to pull away.

"Unfortunately, no. I mean, I tried, but River told me that there's someone else."

Tess swallowed, hope lifting her heart out of the pit of her stomach. "Someone else? Did he say who?"

Heather tilted her head, narrowing her eyes. "You're acting weird. Why?"

Tess swiped at a dark curl that had fallen against her cheek. "Am I? I don't think so. I'm just trying to ask about your night. If you and River didn't hit it off, why did he drive you home just now?"

Heather grinned. "You were watching us out the window? You're jealous, aren't you?" She laughed a little, and Tess felt her cheeks flare hot. "He took me home because I'd had too much to drink to drive safely, and River is a good guy. I always knew he was. It was you who thought otherwise. And my brother." She looked down for a moment.

Tess reached a hand across the space between them and grabbed hold of Heather's fingers. "It's okay to miss him."

Heather looked at Tess with a meaningful expression. "Right back at you, sis. It's okay to miss him and still move on. With River, if that's who you're eying. He says there's someone else. Maybe that person is you?" There was a questioning lilt to her words.

"Maybe." Tess hesitated before saying, "Heather, I need to tell you something."

Heather sat down on the sofa with Tess. "Okay. What is it?"

Tess didn't think Heather was going to like this, but it had to be said. "Well, the thing is, I've hired River to investigate a woman whom Jared was seeing before he died."

"Seeing?" Heather asked, visibly stiffening.

"Dating. He was having an affair."

Heather's eyes went wide. "What?"

"She also has a daughter that she claims is Jared's." Tess held out her phone, and this time she flashed the correct photo of Mia on the first try.

Heather's lips parted as she looked at the phone's screen. "I can't believe you would do this to Jared. He was your husband, Tess. He loved you."

Tess lowered the phone. "Didn't you hear what I said? He was cheating on me."

"No. I don't know what you found out in this investigation you've been doing with River, but my brother was faithful to you. He would never hurt you like you're accusing him of. Tess, he's dead. He can't even defend himself against these accusations."

"Or cover his tracks anymore," Tess muttered.

Heather rose to her feet. "You know what, I'm not going to stick around and listen to you tear down Jared's reputation.

I've always admired what a great wife you were to him, but this is just wrong. It's not you."

"Heather, think about your director. You didn't know he was married when you became involved with him either. This stuff happens."

Heather's mouth fell open. "I can't believe you're going to use that against me."

"I'm not. I'm just saying, guys who cheat don't wear signs. They're not always the slimeballs portrayed in the movies. Sometimes they're the guys we least suspect."

"I know that life isn't like the movies." Heather held up a hand. "I'm done with this conversation." She walked around the couch and snatched her keys and purse from the counter before heading toward the door.

"Where are you going?" Tess asked.

"To my parents' house. At least they know my brother was a good guy." Heather frowned at Tess. "I'm so disappointed in you."

Tess felt gut-punched by that comment. She took a shuddery breath, trying not to cry as Heather slammed the door behind her. Well, that conversation had gone even worse than she'd thought it would.

Tess sat behind the counter of Lakeside Books and opened her laptop. Lara had taken the morning off for a doctor's appointment. Tess had gotten used to having someone else in the shop with her. Now the store felt oddly quiet, which she'd always loved. She still did, but the quiet that happened with another person in the same room was nice too.

Business usually ebbed and flowed on the weekdays. That was fine because Tess needed to check her email in-box. When she opened the app, she found an email from Jaliya's publicist waiting for her.

Tess clicked quickly and read with eager eyes.

Hi Tess!

I've put a box of bookmarks and pens in the mail for the June 23rd event! The warehouse is shipping you boxes of Jaliya's books directly. You should be all set for the event, but please contact me if the books or swag don't arrive in the next week. Also, be sure to take lots of photos at the signing and tag @SunrisePublishing.

Cordially,
Ramona Gibbs
Senior Publicist for Sunrise Publishing

Tess let out a little squeal.

"Must be good news," a deep voice said.

Tess hadn't even realized that a customer had walked in. Least of all, River. "Hi." She was still grinning from ear to ear. "It's just thrilling to have one of my favorite authors coming to my store to sign. I keep pinching myself because I can hardly believe it."

River approached her counter. "I'm excited too. I finished her book last night, matter of fact. I'll be counting on having her sign my copy."

Tess lowered her arms. "I can't believe you read her entire book."

"I might even read it a second time. Maybe we can quiz each other on it." He leaned forward, resting his elbows on the counter and coming closer to her.

Tess felt her body warm. "I'd ace that quiz. So what brings you here?"

"A number of things. Did you talk to Heather?" he asked.

"Last night. After you dropped her off," Tess said.

River's gaze was steady. "It wasn't like that."

"I know. She told me. She said she tried, and you told her there was someone else." Tess's heart thumped erratically. She wasn't asking, just fishing, and now she regretted even bringing it up.

River looked a little taken aback. "I had to let her down gently. I didn't know what else to say."

"Oh." Tess swallowed. "That makes sense." Even if it was slightly disappointing to know she wasn't the one he'd been speaking of. "So yes, I did speak to her, but I didn't get a DNA sample. Instead, I got chewed out and she slammed the door as she left my house."

"She's mad at you?" River asked, brows gathering in concern.

"You could say that." Tess shook her head. "I'm sure she left DNA behind at my home that I could use, but I just wouldn't feel right without her permission."

"Do you want me to talk to her?" River asked.

"No." Tess folded her arms over her chest. "I'll try again, I guess. Sometimes Heather just needs some space to cool down."

River nodded. "I guess that's true for everyone."

Tess looked at River. He didn't ever seem to need time or space. He was always even tempered. "You said you had several reasons for being here?"

"Yeah. I'm working another job, actually. It means I'll be at the Somerset Summer Festival all weekend."

"Not exactly your kind of scene, I'm guessing."

River shook his head. "Not really. I'm looking for clues into the person who stirs up mischief at the festival every year. They've eluded the sheriff's department, so Mayor Gil has asked me to do some private investigative work on the side. He suggested that I would look less conspicuous if I had a date."

Tess straightened. "A date?"

"Well, most dates don't last an entire weekend. I know I'm asking a lot. But I need my Watson."

Being called Watson never would have struck Tess as romantic, but endorphins flooded her system. Her mom and everyone in her life had been telling her it was time to date again. Maybe they didn't mean River Harrison, but why not River? Perhaps a weekend-long date would make up for years of being single.

"Of course, I understand that you have the bookshop to run. You can't just close it for the weekend." He rubbed the side of his cheek absently.

"I'll see if Lara can work. She was already planning to work all weekend, just not alone. I'm sure she'll be okay with it though."

River's eyes seemed to twinkle under her store's low lighting. "So you're tentatively saying yes?"

"People will see us together," she warned. That was one

difference between last weekend and this one. And she was already on Heather's bad side.

"Yeah. I already thought of that. And that's kind of the point for me. It makes me less conspicuous, remember?" He bobbed his head from side to side. "One of the points, at least."

"What's the other point?"

His gaze held hers. "I get to spend more time with you."

Chapter Nineteen

River headed home to change into fresh clothes and take Buddy for a walk down by the creek before it was time to pick up Tess. This felt wrong in some ways. She was his best friend's girl. Kind of. But it felt right because she was also the girl he'd fallen for at first sight there by Somerset Lake. River couldn't remember the last date he'd been on. Not a real date at least. Sure, he'd been to the tavern, and he'd had women sidle up to him where they'd spent an hour or two drinking and talking. He'd had fun, but there'd never been real sparks. None that he wanted to follow through on at least.

He wanted to follow through with Tess. She made him visualize things for himself that he couldn't imagine with anyone else. Going to this weekend's festival didn't even sound so bad if he was attending with her. In fact, he was looking forward to it.

Who was he? Tess made him feel like a whole new man, and he'd barely even cracked the surface of what they might become.

As he walked his dog, he found himself picking a bright purple flower down by the creek and then one with a vibrant yellow color. Before he knew it, he had a whole bouquet of wildflowers in his hand.

"All right, Buddy, wish me luck," River told his dog as he opened the back door of his home and let Buddy run ahead of him.

Buddy glanced back with soulful eyes. For a long time, River had thought a dog was all he really needed. But here he was picking flowers, heart racing over a woman, and considering sending off his DNA to look for even more people he might open up his world to. He grabbed his keys as he cut through the house and headed out the front door toward his truck.

Fifteen minutes later, he turned into Tess's driveway. His palms were damp. He was a former Marine. He wasn't really a guy who let his nerves get the best of him, but Tess made him anxious in a good kind of way.

He blew out a breath, debating on the flowers once more, but he forced his hand to grab them. A woman like her deserved flowers. She deserved the whole world on a platter. And he wanted to kick Jared's butt for not giving her that when he had the opportunity.

River headed up the steps and rang the doorbell.

Tess appeared a minute later, looking at him first and then the flowers. "You brought me flowers?"

"Well, I didn't want to come empty-handed. They're from the creek behind my house."

"Wildflowers." Tess nodded. "No one has ever picked me wildflowers before."

River stood and found himself stepping toward her. She was wearing white Converse sneakers with a pale blue dress. That was good because they'd be doing a lot of walking at the festival.

She glanced down at her outfit. "So is this appropriate attire to be your Watson? Or do I need some kind of pipe in my mouth?"

"You look great. In fact, I might have a hard time investigating who's plaguing the festival due to admiring my date."

She laughed. "Just let me grab my bag." She walked over to the kitchen counter and picked up a small black purse. Then she turned back to him. "All right. Let's go on a date."

Tess was very aware that everyone she knew was in this crowd tonight. The whole town came out for the Somerset Summer Festival.

"You okay?" River asked, glancing over at her.

Tess pulled her eyes from the dozens of familiar faces in the crowd to look at him. "People will see us together. They'll ask questions."

"People always ask questions. You can still change your mind if you want. I'll take you right back home and do this on my own."

Tess liked that River would say so. She liked that he'd brought her flowers, and that he looked adorably nervous tonight. "No. It's fine. We should know what we're going to tell them though."

"We can say we're here as friends," he suggested.

She'd tossed that word at him last week after they'd kissed, and she was pretty sure it had hurt his feelings. And she didn't want to just be friends. She wanted more. It was time. "We'll just tell them the truth. That we're here on a date."

River's eyes twinkled under the star-spangled mountain sky. Yeah, being friends was overrated when you could have more.

"All right then." He gestured forward. Friday night traditionally kicked off the Somerset Summer Festival with music and food, which was what happened on Friday summer nights anyway, just on a larger scale. "Come on. I'll buy you a hot dog."

"Big spender," Tess said on a laugh.

They navigated through the crowd, saying hello here and there.

"Are you two together?" Reva Dawson, town blogger extraordinaire, was the first to ask.

Tess shot River a look. Whatever was told to Reva was told to the entire town in one quick swoop of a blog entry.

"Um. Well, we did drive here together," Tess agreed.

"So it's a date?" Reva clapped her hands with delight.

"Tess is helping me with something," River said.

"An investigation?" Reva asked.

"No." River shook his head quickly, no doubt not wanting to ruin his cover before the weekend had even gotten started. "We're, um…"

"Yes, Reva. I guess you could say that this is a date. But if you don't mind, it's my first date since Jared passed away. I really don't want it announced to the entire town on your blog," Tess said pointedly.

Reva stiffened and pressed a hand to her chest. "Oh, I would never."

Even though Tess was quite sure she would. Reva was a sweet woman who probably wouldn't see any harm in her actions. That's why Tess was spelling it out for her.

"I'm so glad to hear that. Thank you, Reva," Tess said.

"Of course, dear. But if you're trying to be private, this is not the place." Reva's eyebrows lifted toward her rose-toned hair.

"We're not trying to be secretive. We're just asking that our privacy is respected."

"Of course." Reva looked between Tess and River. "I never would have placed you two together in my head, but you make a very nice couple. River, are you ever going to tell me how you got that scar beneath your eye? For my blog. I think most people in town wonder about it."

Tess felt embarrassed on River's behalf. Did the woman have no boundaries?

River slid his gaze over to Tess. "I'm afraid only Tess knows the truth about that. I kind of like to keep people guessing."

Reva looked at Tess. "You already know his secrets? That's a big deal."

"Here's something for your blog, Reva. Bestselling Author Jaliya Cruise has agreed to do a signing at my bookshop on June twenty-third. I just set it up and haven't even announced it yet. It's breaking news."

Reva clapped her hands together at her chest. "Oh, this is fantastic. A bestselling author here in Somerset Lake. Do you mind if I put it in my blog tomorrow?"

"I would love that." Tess fed the woman the quick details, and then she and River continued walking through the crowd. "Am I really the only person who knows how you got that scar beneath your eye?" she asked as they drew closer to the music.

"Well, Douglass knows, of course. But yeah. I kind of like

to keep people in suspense. The stories they make up in their head are much more exciting than the truth."

"A bobcat attack to save your dog is pretty exciting." Tess turned toward him. She hadn't realized they were standing so close, but it was the only way to hear each other over the crowd.

River's eyes lowered to her mouth. He wasn't going to kiss her out here in front of all these people, but he was thinking about it. Those thoughts were circulating around in her mind as well.

"Tess?"

Tess recognized her mother-in-law's voice before she turned to look at Mrs. Lane. Jared and his mom looked so much alike. Mia kind of looked like them too. "Marjory. Hi."

Marjory looked at River. "River," she said, lips pursing.

River was enemy number one in the Lane family. That's how Tess had thought of him until a couple of weeks ago too.

"Hello, Mrs. Lane. How are you?"

She ignored him and looked at Tess. "What are you doing here with him?"

Tess guessed she was just coming out with a bang tonight. "We're actually here on a date."

Mrs. Lane frowned. "After what he did?"

"I understand your reservations, but yes. You don't understand the circumstances."

"The circumstances?" Mrs. Lane shook her head. "My son would be so disappointed in this decision."

"Well, Jared's decisions weren't always the best in my opinion either," Tess said quietly.

"You're talking ill of the dead now?" Mrs. Lane drew her hand to her chest.

"No." Tess shook her head. "I'm just saying that maybe River had a reason for objecting to the wedding that we didn't realize at the time."

Mrs. Lane turned to glare at him. "Well, let's finally hear it, shall we? Jared said you were jealous of him. Is that the truth?"

River shoved his hands into his pockets. Tess felt criminal for putting him in such a position. "I guess some part of me was," River agreed.

Tess's jaw dropped. She couldn't believe he would say so.

Mrs. Lane pointed a finger. "And now that my son is gone, you're moving in on his wife. You should be ashamed of yourself, River Harrison. What kind of friend are you? And you," She turned to Tess. "Let me know when you come to your senses."

"I will likely call you very soon," Tess said.

Mrs. Lane looked perplexed by that remark. Then she glared at River one last time, turned on her heel, and left.

Tess blew out a breath. "She's actually quite warm and fuzzy once you get past the tough shell. A lot like you."

River chuckled. "You think I'm warm and fuzzy?"

"Somewhat. I think it's a well-kept secret though. You seem to have many secrets, don't you?" Like the one he'd told her about the first night they'd met. She wondered if she would've made a different choice. She'd been so in love with Jared, yes, but she'd felt something that night she'd met River on the lake too. Even if she'd done her best to ignore it.

"I think you know all my secrets now," he said.

Tess was tempted to lean forward and kiss him right now but then considered all the people around, seeing them together for the first time and wondering what they were to each other. They'd already been approached twice. No doubt, they'd be approached ten more times before they left. She lowered her gaze and looked around, remembering the other purpose of the night. "So how do we go about catching our guy?"

River exhaled. "Or woman. We can't rule that out."

"Of course," she agreed.

"Sabotage of this festival seems to be the motivation, and Gil has a suspicion that makes sense to me."

"Teenagers." Tess shook her head. "I'm not sure though. I think you should also keep an eye on the former mayor Bryce Malsop. He's always been bitter toward Gil. Bryce Malsop can't stand the fact that Gil is more popular than he ever was."

"That's an interesting theory. Thanks for the tip, Watson." River nodded. "If we see him here tonight, maybe we'll surveil him a little bit too."

"Perfect way to spend our first date," Tess said.

River gave her an apologetic look. "I'm striking out, aren't I?"

Tess swatted a soft hand across his arm, the touch zinging through her body. Forget about the crowd and what people were thinking. She leaned in. "Not at all. You brought me flowers, and we're having an adventure, which seems to be a theme when I'm with you. You're scoring." She went on her tiptoes and brushed her lips to his in a brief kiss.

River's arms wrapped around her waist and stayed there as she leaned back to look at him. Then he tugged, and she surrendered to another longer, deeper kiss that made her body feel like it was floating.

"I guess no one else is going to be asking what we're doing here together now," she whispered.

"They'll just be wondering the same thing I am," he said.

She lifted her brows in question. "What's that?"

"How'd a guy like me get to be so lucky?"

Tess grinned up at him. "I had no idea you had this side to you. Warm, fuzzy, and romantic."

River's gaze was so intense. "Neither did I, until you."

Chapter Twenty

River usually kept a one-track mind, but tonight his thoughts were divided between Tess and the investigation of the festival.

"Do you see anything suspicious?" Tess leaned into him as they sprawled out on a blanket in front of a live band.

"Not yet. I need to walk around. How about I finally get you that hot dog I promised?"

Tess grinned. "Why yes, I would love a hot dog. No onions. I love onions, but I'm planning on more kissing with my date tonight."

Who could work a case with that kind of talk? What was he thinking asking Tess to join him? "One hot dog, no onions. Dr Pepper?"

She tilted her head. "How do you know what kind of soda I like?"

"I'm a PI, and rumor is that I'm pretty good at my job." He winked and stood. "Be right back."

As he walked, he looked around for anything noteworthy. He walked up to the hot-dog vendor and fished his wallet out of his back pocket. When he looked up, he realized that Bryce

Malsop was the customer right in front of him, ordering two hot dogs of his own. Bryce had been the mayor of Somerset Lake for more than fifteen years, and he was grumpy to put it mildly. Tess was right. When Gil Ryan had come into office with new energy and ideas, Bryce was vocal about his dislike for all of them. If River remembered correctly, Bryce had blasted his views to anyone who would listen that this festival was a waste of the town's money. Of course, the truth was that the festival brought in revenue for the town. It brought in tourists and publicity, and Bryce couldn't stand it.

River's pulse jumped a notch. Perhaps Tess was onto something and the former mayor was a viable suspect.

When Bryce had gotten his order and stepped away, the vendor gestured River forward in line. "And you? What would you like?" the woman asked.

"I, uh, changed my mind. Sorry." River turned to follow the former mayor instead. He didn't want to lose track of where Bryce went, and in this crowd, that was likely. River's stomach could wait, and hopefully Tess's could too.

River pulled the festival's agenda out of his pocket and pretended to peruse it as he trailed Bryce, following him to a sheltered area near the back, where a man River recognized as Devin Banner was standing. The former mayor shook Devin's hand but didn't offer him one of the two hot dogs. Apparently, both were for Bryce.

River ducked to the other side of the shelter and leaned against the post, looking at his schedule. He fished his cell phone out of his pocket. He turned off his flash, angled his phone, and snapped a quick picture, and then another.

The conversation didn't appear like that of two friends

catching up. Instead, it looked more like a business exchange. No overly friendly smiles. Bryce's gaze kept darting around as if he were staying aware of his surroundings. That was the behavior of someone who was engaged in something they didn't want anyone to know about.

The two men shook hands again. River snapped another picture with his phone. And...was something passed between them? He snapped more photographs. Devin shoved something in the front pocket of his shirt. A payment maybe? This could be good evidence, depending on what went down between now and tomorrow night.

Thunder boomed overhead, and River placed his phone back in his pocket. He better get back to Tess. She was probably wondering where he went.

Just as he had the thought, the skies seemed to break open, and rain poured down in heavy sheets. River darted for the shelter, where the former mayor and Devin had been meeting. They were no longer there. They'd parted ways. River seriously doubted that Tess would be sticking around on their blanket to wait for him in this sudden summer storm either. And after all the time he'd been gone, she might have already left him anyway.

He jogged through the storm, keeping his head low so he could see as much as possible, scanning faces and looking for Tess. Where was she?

He dipped into another sheltered spot and took out his cell phone to call her. No answer. Likely she was running, and there was no time to stop in the downpour to answer her phone. River found the spot where he'd last left her, but she wasn't there. Of course not. He continued toward his truck.

He'd left it unlocked, which she knew about him after his emergency at her bookshop the other week. Hopefully she'd gone to his truck for shelter.

By the time he reached his vehicle, he was soaking wet. He ducked into the driver's seat and slammed the door shut behind him.

"Hey," he said, glad to find that Tess was in fact taking shelter there.

She cleared her throat. "After all that, you don't even have my hot dog and Dr Pepper?"

He wiped the raindrops off his face with his hands. "Would you like me to go back and get them for you? Because I would if that would make this situation better."

A small smile upturned her lips. "Do you have a good excuse at least?"

"Bryce Malsop was standing in front of me at the hot-dog stand."

Tess's eyes lit up. "And?"

"And my gut tells me he was up to no good here tonight. I trailed him and watched what appeared to be some kind of business interaction."

She smiled back at him. "Interesting. Is this a possible lead then?"

"I think so. He met up with Devin Banner and handed him something, maybe a payment. I got pictures."

River noticed now that Tess's curly hair was soaked, and she had dabs of mascara beneath her eyes. He was a miserable date. "Good job, Sherlock," she said.

"Even though I ruined our date?"

"I wouldn't say it's ruined. But I'm drenched, and I'm

afraid I don't look appropriate to go anywhere else. This dress is sticking to me. It's kind of gross." She looked down at her wet clothing.

"You look beautiful to me."

She lifted her gaze and shook her head on a laugh. "I can't get used to this side of you."

More rain dripped from his hair onto his face. He wished he had a towel. "I guess I'll take you home then. For what it's worth, I'm sorry."

"No need to apologize. You didn't cause the storm. And whoever you're trying to catch didn't cause it either, even though it successfully put an end to tonight's festivities."

River chuckled. "Yeah, it sure did. Gil won't be thrilled with that. Poor guy. This festival means a lot to him. Maybe the rumor that it's cursed is true."

"Hm," Tess hummed. "I don't believe that for a minute. And despite all the unfortunate things that have happened at the summer festival, people still come out for it. Its reputation doesn't precede it just yet."

River cranked the truck's engine. "Home?"

She nodded. "Yes. Thank you."

They were quiet for a couple of minutes as River navigated through the storm, driving more slowly than usual due to the downpour. When he finally turned into Tess's driveway, he put the engine in PARK behind a red mustang. "Looks like you have company," he said.

Tess looked out the windshield at Heather's car. "Great. Hopefully this will be a friendly visit. See you tomorrow?" she asked. "The festival starts at noon, right?"

River hedged. "I think I need to focus on the job at hand

and go it alone next time. A divided mind isn't as sharp. How about Sunday though? I need a chance to redeem myself."

Tess looked like she wanted to argue but then agreed. "Okay. Sunday it is."

"I'll make you dinner at my place," he offered.

"Deal."

He turned to look back out the window, where the rain was still coming down in heavy sheets. "You're going to get completely soaked all over again." He reached across her and opened the glove compartment of his truck. "Ah, there it is." He grabbed an umbrella. "I was hoping I had one for you to use."

"You don't mind if I take it?"

"Of course not." He handed it to her and then reached for his door handle.

"Wait. You don't have to walk me to the front door, River. It's raining. Don't be ridiculous."

He looked at her. "I've messed this first date up enough without letting you walk to the front door alone."

She reached for him and tugged on his shirt. "This is where I'm drawing the line with your noble act, okay? You are staying right here and kissing me good night in the truck."

River's gaze dropped to her lips and lifted back up to meet her brown eyes. "Well then, if you insist."

"I do," she said before pressing her mouth to his.

Tess closed the umbrella and left it by the front door as she stepped inside.

"Hi," Heather said from the couch.

Tess closed the door behind her. "Hi, Heather. What are you doing here?"

"Waiting for you." Heather gave her a sheepish look. "I had time to think, and I wanted to say that I was sorry for reacting the way I did the other night."

Tess crossed the room, set her purse down on the counter, and joined Heather on the couch. "It's okay. I understand. Jared was your brother. He *is* your brother."

Heather nodded, still keeping her head down. "Yeah, but I know he wasn't perfect. Can I see that picture of the little girl you showed me again?"

Tess grabbed her phone from her pocket, brought up the picture, and handed it to Heather. Heather zoomed in on Mia's face.

"She's beautiful," Heather said quietly.

Tess expelled a painful breath. "She really is. She doesn't look at all like him, so she might not be Jared's. River needs a DNA sample to run a paternity test."

Heather looked up. "How will you get one if Jared is gone?"

Tess grimaced. "I was hoping you would offer one. I don't want to have this conversation with your parents just yet."

"My mother would flip at that request." Heather nodded as she looked at the photo again. "Of course. I'll provide whatever you need. Just tell me what and when."

Tess shrugged. "I actually have the DNA kit in my purse."

Heather looked from Tess to the counter, where Tess's purse was lying. "Let's do it. I know my brother wasn't perfect. I never would have suspected him of cheating on you, but then again, I never would have thought I'd be an accidental mistress in my director's marriage." She laid her other hand over Tess's, sandwiching Tess's hand between hers. "All I know for sure is that Jared loved you."

"He had a funny way of showing it."

Heather leaned in and wrapped her arms around Tess, giving her a hug that she didn't realize she needed until she was fully enveloped in it.

When she pulled back, Heather eyed Tess. "Okay, let's take care of that DNA sample right now. Tonight. Then there's wine in your fridge. Let's have a glass and sit while we talk about happier things. Like what's going on between you and River."

It was strange that Tess was torn between mourning the idea of the perfect husband she'd had and moving on with someone new. But that's exactly where she was right now. In *A Woman's Journey to Joy*, Jaliya said there was no right or wrong way to mourn. It was okay to be where you were. To acknowledge and accept it. To celebrate it even.

"That sounds good," Tess told Heather. "First, I need to detangle my hair. The rain didn't do it any favors." She stood. "Nothing a wide-toothed comb and detangling spray can't fix. Give me five?" she asked.

Heather grinned. "I'll grab the bottle and glasses."

The next morning, Tess awoke with renewed energy. She felt recharged even before she drank her first cup of coffee at Sweetie's Bake Shop, where she was meeting Moira for breakfast.

"You have a certain glow about you this morning," Darla commented from behind the counter. "That must have been some date last night."

"How did you know I was on a date?" Tess asked. "Did Moira tell you?"

"Nu-uh. I read it in the town blog earlier."

Tess felt her body deflate. "Reva didn't."

"Oh, she did. Would you expect anything less?" Darla laughed lightly and slid two coffees across the counter, one for Tess and one for Moira when she arrived. "She was tasteful about it though. Just mentioned that she saw you two kissing right before the rain washed everyone out."

Tess nearly dropped the cup of coffee that she'd just picked up, making Darla cackle.

"It's just a kiss, sweetie. And I for one am so happy to know you're out there kissing people. Especially River Harrison." She offered a dreamy look. Then she leaned in. "You don't know how he got that scar under his eye, do you?"

Tess pinched her lips together. "Unlike Reva, I try not to tell everyone else's stories."

Darla shrugged. "It gives him a mysterious look. And I've never liked a man who was too pretty. River is a handsome man. The scar offsets him being too handsome, if you know what I mean."

The bell on the front door jingled, and Darla's face lit up. Tess knew before she turned around that Moira was here. Tess picked up the other cup of coffee and thanked Darla again. Then she turned to one of her very best friends, who undoubtedly had just as many questions as her mother this morning.

Tess headed over to an empty table by the wall.

Moira waved at her mom and sat down across from Tess. Now that she was on the day shift, she looked refreshed. That was a nice change for her. "So? How was the date?" she asked, her voice rising an octave as she settled into her chair. "You and River. I want all the details."

"Didn't you get enough from Reva Dawson's blog?"

Moira's face scrunched. "You made a bullet point in the blog?"

Reva's gossip came in quick bullet points so it was easier to remember and pass along. That was the running theory of the bullet points at least.

"Apparently." Tess rolled her eyes and sipped her coffee. "But last night was wonderful, if you must know. River brought me wildflowers that he picked himself."

Moira sipped her coffee too. "What? Really? That's kind of sweet."

"I know. And we enjoyed the music for a little while until we ran into Reva and then Jared's mother."

Moira's face twisted. "Ouch."

"Yep. And Mrs. Lane wasn't happy about us being there together. Then River left to go get us a hot-dog dinner, and he got sidetracked on a case he's working," Tess explained. "That's when the storm hit and I got drenched. I had to run back to his truck and pray it was unlocked."

Moira blinked from behind her cup of coffee.

"What?"

"Hmm. Yeah, that sounds like a fantastic date," she said sarcastically, taking another sip of her coffee.

"It actually was." Tess sighed. "Despite all of that, last night was wonderful. Because of him."

Moira's lips parted. "Oh, wow. Don't tell me you're falling for River this fast. You've had one date. Slow down, Tess. He's the first guy since…"

"Since my husband? Yes, I know. But all we've done is kiss, okay? I am going slow. And I'm not falling for him," she lied. She totally was, but she couldn't seem to help herself. "I'm being careful with my heart. I'm just happy, that's all."

"Well, I'm happy for you," Moira said. "It's about time."

"Look who's talking." Tess tilted her head. "At least I have an excuse for being single so long."

Moira swatted that comment away with a wave of her hand. "I've been working the night shift for years. Do you know how hard it is to date when you work the night shift?"

"But you're day shift now."

"And loving it. Except I will say, the dispatch is significantly more boring during the day, if that's possible."

The conversation continued to ebb and flow around their personal lives. Then a customer walked in to the bakeshop and headed to the counter.

"What's wrong?" Moira asked.

"Devin Banner is here," Tess whispered. "River is trailing him for a case. But you're not supposed to know that, so shhh."

Moira lifted her gaze to look at Devin. "Really? His name has never crossed my dispatch."

Tess straightened. "He's taking a seat on the other side of the shop. We should sit behind him, right? In case he makes a phone call. So I can hear what he says."

Moira lifted a brow. "You're a bookstore owner, not a PI, Tess. Leave the detective work to your boyfriend."

"River is not my boyfriend," Tess argued, glancing at Devin again. She took out her phone and tapped out a text to River.

> **Tess:** Devin Banner is eating at Sweetie's Bake Shop right now.

The dots started bouncing. Maybe she should have been a detective. Investigating was kind of fun.

> **River:** You're off the case, Watson. But thanks for the information.

He followed that with a winking face emoji.

When Tess looked back up, Moira was shaking her head.

"You're blushing over there. What did River say?"

"The same thing you did. To leave the PI work to him," Tess said.

Moira frowned. "Good. So why do I have a feeling you're not going to listen to either of us?"

Tess glanced over at Devin. "I'm just keeping an eye on River's suspect, that's all."

"A lot of my dispatch drama starts off this way, you know?"

Tess laughed quietly. "Speaking of, don't you have a shift to get to?"

"Yes, and if I hear your name cross the dispatch, I'm not going to be happy." Moira pointed a finger as she stood and collected her things. "Leave that man alone," she whispered.

"Which one? Devin or River?" Tess asked.

To this, Moira grinned. "Of River, I now approve."

Chapter Twenty-One

River sighed as he stared at his cell phone. Ever since he'd gotten out of the Marine Corps, he'd worked alone. He didn't have a boss or keep employees, and Tess's behavior right now was why. He'd included her on this case with the festival, and she had taken the ball and run with it. In fact, River didn't have any control of the ball right now.

There were three photographs on his phone from Tess. One of Devin at Sweetie's Bake Shop. Another of Devin walking down Hannigan Street and drinking his coffee. A third of Devin getting into his car. That's when the messages had stopped.

River had texted Tess not to follow Devin. She hadn't answered. He'd texted her that she was technically stalking the man. No response.

River's blood pressure felt elevated, and a small headache thrummed at his temple. He didn't think Devin was a dangerous guy by any means, but Tess shouldn't be following around a suspect in a crime. She wasn't even heeding his advice or warnings. What had he been thinking, asking for her help? Yeah, he knew what he was thinking. His mind had been on the possibility of an actual date. His thoughts had circled around the possibility of sharing another kiss.

He growled in frustration now.

"You okay?" Gil Ryan headed in River's direction. River had gone straight to Sweetie's Bake Shop when Tess didn't answer, hoping she hadn't left the area. But her car wasn't parked along the street, and when he'd stepped into the bakery, Darla confirmed that Tess had been gone for at least fifteen minutes. Then she'd given River a coffee on the house.

River noted the coffee in Gil's hand too. Everyone around here loved Darla's brew. "Not really. Tess seems to have taken over my latest investigation."

Gil's eyebrows lifted. "That was supposed to be kept between us."

"Yeah, well, feel free to fire me. I agreed with you that bringing a date to the festival might make me look less suspicious," River said.

Gil chuckled. "Yeah, that's the excuse you sold yourself to finally ask Tess out like you've been wanting to for a while." He sipped his coffee. "She's taken over the case?"

"She's following Devin Banner around." River had already filled Gil in on seeing Devin and Bryce meet up last night at the festival, and about his gut instinct telling him that maybe the culprit was the former mayor instead of a few bitter teenagers. "She was texting me pictures of Devin at breakfast, and now she's not responding to my texts."

"She's probably just driving. Not texting while driving is a good thing. As mayor of this town, I approve."

"Yeah, well, it's making me nervous. And it's my case. I work alone. Always. I never should have told her anything."

Gil laughed softly. "Tess has always been a take-charge kind of girl. Even in high school. I've always thought it was funny that she became the owner of a bookstore. She's so outspoken and adventurous."

"You don't have a thing for her, do you?" Because River really didn't want to bump heads with another friend over a girl.

"Nah. I mean, Tess is beautiful and smart; she's nice and amazing."

"You're sure you don't have a thing for her?" River teased. Then his phone buzzed with an incoming text. His pulse jumped.

"Is it from her?" Gil asked, leaning in.

"Yeah. She says that Devin stopped at Blue Peaks Park and met with Bryce Malsop there." River flashed the picture that Tess had attached.

Gil's brows furrowed. "That's fishy, huh?"

River started tapping a text to Tess.

> **River:** You're off the case, Watson.
>
> **Tess:** ...
>
> **Tess:** You're firing me before our second date?
>
> **River:** I never should have asked you to help me. That was poor judgment on my part.
>
> **Tess:** I'm helping you.
>
> **River:** What if Devin sees you? This is an unnecessary risk.
>
> **River:** Get back in your car and leave. Please.
>
> **Tess:** ...

> **Tess:** Fine, Sherlock. You win. Good luck with
> your case.
> **River:** Thank you.

River shoved his phone back in his pocket and exhaled.

"Everything okay?" Gil asked.

"Yeah. She's off the case."

"That's good, although she might have just gotten us some very important information." Gil shrugged. "Maybe having a partner isn't such a bad thing, buddy. Just saying."

At noon, River showed up at the Somerset Summer Festival alone, which was how he intended to work all his cases from now on.

"River!" Reva Dawson said with exaggerated cheer. "No date on your arm today?"

River frowned at the town's blogger. "No comment."

"Oh, you're not mad at me for putting you in my blog, are you? It's so seldom that I get to include your name. I thought it would be good fodder."

River kept his eyes moving while he chatted with the older woman. "I prefer not to be the town's fodder," River said. "Maybe you can help me though, Reva. Has Devin Banner ever been fodder for your blog before?"

Reva's forehead wrinkled at the name. "Oh, Devin? Yes, of course. Everyone has been in my blog. I don't leave anyone out, you know."

"What did he do to make a bullet point in your blog?"

Reva tapped an index finger to her chin. "Let's see. Well, last year he moved his mother to that assisted living facility where your father stays. It's not cheap to live there, so Mr. Banner has been working odd jobs ever since. He asked me to put him down as a bullet point to let the town know he was looking for side hustles." She shook her head. "I'm not in the business of finding people jobs, but I did that for him because I'm good friends with his mama. She loves it there at Weeping Willows Assisted Living Facility, and I want the very best for her, so I said yes."

River had his notepad out and was writing all the details down. This was good information. A need for money was motivation for seedy activity.

"Why are you writing all this down? What are you investigating?" Reva asked.

River lifted his gaze. "If you promise not to mention this conversation to anyone, Reva, I'll give you"—he cleared his throat—"fodder on my second date with Tess tomorrow."

Reva's eyes lit up. "Is that a promise?"

"It is, and I never break a promise," he said. "But it's dependent on you not sharing that Devin's name ever came up between us."

She lifted her hand to her lips and pretended to zip them. "I love to gossip, River. But I don't break a promise either." She offered her hand for him to shake. "You have yourself a deal."

River slipped his hand into hers and shook, wondering when he'd started taking on partners and making deals with the town's gossip blogger. What was going on with him these days?

∞

Tess didn't really feel like walking through the festival alone. Sure, she had friends she could call, but she didn't feel like mustering the necessary energy to be with them either. So instead, she returned to Lakeside Books. She needed to keep herself occupied so that she didn't think about her life situation all day, wondering what the DNA results would say. No matter what, Jared had betrayed her. Had their whole marriage been a lie? Maybe Jared really had loved her but had just struggled with remaining faithful.

Lara looked up from behind the counter as Tess walked through the door and headed her way. "I thought you were taking the day off."

Tess shrugged. "I changed my mind. And actually, I think you should be the one to have the day. Go enjoy the festival."

Lara looked unsure. "That festival has bad luck, doesn't it? Last year, the food had worms in it, right? And the year before the sprinkler systems went off and doused everyone on the stage."

"Oh, come on. You don't really believe it has anything to do with luck, do you?" Tess asked, approaching the counter.

Lara shrugged. "It poured last night, right? Rain wasn't even in the forecast. I'm kind of leery on going to that festival."

Tess frowned. Poor Gil. He'd poured his heart and soul into that festival, and it was getting a bad reputation. Tess hated that for him. "The festival was great before the rain. And it rains unexpectedly half the days of summer around here."

Lara smiled. "Well, I won't turn down a day off if you want to work today."

"I do. The festival always brings in lots of business. It should be a good sales day." Tess put her bag down. "Enjoy your free time, festival or not." She plopped onto the stool behind the counter.

Lara looked at her more closely. "Are you okay?"

Tess glanced over. "Yeah. It's just all the stuff I mentioned at book club the other night about my late husband." Tess sighed heavily. "If he really was having an affair, how could I be so clueless?"

"Because we see what we want to see. Maybe you just wanted to see the perfect life you thought you had. Are you sure you're okay? I can stay," Lara offered.

"No." Tess forced a smile. "I'm fine. I'll probably pick a book off the shelf and start reading it. Really."

Lara nodded reluctantly. "Okay. Well, call me if you change your mind. I don't have any plans."

"Thanks." Tess watched Lara leave the store and stared blankly for solid minutes, watching passersby on the sidewalk outside. She was feeling sorry for herself, and she couldn't seem to help it. It wasn't enough that she'd lost her husband, she'd now lost the way she remembered him.

She allowed herself to wallow in her self-pity for only a few minutes. Then she opened her laptop and checked her email. There was nothing to speak of in her in-box. Against her better judgment, she also checked Reva Dawson's blog, which was speckled with details about last night at the festival. Tess held her breath as she read.

Good Saturday morning, Somersetters! Here's your daily dose of Reva:

* The Somerset Summer Festival kicked off last night with live music, good food (sans worms), and lots of friends.

* Who knew Tori Jacobs could sing like that? I didn't!

* Also, who would have guessed that Tess Lane and River Harrison would have shown up together, holding hands and locking lips? Not me!

Tess groaned out loud as she read the bullet point with her name, even as her eyes continued soaking in the other details.

* Looks like the festival is living up to its reputation of being cursed, because it was rained out after just two and a half hours. I wonder what today will bring for those in attendance at the festival?

Why did Tess read this blog? She knew the answer. She read it because everyone else in town did, and if her name was going to make a bullet point, she wanted to know what people would be saying about her.

With one final groan, Tess closed the browser and busied herself with Jaliya's book signing, which was coming up soon, creating flyers to display at the counter and post in the front window. She also created an email to send out to her store's subscriber list announcing the event.

At midafternoon, the bell on the store door jingled.

Tess looked up from her laptop as Heather walked in. "Hey."

Heather sat on the couch where the book club ladies

usually curled up on Thursday nights. "Hi. Just thought I'd come see what you were up to. My mom came to the house earlier, by the way."

Tess blew out a breath. "I'm glad I decided to work then. I'm sure I'm not her favorite person right now."

Heather curled her legs into her chest. "I told her about the other woman and about Mia, my maybe-niece. Her maybe-granddaughter."

"Oh? How did that go?"

Heather shrugged. "She was adamant that Jared would never do such a thing to you."

Tess lowered her gaze. "I see."

"But after talking to her for a little bit, she agreed that Jared was spending a lot of time out of town that last year before he died. He was acting secretive…" Heather trailed off for a moment. "The point is, my mother knows that Jared wasn't without fault."

Tess nodded, returning her attention to her former sister-in-law. "Well, I'm just now figuring that out."

Heather gave her a meaningful look. "Perfection is over-rated."

"Well, monogamy isn't. Enough about my life. What's going on with yours? Are you going back to LA soon or have you decided that small-town life is for you?"

Heather scoffed. "I need the city. I'm just waiting to see what happens with an online audition I had the other day."

"That's exciting. Do you feel good about it?" Tess asked.

"Yeah, I really do. The part would be a fairly big one, and I'd get to play a role I've never really delved into. That of a loving aunt, which I guess might not be such a stretch." She offered a sheepish look.

"It's okay to be excited about the prospect of a niece you didn't know about," Tess said.

"Maybe Jared wasn't perfect, but he was my brother. Knowing there might be some piece of him out there to hold on to is exciting."

Tess would feel the same way if circumstances were different and if the piece of him didn't mean that Jared had been unfaithful.

"For what it's worth, I'm sorry about all of this," Heather said.

Tess walked around the counter and joined Heather on the couch. "Thanks for saying that."

Heather reached out her hand, offering it to Tess. Tess grabbed it and wondered at the squeeze that Heather placed around her palm, like a tiny hug. "No matter what, you'll always be my sister."

As much as Heather annoyed Tess, Tess appreciated that comment. Maybe Heather was the tiny piece of Jared that she could keep.

Chapter Twenty-Two

River was beginning to think his investigation into the festival was a dead end until he heard sirens screaming in the distance. He followed the sound, instinctively knowing that whatever was going on had to do with whatever he was looking for. Not that he even had a good idea of what that was exactly. Just something awry.

The lights of the sheriff's car caught River's eye. He made out Sheriff Ronnie Mills cutting through the crowd. A park ranger's truck was also parked haphazardly behind the deputy cruiser. River remembered that Tess had seen Bryce and Devin talking at Blue Peaks Park. The clues were falling into place.

River jogged over to catch up with Ronnie. "What's going on, Sheriff?"

Ronnie glanced over but didn't slow his pace. "Are you working a case here?"

The sheriff knew River better than to think he'd be here on his own for the fun of it.

"Kind of. Did something happen?" River asked.

Sheriff Ronnie gave a nod. "Park Ranger Devin Banner

reported seeing a black bear on the grounds. We have to contain the crowd and send everyone home."

"Devin Banner? Did anyone else see it?" River asked.

The sheriff continued walking. "If you want to help, keep people moving toward their vehicles once I make the announcement. I don't want anyone lingering while there's the potential for a wild animal roaming out in the open."

River stopped walking short of the festival's outdoor stage. The sheriff wasn't going to give him any more details, but something was off.

The sheriff stepped behind a podium and took a microphone that was set up for a talent show later. "Attention, everyone. I need you to stay calm and head back to your vehicles. I'm sorry to say that the festival is being cut short. Please don't have conversations, just go directly to your cars and trucks, and leave in an orderly manner."

"What's going on, Sheriff Mills?" someone called out from the crowd.

He hesitated as he propped his hands on his hips. "Well, our local park ranger has spotted a bear roaming the grounds. He and a team are working on catching and containing it right now. If you see the bear, don't interact with it, just depart and call nine-one-one."

The rumble of the crowd grew loud with nervous chatter. Then everyone started hurrying toward their vehicles in the parking lot. River didn't, however. He somehow suspected that there was no bear. Instead, he suspected a snake in the grass. Or two.

∞

An hour later, River caught up with Sheriff Ronnie again.

"Did you locate the bear?" he asked.

Ronnie looked up and shook his head. "Nah. It must have gotten scared off by the commotion of the crowd heading back to their vehicles."

"You sure there was ever a bear at all?" River folded his arms over his chest. "I mean, did anyone other than Devin see it?"

Ronnie frowned over at him. "Why would Devin make up something like that?"

"Oh, I don't know. To end the festival early. To continue on with the festival's reputation of being cursed."

Ronnie chuckled. "Don't tell me you believe that garbage."

"No. But I do believe that someone is feeding that nonsense to the town."

Ronnie seemed to consider this. "You think Devin reported seeing a bear in order to get the festival shut down? You suspect him of being behind all the past sabotage of the summer festival?"

River shook his head. "No. I suspect someone else. I think Devin was just roped in for this year's sabotage."

"Do you have a name for that other person?" Ronnie asked.

"I'm not one to point fingers without solid proof," River said.

Ronnie grinned. "I respect that. I've told you before, but if you ever want a job, come talk to me."

"I appreciate it. I like to work alone though," River said, even though his mind went to Tess. He hadn't completely worked alone on this case. She'd helped him, and he hadn't minded as much as he would have thought. "Mayor Gil puts so much time and effort into this festival. It's a shame that it gets marred year after year."

Ronnie blew out a long breath. "He's a good mayor. I like him a lot better than Bryce Malsop, that's for sure."

River had to hold his tongue so he didn't give away his suspicions about the former mayor. Instead, he shook Ronnie's hand. "Thanks. Good luck catching the bear," he teased.

"Thanks. Good luck with whatever, or whoever, you're chasing," Ronnie said back.

"Thanks." Although River had never believed in luck. He believed in right and wrong, in keeping your word, and helping others as much as possible. He couldn't imagine ever falling into a pattern where he did the wrong thing and needed to search out lawyers to hide his secrets. What kind of secrets had Jared been hiding? River liked to think that if he and Jared were still friends when he'd died, Jared would have confided in River. Maybe River could have helped him sort through whatever he was dealing with.

As River headed back to his truck, he texted Tess.

> *River:* Looks like the festival is over.
> *Tess:* I heard. A bear?
> *River:* That's the story at least. Are you home?
> *Tess:* The bookshop. I gave Lara the day off.

Disappointment settled in River's stomach. He'd kind of hoped to see Tess. Spending a Saturday night alone had never bothered him before, but tonight he didn't want to.

> *Tess:* You can grab dinner and come to the store.

River smiled at his phone.

> **River:** Sounds like a plan. I'll see you soon. Any
> requests?
> **Tess:** Surprise me.

∞

"How did you know I have a weakness for sushi?" Tess asked as she used her chopsticks to claim another piece.

"I didn't. I just guessed that you would."

Tess closed her eyes as she devoured another piece. When she opened them again, River was watching her with an undeniable look of attraction in his eyes. She should probably feel self-conscious about the way she was moaning over the sushi, but she was so relaxed around River. "I know you said we'd have our second date tomorrow night, but this totally counts as date number two."

River picked up a piece of sushi with his own chopsticks. "Yeah? Even though I didn't pick you up at your front door or bring you flowers?"

"I don't need that stuff," she said, smiling at him.

"No? What do you need?"

"How about honesty?" She let out a humorless laugh. "I always valued that, but now it's everything. More than flowers or chocolate."

River nodded at her. "I can give you honesty."

"Mm, I know. You are George Washington himself. I'm not sure you're capable of telling a lie."

"That's a plus when it comes to you, right?"

She laughed. "Yes. A definite plus. You know what? I bet you'd be horrible at playing Two Truths and a Lie."

He lifted a brow. "What's that?"

"Don't act like you've never heard of it. It's a drinking game. You tell someone two truths and a lie, and the other person has to guess which is the lie. But since you don't lie, you'd lose for sure." She grinned over at him, reaching for another piece of sushi. "Let's play it."

"Now?"

"Well, minus the drinks, of course. I have no customers. It'll be fun. And we might learn something about each other."

He smiled quietly at her. "I wouldn't mind learning more about you."

"Okay then. I'll start. Here I go." She took a moment to collect her thoughts. "My first movie crush was Indiana Jones. I despise eating avocados because of the color. And I cut all the tags out of my clothing because they make me itch."

River's brows lifted. "Wow. Those are very specific things."

"That's how you play. Details make it seem more convincing."

"I see." He scratched the side of his face, where stubble was growing. "I'm going to go with the lie being the avocado. Everyone loves avocados."

She shook her head and laughed. "Not me."

"You don't like avocados?" he marveled.

"Nope. The color is not something one should eat." She grinned. "My first movie crush was River Phoenix. So when I met you, I was intrigued by your name."

"River Phoenix, huh?"

She nodded. "Yep. He played the young Indiana Jones in *The Last Crusade*."

River pointed. "So it wasn't a full lie. That doesn't count then. You should have specified Harrison Ford."

Tess laughed. "Argh. You got me. Okay, your turn."

River pinched his chin thoughtfully. "I sing in the shower, and Buddy howls at me through the curtain. I talk to myself when I'm camping on my own. And I, uh, sleep in the buff, except when I'm camping."

Tess felt her lips part. "Two of those three involve you being naked."

River dropped his face in his palm and then looked back up at her. "They're the first things that came to my mind."

"Shows where your mind is," she said on a small laugh, teasing him.

He continued to watch her. "Which one is the lie, Watson?"

At this, she grinned. She loved that he had a nickname for her. It felt intimate, just like everything else between them. Even this simple game. "I've been in the same room while you slept and while you showered."

He shook his head. "I beg to differ. You were not in the same room while I showered."

"Right." Her cheeks warmed. "But I was in proximity, so maybe you changed your habits for my benefit. I think the lie is that you talk to yourself while you're camping. People who talk to themselves typically aren't comfortable with quiet. That's not you. You're at home in silence."

He stared at her for a long moment. Then he nodded. "You're right. I don't talk to myself."

She pumped a fist in the air. "Yes." Lowering her arm, she asked, "So you really sing in the shower? That is surprising. What do you sing?"

He shook his head. "I'm not sharing all my secrets tonight. You'll have to stick around to find out."

Tess leaned toward him, prepared to kiss him, when the bell over her store's door jingled. She'd almost forgotten that she was working. She turned to look at her incoming customer, and everything inside her froze. "Mrs. Lane. How are you?"

Jared's mother continued walking until she was standing right in front of Tess and River. She briefly glanced at River. Then her gaze stayed on Tess. "I had a talk with Heather this morning, and I felt like I needed to come down here and see you."

Tess braced herself. She wasn't sure what Mrs. Lane was about to say. Was she going to defend Jared? Or ask how dare Tess accuse Jared of doing something so horrible?

"If Jared did in fact have a lover somewhere else, I just want to tell you how deeply sorry I am on his behalf. I know what an amazing wife you were to my son. You were always so good to him. I just..." She shook her head as tears filled her eyes. "I hope this isn't true for your sake." She glanced over at River and back to Tess. "I don't blame you for moving on with your life. It's time for that. Long past time, and who you move on with is your business."

"Thank you, Mrs. Lane." Tess stood and opened her arms for the older woman to step into. The hug was awkward at first but melted into something less so.

Mrs. Lane stepped away and wiped beneath her eyes. "You'll come over to dinner very soon?"

"Yes. That would be nice."

Mrs. Lane finally looked at River for more than a second.

"And if Tess should ask you, you're welcome to come as her date. She will always be family at my house, so whoever she chooses to be involved with romantically is welcome in my home too."

River nodded. "Thank you, Mrs. Lane."

"You were a good friend to Jared until the wedding." She pursed her lips. "But that's the past. I don't guess I'll hold that against you any longer."

River nodded again.

Tess supposed this was as close to a truce as she would get, and she was glad for it. She didn't want to lose Jared's family. They were a huge part of her life and always would be.

"Okay, then. I will be attending this book signing that you've set up here in the store. I think that will be exciting. I'm sure your aunt Sheila is so proud of what you're doing with the store."

"I hope so," Tess said, refraining from mentioning that some folks in town weren't in favor of some of the changes she'd implemented.

"This is that author that you enjoy so much, yes?" Mrs. Lane asked.

"It is," Tess confirmed. "I've read her book a half dozen times. I got you the book for Mother's Day last year."

"Yes, that's right." Mrs. Lane didn't add that she'd read it. She probably hadn't, but River had. Just another reason that Tess was falling hard and fast for him. She couldn't stop herself even if she tried, and she didn't want to. Mrs. Lane was right. It was time to move on with her life, and River was the perfect person to do it with.

Chapter Twenty-Three

On Monday morning, River put the sealed DNA samples from Mia and Heather in a biohazard bag and dropped it off at the medical lab where he had tests like these run. He dropped his own sample in a biohazard bag as well and sent his off to 23andMe. He wasn't above using a commercial company to do his detective footwork for him. It would be the quickest way to locate any matches to his own familial roots.

He didn't have to decide if he was going to go through with anything until potential relatives' information showed up for him in the system. *If* it showed up. Then he could do his due diligence. He could investigate the names if he wanted to. That's one advantage he had over others who used the company. River knew how to follow an online footprint. He could find out everything there was to know about a person before he even met them.

With the samples dropped off, he headed toward his truck in the parking lot. Tess was on his mind. He was falling for her more every day, which was why he needed to come clean with her about visiting Mr. Browning and discovering that Jared was in the process of filing for divorce. It was one more thing that would devastate her, but keeping this secret would ruin whatever chance they had at a real relationship.

As if hearing his thoughts, his cell phone rang, and Tess's name popped onto his screen.

"Hey, I was just thinking about you," River said in answer.

"Oh? What about me?" Tess asked.

"The case actually."

"Which one? The festival or mine?"

River chuckled. "I don't have any new leads on the festival case. Unless you do," he said. "You're quite the detective these days."

"Sorry. You're on your own, Sherlock. I'm going to stick to my day job. So you were thinking about my case?" she asked. "What about it?"

River hedged. This would be better said in person. "Just following up on a few things. We can meet up to review the last details this week. I guess once we get the DNA results, it's case closed."

"Mm-hmm," she agreed, voice going quiet.

River's gut told him that Tess wasn't doing as well as she had seemed to be. Maybe the realization of everything was slowly sinking in. "Hey, I have an idea. Why don't we go camping?"

"What? When?"

"Today. Can you get away from the bookstore? It'll take your mind off waiting for the results. I read your favorite book, which is your thing, so I think you should go camping with me, which is my thing."

"On a weeknight? I don't know. I've already asked a lot of Lara lately."

"You worked Saturday and gave her the day off. And you're closed on Sunday. She can work for one day. It'll be fine," River said. "Let's go. We can disconnect from the world for twenty-four hours. You'll be a new woman when you come back," he promised.

"I thought you liked this woman the way she is."

"I do. I happen to like her a lot. That's why I want to take her camping. I never got to show you my favorite hiking spot."

"You said it was Jared's spot you wanted to show me."

"True," River said. "But it's also mine."

"In that case, I'll call Lara. I'm warning you though. I don't have good survival skills. I have no idea how to catch my own food or build a shelter."

"I'll teach you. The key to survival in any situation is keeping a clear head." And that's why River thought taking Tess camping was so important. Her head needed to be clear because he suspected, even without the proof, that the case was closed as well. And when the proof came any day now, he wanted Tess to be ready.

Tess knew what River was doing, and she was falling a little more in love with him by the minute for it.

Love? Had she honestly just thought that?

Here she was, having her own personal crisis. Her late husband wasn't the man she'd thought he was. He had been having an affair. And he may have had a child with some other woman. Yet, here Tess was falling hopelessly in love with River Harrison. Her emotions were at war, but out here in the great outdoors, she really could see things more clearly. No matter what had happened three or four years ago, it was still in the past. This was now, and she was here with River. There was nowhere else in the entire world she'd rather be.

His gaze slid toward her. "Usually when I'm out here, I think about life. Douglass, Julie, the parents I never knew. Jared," he said quietly.

"Not this time?" she asked, leaning into him.

"This time, all I can think about is you."

She laughed out loud, the sound carrying deep into the woods. "Sorry?"

"No, it's good. I like thinking about you. You're one of my favorite subjects these days."

She thought that she should feel guilty for being this happy when the life she knew, the one she'd thought she had once upon a time, was crumbling somewhere in her subconscious. She didn't want to feel guilty though. "Thanks for taking me out here."

"You thank me now. Later, when there's no bathroom or shower and you're hearing frightening nighttime noises, you might be cursing me."

"You'll protect me, right?" she asked.

"Yep. And bathrooms and showers are overrated."

She lifted a brow. "Really?"

"We'll only be here for a night. You'll be fine." He bumped his shoulder next to hers. Then he stood and extended his hand to her. "A hike?"

She allowed him to help her stand. "Okay. Let's go."

Three miles later, Tess was breathing deeply, and her only thoughts were on the next step. She and River had seen deer tracks, an eagle and its nest, several rabbits, and then they'd stopped and stared down a mother deer and her doe. It took Tess's breath away completely. She didn't pull air into her lungs until the mother and its doe finally ran off into the woods, their steps breaking twigs in the distance.

Tess pressed a hand over her heart as River turned to her. "I understand why you love this area. It's so serene out here."

"I'm glad that I get to share it with you." He stepped toward her and wrapped his arms around her. Then he lowered his face to hers. "Mind if I kiss you, even though I'm hot and sweaty?"

She smiled. "I'm also hot and sweaty. I never in a million years would have said this was romantic. It's not in any of the romance novels I've read, and I've read a lot of them."

River looked at her, waiting for her answer. "So the answer is no?"

"I didn't say that. My answer is yes. Maybe I've never read a hot, sweaty hiking scene in a romance novel before, but this is undeniably romantic," she whispered, drawing closer to his mouth.

"Yeah? Just wait until we're lying under the stars tonight. I plan on impressing you with my knowledge of constellations. I hear women like that."

Tess grinned. "That does sound romantic." She lost her breath again as River finally leaned in and kissed her. Her heart pounded beneath her cotton tee. Had she ever felt this way before? If she had, it'd been too long ago to remember. The feeling was dizzying. Amazing.

River stepped back and looked at her. "Wow."

"What?"

"I never believed those people who said things were better when they were shared. But it's true. When shared with the right person, everything is better. Especially this."

Tess gave his chest a little push. "I will never get used to the fact that you are a romantic. Did Jared know that about you?" As soon as she asked the question, she regretted it. Even though they'd both had a relationship with Jared, she didn't want to keep bringing his name up.

River reached for her hand. "You can talk about him. It's okay, you know? It doesn't bother me."

She turned and started walking on the path again. River followed beside her, reaching for her hand. "Maybe it bothers me. How can we be together and have him between us?"

"He's not between us. He's not here," River said gently. "We're here. He was your husband. He was also my best friend. We can't change that, and I wouldn't want to. Would you?"

Tess offered up a humorless laugh. "Ask me in a couple days when I have that evidence we're waiting for."

River squeezed her hand. "You don't mean that. There were good times. And none of us would be the person we are without the bad times."

She sighed as she glanced over. "So did he? Did he know that you were a romantic?"

River shook his head. "No way. Jared would have teased me mercilessly. Men don't let each other know they're romantics at heart."

"In my experience, most men aren't."

River gave her a questioningly look. "No?"

"You're special." She squeezed his hand back. "My very own hero straight out of a romance novel."

River groaned. "Please don't let that get out. Especially not to Reva Dawson."

Tess grinned. "I won't. But the main reason is because then I'd have to fight all the women in Somerset off you. A romantic man is hard to find."

"A woman who brings the romance out of me is even harder."

"Guess we should stick together then," she said.

"At least until we're out of these woods," River suggested with a teasing bump against her shoulder. "I don't think you'd make it out without me."

She laughed some more. "Very true. I'll stay by your side at least until then. Maybe longer."

As night fell, Tess did draw closer to River out of necessity more so than attraction.

"That was a coyote. I know it. Are they howling because we're out here?"

River reached for her and rubbed her arm. "No. They don't care about us. And I've fought off bobcats before, remember? You're safe with me."

She snuggled into his side, feeling reassured and safe. She loved that about him. He made her feel so many things. She took feeling safe for granted, but out here, she realized just how nice it was to have someone who was capable of fighting off wild animals. "I could probably fight a coyote if I had to," she mused into the night.

"I'm sure you could. This scar below my eye would look sexier on you."

She rolled into him, going up on her elbows to kiss said scar. Then she gazed down on him. "An inch higher and you would have lost that eye. A patch would have been interesting."

"Would you date a guy with a patch?"

"If he was you, yes."

River continued to look at her. "For clarity's sake, are we dating then?"

"It sure feels that way to me. I don't want to go out with any other guy, and trust me, my mom has tried to push them on me."

"Just me?" he asked.

"Just you."

"That's good, because I don't want to go out with any other woman."

"Just me?" she asked, following his lead.

"Just you."

She rolled back into the crook of his arm. "Okay. Prove your knowledge of constellations. Or were you just saying that to impress me?"

"I don't tell fibs," River said. "I do know the stars." He pointed into the sky. "See that one right there?"

"Mm-hmm."

"That's River."

She swiped her gaze to look at him. "River?"

"And that one right there is Tess."

She shoved her hand against his side. "You just said you didn't tell fibs. How can I ever believe what you say again?" she teased.

He looked at her seriously. "You just called me on my fib immediately. I think you can trust yourself to know when to believe what you're hearing is true."

"I'm not so sure," she said quietly. She wasn't sure she could ever trust herself again.

"Let's test it out. Two Truths and a Lie." River reached for her hand. "I'll start. One: If love at first sight is a thing, I fell for you that first night at the lake. Two: I haven't been in love since. Until now. And three: My favorite thing to do is drink beer and watch TV."

Tess's eyes burned. "I've never known you to drink beer and watch TV."

"Maybe you don't know me as well as you think you do," he said, looking over at her.

"I think I know you pretty well." She ignored the coyote's howl in the distance this time. She was safe with River. She believed that. She trusted that she could believe everything he said, including that the two stars above them were named River and Tess. Why not? "You're in love with me?" she asked, suddenly realizing the weight of what he'd just said.

"You tell me. Is that the truth or is it the lie?"

She searched his eyes, pinning all the facts she had into place. The proof, as River would say. He had read her favorite book. Taken her camping. His romantic side was showing even though she was pretty certain a man like him didn't show it easily. "I think I'm falling for you too," she said instead of answering his question.

The faintest smile crept up on his mouth. Then he leaned in and kissed her. The kiss stretched across the night. It was just a kiss, but it was so much more than that. By the time she fell asleep on his shoulder, she was sure. She didn't just think she was falling for River Harrison. She was certain she already had.

Chapter Twenty-Four

On Wednesday afternoon, Tess stared at a text she'd received from River.

> **River:** Can we see each other tonight? I'd like to review the case.

Reviewing the case meant that the results were likely in. Mia was either Jared's daughter or she wasn't. But Tess already knew the little girl was. Didn't she?

Her fingers tapped out an answer.

> **Tess:** Sure. I'll cook you dinner at my place.
> **Tess:** Heather is staying with the Lanes this week so we'll have the house all to ourselves.

Not that this would be a romantic evening. River was already prefacing that he wanted to discuss business. She wanted to ask what the results were right now. She didn't want to wait any longer. Just tell her what he knew.

She knew River wouldn't reveal one way or the other

over the phone though. He would want to be there with her in case she freaked out. Panicked. Cried. What? How did one react to proof that their late husband had a child with another woman?

Ignoring the worries and fears floating through her mind, Tess texted another upbeat message that was meant to relay *I'm fine. Totally fine.*

> **Tess:** You can bring Buddy, of course. I miss my furry friend.
>
> **River:** He misses you too. Your place around 7?
>
> **Tess:** Looking forward to it.

Tess stared at her screen, waiting to see if River would send her another message. When he didn't, she busied herself in the bookstore for the rest of the afternoon so that she didn't have to think about what he might tell her tonight. Jaliya's book signing was this weekend, so there were lots of finishing touches to be completed, including sending a reminder email to all the bookstore's subscribers about the event and updating the website.

Tess wanted to attract a huge turnout for Jaliya. Hers was a small bookstore, but she had loyal customers whom she knew would love Jaliya's book if they gave it a chance. It had breathed life into Tess when she needed it most, right after Jared's death. Tess had mourned the loss of her husband, yes, but also the future she was going to have with Jared. The happily ever after. Would they have had it if he'd lived? Would Jared have ever told her about Ashley?

One of Tess's biggest pet peeves in a book was an ending

that didn't fully resolve the story. Loose ends left her feeling anxious and unsatisfied, and that's what she felt with her marriage to Jared now. It was unresolved. There were loose ends that she wasn't sure she'd ever clear up, even with River's help. She'd have to accept that. Put the book that was her and Jared's love story on a shelf in her past and leave it there.

At six o'clock, she closed the bookshop and headed home. She'd promised to cook River dinner, which had been an impulsive offer. She hadn't had time to go to the grocery store, so she had only what was in her fridge to work with. She grabbed some ground beef she had thawing and decided to go with tacos. Quick, easy, and hard to mess up.

She prepared some bowls of shredded cheese and lettuce, diced tomatoes, and sour cream so that they could build their own tacos and then made a pitcher of sweet tea. The doorbell rang just as she was putting it on the table.

"Perfect timing." She opened the door to the most handsome man in Somerset Lake—hands down. And the cutest dog. "Dinner is served. For us. I'm afraid I don't have anything for Buddy."

"I brought a treat for him. He'll be happy." River stepped inside with Buddy and his gaze moved to the dining room table. "Mexican. Nice choice. I was craving that kind of cuisine today."

"Yeah?" She narrowed her eyes. "Are you just saying that?"

"Nope. I would never lie to you."

And Tess found that statement very comforting. Who knew honesty could be such a sexy quality in a man? She'd never considered it before, but now it felt like one of the most important qualities. Back in her twenties, she would have said she found the eyes and shoulders most attractive in a romantic interest.

"Let's eat before it gets cold," she said.

"I'll just go wash my hands."

She gestured. "The bathroom is down the hall. Second door on the left. I'll pour our glasses of tea."

"Thanks."

Tess went to the kitchen to grab two glasses from the cabinet. Her hands were shaking. Her whole body was shaking. If she was so certain she knew what River was going to tell her, why was she nervous?

She braced her hands on the counter, closed her eyes, and took a couple of calming breaths. Whatever River told her wouldn't change anything now. Jared was already gone. She'd already moved on. She was falling for River. Whether or not Mia was Jared's daughter was just a fact. Plain and simple.

"You okay?" River asked, coming up behind her.

She hadn't even heard him leave the bathroom. She opened her eyes and willed herself to relax as she turned to face him with the two glasses in hand. "Yep. Just getting these for our tea."

River's expression told her he wasn't buying it. He stepped up to her and took the glasses from her hands, putting them on the counter at her side. Then he wrapped his arms around her waist. "Talk to me."

"I'm shaking. I don't know why I'm shaking, but I can't stop. I just need to know what the results say. Is Mia Jared's daughter or not? I mean, I know she is. Isn't she?" Tess's words were coming quick, stumbling over each other. Tears sprung to her eyes as she looked at River. "I wish I didn't care so much."

"Hey. Of course you care. I'd be worried if you didn't. Jared was your husband."

She swallowed back the onslaught of tears. "So?"

River hesitated. Then he reached into his pocket, pulled out a folded piece of paper, and handed it to her. "Here. This is for you."

The tears wouldn't hold. They started slipping down Tess's cheeks as her shaky hands struggled to unfold the paper. She opened it and blinked past her tears so she could read: "Ninety-nine point five percent probability of paternity."

She swallowed a sob and felt River's arms go around her, hugging her tightly or maybe holding her up as her knees buckled. "Mia is his daughter?"

"Yes," he said simply.

There was no more conversation for a long time. River just held her while she cried. She hadn't thought she'd cry. She'd prepared herself for this outcome. She'd expected it even. But it still surprised her. Still hurt. Her heart felt like someone had broken it open, and grief spilled out of her.

"I'm sorry," she finally said, looking up at River.

"For what?"

"Crying on you. Ruining dinner. It's probably cold by now."

"I like cold tacos."

She cocked her head to one side. "I thought you said you'd never lie to me."

"And I won't. If you made the tacos, I will love them. Hot or cold."

She rolled her lips together, feeling foolish and spent. "I probably look a mess, huh?"

"You look absolutely beautiful to me, Tess." He stroked her

cheek with his finger. "What do you need from me? I'll do anything to make you feel better."

"I just need you to stay awhile. Otherwise I might cry all night, and I don't want to do that."

River nodded. "I'll stay all night then. We've shared a room before. You know you can trust me."

"Yeah. I do know that." And considering what she'd just learned about her husband, that was saying a lot.

"So? Do you want me to stay?" he asked.

Tess didn't even have to think on her answer. That's the only thing she wanted right now. "Yes."

The next morning, River got up quietly and moved through Tess's house, not wanting to wake her. He'd stayed the night, but now the sun was up and he thought it was best if he made himself scarce.

Buddy's feet were loud on Tess's floor. You couldn't tell a dog to tiptoe or to be quiet. They didn't understand. River was searching Tess's kitchen for a piece of paper to leave her a note when Tess shuffled into the kitchen.

"Trying to leave without saying goodbye?"

River turned in her direction. "Just trying to give you privacy." He stepped toward her and dipped to kiss her forehead. "I have some errands to run this morning. I'm going home to shower and change."

She nodded. "Okay."

"You're all right?" he asked.

"Yeah. Thank you for staying last night."

He'd slept right beside her, with her under the covers and him over. He hadn't wanted to make any moves when she was vulnerable. That wasn't why he was here last night. His sole job was to comfort her. "Anytime. I guess I won't see you tonight since you have book club and I'll be at the tavern."

Tess frowned. "Right. Want to meet tomorrow morning for breakfast?"

"As a date or to discuss the case?" he asked.

"The case is closed. Your job is done. My husband had an affair, and Mia is his child." She audibly swallowed.

There was more that River hadn't told Tess. About Jared's plans to divorce her. He'd been convinced that she needed to know that as soon as possible, but after seeing how devastated she was last night, he'd changed his mind. Maybe some facts weren't meant to be out in the open. He didn't want to be the one to hurt her yet again.

"So from here on out, it's just pleasure between you and me. No more business."

He tugged her toward him. "No more Watson? I might need to call on you for your help again at some point."

This brought a glimmer of a smile to her mouth. "On a case-by-case basis maybe. I wasn't much help with the festival case."

"Well, I'm still working on that one. I'm meeting with Sheriff Mills today, actually. Some of the pictures you took might come in handy, Watson." He bent and kissed the smile on her lips, unable to resist. "Breakfast tomorrow. Sweetie's Bake Shop?"

Tess kissed him back. "How about you get it and bring it to the bookshop? It's more private. We can sneak in more kissing."

"I like the way you think. You sure you're okay?" he asked before leaving.

She gave his chest a little push. "I'm fine. Really."

River headed out the front door, locking and closing it behind him. Before getting into his truck, River took Buddy for a walk to relieve himself among the trees. He was very aware that neighbors were already out and about, walking their own dogs and getting into their vehicles for work. Heads seemed to swivel toward him in Tess's yard. It was barely seven a.m. At least none of the neighbors were Reva Dawson, but he didn't really mind one way or the other. He and Tess were more than a fleeting thing. In some ways, it felt like he'd been waiting for her since he was nineteen. He just hadn't realized it.

After Buddy was done with his business, River got into his truck with his dog in the passenger seat, and he drove home to shower and change clothes. Once he'd freshened up, he drove to the sheriff's department. He had the pictures of Bryce talking to Devin at the festival and at the park right before Devin called in the bear sighting. Maybe it wouldn't be enough evidence to prove the former mayor was the one trying to run the festival into the ground, but it would be a leg to stand on in order to have a talk with the sheriff.

After laying out his case before Ronnie, River nervously waited.

"I always suspected Bryce myself," Ronnie finally said. "He has motivation. Who else would want to sink the town's festival?" Ronnie shook his head. "It'll be hard to prove though. I'll need solid evidence to move on this case."

River nodded. "I'm working on it."

"Mayor Gil is a good guy with a good heart. I don't know why Bryce would hold that against him."

"Because Gil is the fun mayor. Reva dubbed him that in her blog from day one, and it stuck. She didn't exactly spell out that Bryce had been the antithesis, but…" River trailed off.

"Bryce isn't a fun guy at all," Ronnie mused. "He's Mr. Fuddy-Duddy himself."

River stood and prepared to leave.

"So, uh, Tess Lane, huh?" Ronnie asked.

River felt taken aback by the question. "Yeah. We've been seeing each other lately."

"I think that's great. For both of you."

"Thanks. We'll see where it goes," River said, keeping the conversation casual. He already knew where he wanted things to go. He saw a future with Tess. Something he'd never seen with anyone. It scared and excited him. He just didn't want to mess things up somehow with her. That's why he was taking things slow. This was her first relationship since Jared had died. River didn't want to be the rebound guy. He wanted to be the forever guy.

Tess cradled her cup of hot tea in her hands. She loved book club nights with her favorite ladies. It was a chance to catch up, relax, and talk about Tess's favorite subject, which these days wasn't just books.

"So you and River are still going strong, huh?" Lucy asked from the chair across from Tess.

"He's pretty wonderful," Tess gushed. "Every time I think he can't be more amazing, he surprises me."

Moira reached for a lemon square off the plate on the coffee table. "Sounds like true love to me. Not that I have experience. I've read about it in a book though."

Tess nibbled on her lower lip, debating how open she would be with her friends. Then she decided to tell them everything. "He actually told me he loved me the other day."

The women all gasped in unison.

"He said the L-word?" Della Rose lowered the lemon square in her hand. "That's fast, isn't it?"

"River apparently has had feelings for me for a while," Tess told them. "He had feelings for me before Jared and I got married."

Moira's eyes widened. "Is that why he tried to stop your wedding?"

Tess sipped her tea. She looked around the group. "He caught Jared with Ashley before the wedding."

"Caught him?" Moira asked.

Tess nodded. "In an intimate position, I guess. He didn't elaborate. He warned me that, once I knew the truth, I couldn't unknow it." She sucked in a shaky breath.

"If Jared were alive right now, I'd pour a hot coffee on him. Not scalding, because I would never hurt someone. But I'd want to for what he did to you." Moira reached her hand toward Tess.

Tess took it and squeezed. "Thanks."

"I'm so impressed that you're able to know all this and still move on with River," Lara said. She'd joined them again tonight.

Tess looked at her as she brought her hand back to her side. "River is a different person."

Lara nodded. "Of course he is."

The others nodded their reassurance. Tess didn't feel reassured though. Instead, discussing this out in the open made her feel less assured. She never in a million years would have thought Jared had cheated on her before their wedding. She wouldn't have married him if she had. She wouldn't have suspected he'd had an affair later in their marriage either. Apparently, she was clueless and couldn't trust her own judgment. What made her think her impression of River was any different?

She blew out a breath.

"You okay?" Lucy asked, looking worried.

"Yeah. The truth just keeps hitting me at random moments. I think all the stuff with Jared is slowly sinking in."

"That's natural," Trisha said. "That's how I felt when I learned my ex-husband had a hidden side of his life that I wasn't aware of. It takes time to process. And you can't even begin to deal with it all until you've processed everything."

Trisha's ex was a financial advisor who'd scammed his clients out of thousands of dollars. He was currently serving a lengthy prison sentence, which was part of the reason Trisha had come to Somerset Lake for a fresh start. "I'm glad I have you guys here to help me process. I wouldn't want to go through this alone."

Della clucked her tongue. "You didn't let me go through my divorce alone."

"Or let me go through my mom's passing alone," Lucy added. "We're here for each other. Always. No matter what."

Tess turned to Lara. "See? This is more than a book club."

"I'm seeing that. And I'm glad you've invited me in. I could use friends like you all," Lara said.

The conversation eventually moved on to the book selection, but Tess's mind was on Jared and River, Ashley and Mia. She'd thought finding River right now was perfect timing, because he could distract her from her emotions. But what if the opposite was true, and it was bad timing, because she was dealing with too much all at once? A perfect storm of bitter and sweet.

When Tess got home that night, she was almost sad that Heather was staying the night at the Lanes' home. Part of her didn't want to be alone with her thoughts and feelings, because they kept turning on her. Maybe she didn't want to process anymore. River was right. Once you knew the truth, you couldn't forget it. The door had been opened, and now it couldn't be closed.

Tess washed her face and changed into her pajamas before spending some time tending to her hair. She collected her curls in a loose ponytail at the top of her head and then generously sprayed her favorite macadamia nut oil over the ends before pulling on her satin sleep cap.

A yawn stretched her face as she headed to her bed and sat on the edge, reaching for her phone. She tapped out a quick text to River. He might still be at the tavern with the guys. She wasn't sure.

Tess: Hey. Hope you had fun tonight.

She waited to see if he would respond immediately. When he didn't, a thought poked through her mind before she could censor it. Maybe he'd met someone at the tavern. A woman. Maybe he was at the bar talking to her. Getting her number.

Tess blinked, and tears rushed to her eyes. She wasn't a jealous or paranoid person. That wasn't her at all. Jared put those thoughts in her mind. How dare he? Her tears weren't sad this time. They were angry. How could Jared have done this to her? How could he have gotten Ashley pregnant when he was married to Tess?

Hot tears streamed down Tess's cheeks, and her breaths started to quicken. She braced her hands in front of her, struggling to catch her breath. *Is this a panic attack?* She'd only ever had one once before, when she'd learned of Jared's death. But this was the same sensation. She couldn't control her breaths, her tears, her body from shaking. She wanted to scream and yell at Jared, but he'd taken even that from her.

Sobs poured out of her. They were loud and ugly. Then she heard someone say her name, and it all stopped. She gasped and looked up at Heather.

"What... What are you doing h-here?"

"My mom is driving me insane so I decided to come crash at your place tonight." The skin pinched between Heather's brows.

Tess wiped at her eyes but it was futile. Her face felt swollen. She couldn't hide this. "You know the stages that people go through after some kind of trauma or loss?"

"Yeah." Heather walked over and sat on the bed in front of Tess, reaching for her hand.

"Apparently, I'm in the anger stage...Sorry. I know he's your brother."

"Yes, but I'm angry at him too," Heather said. "Because you're my sister."

Tess sucked in a deep breath, filling her lungs. "What comes after anger?" she asked, afraid to know.

Heather shook her head, the pinched fold of skin deepening between her eyes. "I'm an actress, remember? Psychology isn't my specialty."

Tess laughed. "I'm glad you came back. Now I don't have to drink alone tonight."

"Wine?" Heather asked. "I'm always up for a glass."

"Yes, please." Tess sniffled. Her phone buzzed on the nightstand as she got up to go into the kitchen with Heather. She picked it up and read the text from River.

> *River:* I had fun with the guys, but I would have had more with you. How was book club?

Tess tapped out a text.

> *Tess:* Enlightening. I'll fill you in tomorrow.
> *River:* Can't wait. Night. Sweet dreams.
> *Tess:* Night.

Heather glanced over her shoulder. "Messaging River?"

Tess sat on the barstool. "Do you think it's too soon for us? Considering what I just found out about Jared?"

Heather set a glass in front of Tess and poured a deep glass of red wine. "That's your mind talking. Only the heart knows the answer to that question. If it was too soon, you wouldn't be falling in love with him."

Tess reached for her glass. "That thing you said about being just an actress. There's more to you than that. Those were pretty wise words."

Heather lifted her glass high in the air as if to make a toast.

Tess lifted hers as well and gave Heather a questioning look.

"Jared gave me a lot of grief when he was alive. But he also gave me my one and only sister. Technically sister-in-law, but I'm not concerned with technicalities."

Tess smiled. "Me either."

Heather bumped her glass to Tess's, making the wine swish around in the glass. "To sisters forever, no matter what."

"To sisters," Tess said, feeling thankful that she could keep this relationship intact. She loved the Lane family. She enjoyed being a part of it.

"And to moving on," Heather said.

Moving on. Tess had done that until she'd happened upon the photograph in River's bedroom a few weeks ago. Now she would have to work on doing it again. "To moving on."

Chapter Twenty-Five

The next morning, River draped his legs off the bed and rubbed his hands over his face. He still didn't know what to do with the information Peter Browning had given him. Would Tess want to know the rest of the truth? Sometimes it was best to be left in the dark.

Buddy pressed his wet nose against River's knee, urging him to get up and take him out.

"All right, Buddy. I'm coming." River changed into some jeans and a T-shirt and slipped on his sneakers. Then he and Buddy took a walk along the creek.

Keeping something so big from Tess would drive a wedge between them. She had a right to know. He just wished he didn't have to be the one to break it to her. But it had to be him. He could take her into his arms and hold her. He could be there for her in whatever way she needed.

His resolve strengthened as he went through his morning routine of showering and having breakfast. Then he headed out to meet with another prospective client who'd contacted him about needing a private investigator. By the time he was through with that meeting, it was noon. He stopped by

Weeping Willows to have lunch with Douglass, which ended up being more like lunch with twelve other men.

"There's a book signing tomorrow," River told Douglass. "At Lakeside Books. I plan to go there and have a book signed by the author. After that, I'll come visit."

Douglass seemed to study him. "Is the author the woman you're seeing?"

"No." River shook his head. "The bookshop's owner, actually."

"Tess Lane." Douglass grinned. "I always liked her."

"Me too," River said.

"So who is the author that's signing at her store?"

"Jaliya Cruise. She wrote an inspirational self-help book that Tess loves. I read it and enjoyed it too."

Douglass nodded. "You're reading her favorite self-help book. That sounds like true love to me."

River looked out on the pond in front of them. "I've got a dilemma."

"Oh? You're not too old to get advice from your old man?"

"I'll always listen to advice from you. The dilemma is that I know something, a piece of information. It's about Tess's late husband. She hired me to look into his background right before he died. There's something I haven't told her yet because, well, it'll hurt her."

"What is it that you know?" Douglass asked.

River blew out a breath. "Remember when I had a falling out with Jared? Because I barged in on his wedding?"

Douglass frowned. "Yes."

"Well, that was because I caught Jared with another woman. He said it was just a one-night thing. Sowing wild oats or something. I don't know. I thought Tess needed to know who she was marrying."

"But you didn't tell her?" Douglass asked.

"No. I asked Jared to tell her. To come clean. It was his secret to tell. Instead, it cost me my friendship, and Jared still married Tess." River looked down at his hands. "My most recent investigation turned up proof that Jared had an affair before he died. He was seeing the same woman from before. They had a child together. Tess knows, and it's been pretty painful."

"I can only imagine. But there's something else?" Douglass asked.

River nodded. "She thinks Jared was just cheating on her. Stringing the other woman along. I found out that Jared was planning to get a divorce before he died though. I think he was in love with this other woman and planning to leave Tess. A physical affair is one thing. An affair that's also emotional is much worse." River shrugged and looked at Douglass. "Does she need to know? I mean, Jared's dead."

Douglass seemed to think on his answer. "It's not that she needs to know that her husband was in love with that other woman. Or planning a divorce. The reason you should tell her is because keeping something hidden from her will tear your relationship apart before it's started. You can't build something lasting on a foundation of secrets. Not even one. It won't work."

River sucked in a breath. "Yeah. That's what I knew you'd say."

"Because you already knew that's what needed to happen." Douglass patted River's leg.

"Okay. I'll tell her. Thanks, Dad."

"You're welcome." Douglass turned and gave River an unexpected hug.

They didn't hug often, but it was nice. River hadn't realized he'd needed a hug from the man who'd raised him. His dad.

After walking Douglass back to the facility, River headed out. He checked his cell phone and realized he'd missed a call from the sheriff. He got into his truck and dialed Ronnie back.

"Hey, River. I was just calling to let you know that I'm planning to pay Devin Banner a visit this afternoon. I'm on my way to his office right now actually."

"Yeah?" River cranked his truck as he listened.

"He was the only person to see the black bear at the summer festival. Combined with the pictures you and Tess took, I think we have enough to warrant a little chat. I'm hoping the good park ranger will throw our former mayor under the bus, but if not, he'll know we're keeping an eye on him. Maybe that'll send Bryce a message to leave the summer festival alone next year."

River turned out of the parking lot as he listened. "Let's just hope Devin cracks under pressure."

"Why don't you come help me lay on that pressure? Meet me at the park?"

River's work didn't often involve any kind of confrontation, but he didn't want to miss whatever was said in Devin's interview. "Sure. Be there asap."

Ten minutes later, River parked beside Ronnie's unmarked SUV and got out. The ranger's office was through the gate and down a dirt path. Ronnie stepped over and shook River's hand.

"Do you want to lead with the questions?" the sheriff asked.

River shrugged. "My questions might come out more as accusations."

"That's fine by me."

They walked through the gate and up the path, stopping at the ranger's office. The sheriff didn't knock. Instead, he opened the door and stepped inside. He was a large man with an intimidating presence.

Devin looked up from his desk. "Hello, Sheriff. This is a nice surprise." He looked at River as if trying to place his name.

"River Harrison," River said, although he was pretty sure Devin knew.

"We were hoping to have a little chat," Sheriff Ronnie said.

"About what?"

"About a black bear," River told him, bringing a chair up to his desk. He pulled out the little notebook in his pocket, along with a pen. He uncapped it and looked at Devin expectantly. "We know there was never a bear and no real reason to shut down the Somerset Summer Festival." River didn't look at Sheriff Ronnie, just in case the sheriff's eyes were wide and disapproving. River didn't want to waste time though. He just wanted his suspicions confirmed.

"What are you talking about?" Devin asked. "Why would I lie about a bear?"

"You tell us. We know about your meeting with former mayor Bryce Malsop. We know about the money exchange." At least that's what River assumed happened last Friday night before the rainstorm. "It's not hard to connect the dots."

Devin looked between River and Ronnie, his gaze finally stopping at Ronnie. "Am I under arrest?"

"Let's just say you're under suspicion," Ronnie said. "The best thing you can do is tell us the truth. I can't promise it'll set you free, but it'll make life a whole lot easier on you."

Devin folded his arms over his chest. "All I did was call in a bear."

"Which was a false report to nine-one-one and law enforcement," Ronnie told him. "Did you also take a bribe from the former mayor to do so?"

Devin's face blanched. "Do I need a lawyer?"

Ronnie shrugged. "Might not be a bad idea. I hope Bryce paid you enough to cover the legal fees."

Devin opened his mouth, but no words came out. Then he sighed. "He paid me five hundred dollars. That's a lot of money for someone like me, okay? I could use it. I have to send child support to my ex every month, and I barely have enough money left to cover the rest of my expenses."

"Just to be clear, who is it that paid you the five hundred dollars?" River asked.

"Bryce Malsop," Devin said. "The former mayor of Somerset Lake."

"Did he tell you why he wanted you to call in a bear?" River asked.

Devin nodded. "To stop the summer festival."

River closed his little notepad, shoved it in his pocket, and looked at the sheriff. "Case closed."

After leaving the park, River found himself driving down Hannigan Street toward Lakeside Books. He just wanted to see Tess. He didn't plan to tell her about what he'd learned at the lawyer's office just yet. But he needed to tonight.

He parked and walked the short distance to the bookstore. Lara was behind the counter when he stepped inside.

"Looking for Tess?" she asked.

"Yeah, I was hoping to see her."

"Well, you just missed her," Lara said. "She was on her way to meet somebody."

"Oh? Did she say who?"

Lara shook her head. "No. She got a phone call that seemed important. Then she asked me to close for her, which I didn't mind at all."

"An important phone call. Hmm." River couldn't think of who that might be from. Maybe Ashley? Or the Lane family. "Thanks," he told Lara. "I'll just text her when I leave here."

Lara nodded. "Good idea. Are you stopping by the book signing tomorrow?"

"Of course. I want my signed copy of the book."

"I am so impressed that you read the book." Lara held up a copy that was lying on the counter. "I'm making my way through it today while I work."

River grinned. "It's a great book. You'll enjoy it."

"I am so far. Well, we'll see you tomorrow then. Have a good night."

"You too," he called behind him. He stepped out onto Hannigan Street and texted Tess.

> **River:** Just dropped in at Lakeside Books, but Lara said you were meeting someone?

He waited for her to reply, but she didn't. Worry crept into his thoughts. Who could she be meeting with? The private investigator in him needed answers. He walked down to Sweetie's Bake Shop and looked around. No Tess.

"Need something?" Darla asked from behind the counter.

"Have you seen Tess?" he asked.

"Not since this morning. She's really excited about that book signing tomorrow, isn't she?" Darla leaned on the counter. "I'm going to try to slip down there and get a book signed. I haven't read it yet, but I've heard that you have."

"It's really good," River said, growing tired of people's reaction to the fact that he'd read Jaliya Cruise's book.

"Must be love," Darla said in a singsong voice. "If I see Tess, I'll tell her you're looking for her."

"Thanks." River left the bakeshop and headed back toward his truck, checking his phone to make sure he hadn't missed a text or call. Nothing. This shouldn't worry him so much. But for some reason, his gut was firing off all the alarms. Something was amiss.

Chapter Twenty-Six

Tess sat nervously at a table in the diner with a Dr Pepper in front of her. The man on the phone had said he needed to discuss Jared. He was a lawyer with whom Jared had worked. Tess knew only of the family lawyer. Peter Browning was not part of that practice.

She fidgeted absently with a napkin as she watched the door. Whatever this man wanted to talk to her about, he'd wanted to say it in person. What else had Jared been hiding from her? Was there more?

She heard her phone ping from inside her purse. She checked and saw that River was texting her again. If he knew what she was doing though, he'd insist on coming with her. He was Sherlock after all. But something told her that she needed to do this alone. She didn't want to wait for River. Didn't want him to shield her. She just wanted answers, and she wanted them now.

As if on cue, the diner's door opened, and a man in a gray business suit walked in. He turned to assess the people dining and spotted her, seeming to recognize her. She'd never seen him before in her life.

"Mrs. Lane?" he asked, stopping at the front of her table.

"Yes. Mr. Browning?"

He placed his briefcase down and slid into the booth. "I'm sorry I didn't choose a nicer place to meet."

"It's fine." Her chest muscles tightened. "What is it you wanted to discuss? You said it was about my husband?"

He took a breath, seeming just as nervous as she was. As he started to speak, a waitress came to the end of their table.

"Can I get y'all something?" she asked.

Tess just wanted the information that Mr. Browning had to give her, but sitting in a diner, she was expected to order more than a soda. "Some sweet potato fries, please. I saw those on the menu."

"Those are delicious," the waitress said, writing it down on her pad of paper. "And for you?"

"A coffee with cream. That's all," Mr. Browning said.

They waited for the waitress to head back to the kitchen. Then Mr. Browning took another breath and met Tess's eyes. "I should have come to see you sooner than this. I apologize."

Tess wrapped her fingers around the glass of Dr Pepper. It was wet on the sides, sweating bullets just like her. She didn't say anything. She just waited.

"When Mr. Harrison came to see me a couple of weeks ago, following a lead on your case, I realized that perhaps I had done you a disservice by not bringing this information to you."

Tess squeezed the glass, needing something to hold on to. "I see," she said. Why hadn't River mentioned this lawyer to her before?

"I thought it best left alone, but, well, I guess that wasn't my decision to make." He turned toward his briefcase and opened it on the booth beside him.

The waitress appeared with Tess's fries and Mr. Browning's coffee. They thanked her, and then Tess slid her tray of fries off to the side. Her stomach was tying itself into tiny knots, waiting to see what was in that briefcase. She heard her phone ping from inside her purse once more. It was probably River, wanting to know what was going on.

Mr. Browning slid his coffee to the side as well. Then he reached back into his briefcase and placed a stack of papers on the table in front of him. "I'm sure your private investigator filled you in, so this shouldn't be a shock."

Tess nodded, doing her best to keep a straight face. She didn't want Mr. Browning to know that she had no idea what he was about to tell her. If he knew, he might hold back, and she was tired of being shielded, lied to, left in the dark.

"This is the divorce document that Mr. Lane had me draw up." Mr. Browning slid it in front of Tess.

She pressed her lips together tightly, reminding herself to breathe.

"I guess the reason I wanted to see you in person is because I wanted you to know that your husband was very concerned about making sure you were well cared for in the divorce settlement. He cared about you, which is something that I don't always see in a divorce. I usually recommend a marriage counselor when I have clients that are so invested in their current partner's emotions and well-being. And I did in this circumstance as well."

Tess couldn't find any words to say. She was speechless.

"Of course, that's when he told me about the other woman he was in love with. And about the pregnancy."

"I see," Tess said, struggling to keep her tears at bay. Jared hadn't just been cheating on her. He had been in love with Ashley.

"I wanted to emphasize to you how much Jared cared about you in this situation. He didn't want you to get hurt. When your PI left my office a couple weeks ago, I wasn't sure that I had relayed that well enough. I felt strongly inclined to tell you this myself. Maybe I should have contacted you a long time ago, but, well…" Mr. Browning offered a weak smile. "You'd already lost your husband. In some ways, I felt like this would be losing him all over again. The fact that you hired an investigator made me realize that you wanted the truth."

"Needed it," Tess finally said.

"I am truly sorry for your loss, Mrs. Lane."

"I appreciate you bringing this to me." Tess looked down at the documents. "Jared already signed them?"

"Yes. He died the next day. I never sent them."

Tess stared at Jared's sloppy signature. She'd been only a couple of days from receiving these papers when she'd gotten the call about his death. She swiped a hand beneath her eye. "Thank you, Mr. Browning."

"Of course." He reached for his coffee and poured in the creamer before stirring it and taking a sip. "Some people want all the facts, and some say ignorance is bliss."

"It wasn't bliss," Tess said.

Mr. Browning shut his briefcase and slid out of the booth, leaving his coffee on the table along with a five-dollar bill. He reached into his pocket and brought out a business card.

"If you have any further questions, please don't hesitate to contact me."

Tess took the card and nodded, doing her best to hold her tears at bay. "Thank you again."

Mr. Browning held his briefcase to his side. "My deepest condolences."

Tess watched the lawyer leave the diner. She sat there and read over the divorce settlement. She would get half of everything they owned. Mr. Browning said Jared had cared about her, but that he had loved Ashley.

Tess blinked past her tears. Her phone pinged inside her purse again. She knew exactly who it was, and she didn't want to speak to him right now. River had known about these papers and hadn't told her. He'd known for weeks now. What happened to never lying to her?

She blinked past her tears, Jared's signature blurring on the paper. Divorcing her was one of his last tasks. His last wish. If she let herself, she'd break down into sobs right here in this diner. It wasn't the place though. She retrieved a ten-dollar bill from her purse and left it along with her untouched fries. Then she collected the papers and walked out, heading to her car. She couldn't break down in her car either. She needed to get home. She needed to be alone.

It was late, and Tess wasn't responding to his calls. He could see on his phone that she'd read the messages, so that meant she was alive. Whoever she'd met with hadn't kidnapped her or worse. But something was wrong. He could feel it.

River headed out of his house and got into his truck. If she wasn't going to answer her phone, he'd go to her home to see her. When he turned into her driveway ten minutes later, her car was there. Thankfully, Heather's was not. Nothing against Heather these days, but he wanted some privacy with Tess. He had a feeling they'd need it tonight.

He parked and hurried toward the door, eager to make sure things were okay. It wasn't like Tess not to respond to him.

He rang the bell and waited. When she didn't answer, he pressed the button again. "Tess?" he called through the door. "It's River. Are you okay?"

His phone buzzed in his pocket. He reached for it and read a text.

> **Tess:**　I would like to be alone tonight.

He tapped back his reply.

> **River:**　What's going on? You okay?
> **Tess:**　No. I'm not okay.
> **River:**　Please let me in. I want to see you.

She didn't respond. He waited on her doorstep, unsure of what to do. Finally, she opened the door. Her eyes were swollen and red, like she'd been crying all afternoon.

"What happened? Who did you meet with this afternoon?" he asked.

Tess lifted her chin and folded her arms tightly across her chest. She made it clear that she wasn't happy to see him right now. "I met with Peter Browning. You met with him as well, correct?"

River swallowed, understanding immediately what the problem was. "I was going to tell you tonight."

"What is it you were going to tell me? That my husband didn't just have a fling? That he was in love with Ashley? That he wanted to divorce me in order to be with her?"

River stepped closer. "I was waiting for the right time to tell you."

She started to close the door. She didn't want him near her. She didn't even want to see his face right now. "Well, while you were waiting, someone else told me. Now I know."

River opened his mouth to speak, but no words came out.

"Answer me this: Why do the men in my life keep secrets?"

"I was going to tell you," River said again.

She nodded. "I want to believe you. I do."

Relief splashed over him.

"But I'm not sure I can trust my feelings anymore. I'm not sure my internal compass works."

"You can believe me, Tess. You can trust me. I would never hurt you. You know that."

She stared at him from inside her house. "I'm not so sure. I just need to be alone."

"For tonight?" he asked.

She hesitated, rolling her lips together. River could feel the unshed tears she was holding back. "I might need to be alone a lot longer than that. Maybe I'm not ready to be in a serious relationship right now. Maybe I never will be again."

River froze; the only part of him moving was his heart, which seemed to shake his body with its forceful beat. "I love you, Tess."

A tear slipped down her cheek and then another. He just wanted to step over the threshold and wrap his arms around her. But he respected the invisible wall she'd built up between them. "I love you too," she said softly. "But I'm not even sure I can trust that feeling."

River swallowed. "I think you can. I've never told a woman I loved her before. Just you. I know what I'm feeling, and I'm pretty certain you feel the same way."

She shook her head as more tears fell. "This is too much, too soon. I can't do this, River. I can't do us," she clarified.

River couldn't stop himself anymore. He stepped toward her, but she stepped back.

"Please leave. I want to be alone. The case is solved. My husband did more than cheat on me. He fell out of love with me and in love with someone else. He broke his promise, his vows, my heart. Even if I could trust what I feel for you, my heart isn't intact. I don't have a whole heart to offer."

"What are you saying, Tess?"

"I'm saying that our business is through. And so are we."

River didn't move. "My birth parents gave me up. My best friend turned his back on me when we didn't agree. I've had my share of people disappointing me, Tess. I'm sure my heart is less than whole. But I'm still here. I'm still willing to risk the heartache and pain again. For you."

Her lips twitched. He could see that she was trying not to cry. "Well, maybe I'm not as strong as you," she said quietly. "Because I'm not willing."

Buddy greeted River with a wagging tail and joyful eyes when he returned home. Unconditional love is what a dog offered.

No matter what. Dogs seemed to have an uncanny way of forgetting their troubles. They lived in the moment. Next life, River wanted to be a dog. Not that he believed in next lives. He was only concerned with this one, and currently, this life was crumbling around him.

He grabbed a soda from his fridge and headed out to his back porch to sit and look out at the creek. That was the selling point last year when he'd purchased this home. He loved a nature view. He loved water and wildlife. He'd thought he loved experiencing it alone, but somehow, he enjoyed it more with Tess. He didn't like the idea of being alone as much now that he'd had her, brief as it was. He had never thought he was lonely. He wasn't. At least not before. But now, being without her, he felt the greatest sense of loneliness he'd ever endured.

He blew out a breath. She'd had a shock this afternoon, hearing that Jared was going to divorce her. Maybe her reaction was just that. A reaction. And tomorrow she'd see things differently. Somehow, he doubted it. He'd seen the lost look in her eyes. She didn't want to go through the pain of another failed relationship, especially when she'd thought everything was okay between her and Jared. River didn't blame her for doubting that she could ever trust herself again. He blamed Jared for making her feel that way.

River tipped his head back and closed his eyes. He had a picture with Jared on his nightstand still because, no matter their disagreements, River always thought of Jared as a friend. He wasn't like his parents, who'd decided they didn't want him. River didn't leave people behind. As if the universe knew he was thinking and resenting his birth family, his email pinged with an incoming email. River tapped his screen and stared at the subject line from a woman named Margaret Thorndike.

I think I might be your sister.

It was Saturday at noon and the book signing was about to start. Tess should be over the moon right now. Jaliya Cruise herself was sitting at a table in the back of Lakeside Books, and the line waiting outside to come in the store stretched all the way to Sweetie's Bake Shop.

Tess couldn't muster more than a smile though. She felt so drained after yesterday afternoon and last night. She'd cried half the night and had slept restlessly. She probably looked a mess today, even though she'd tried her best to hide the bags and reddened eyes.

She was a mess. Maybe even messier than when Jared had died. It felt like she'd lost Jared all over again. And she'd also lost River. It felt like all was lost, even though she knew that was a bit dramatic in reality. She had her health, her family, her friends, and the bookstore. And her favorite author was sitting just six feet away behind stacks of hardcover copies of Tess's favorite book.

Jaliya glanced over. "I'm so nervous."

Tess offered up a smile that was halfway true. "You've done interviews on TV. How can a signing at a small-town bookstore make you nervous?"

"Oh, I get nervous every time. I have a little bit of what's called imposter syndrome. I don't feel like I belong in this seat. All I did was write a book about myself and how I dealt with things. I didn't go to school for literature or do anything that would warrant a line of people standing outside."

Tess headed over to her table. "If you only knew how much your words helped me after I lost my husband." Tess's eyes burned. After she'd lost the husband who was about to divorce her anyway. Now she had a little bit of that imposter syndrome in calling herself a widow. She wouldn't have stayed Jared's wife. He had wanted out.

"Hey, is everything okay?" Jaliya asked.

Tess nodded and then shook her head. "Actually, I think I need to read your book again, because I'm struggling in my personal life right now. That's why you belong in that chair. You have helped so many people. You deserve this, and I'm thrilled that you're here at my store."

Jaliya smiled. "How about you and I go have dinner after this signing? Otherwise I'll just be going to a hotel. I'd love to get to know you better. Maybe you can tell me what's going on." She shrugged. "I can't promise to help, but I'll listen."

Tess was blown away by the offer. "I would love that. My treat, of course." She turned and looked at the door. "It's time for you to meet your fans and fans-to-be. Don't be nervous." Tess held up a finger. "Unless you meet a woman with pinkish-colored hair. She has a blog, and you are sure to make a bullet point tomorrow."

Jaliya's brows furrowed. "Okay. Noted."

Tess laughed softly to herself. "I'll go let your fans in. Good luck and have fun." Tess headed down the aisle of her store, feeling a spark of excitement. And she was looking forward to having dinner with Jaliya later. Who knows? Maybe Jaliya could help her figure out how she should feel, because she had no idea right now.

The customers entered in a line, heading straight toward Jaliya's table. Lara was manning the cash register, and Tess was greeting folks. River had said he'd come today, but after last night, Tess doubted he would. Some part of her wanted him to show up, even after she'd told him to leave her alone. What kind of thinking was that? Wanting him to do the opposite of what she'd said. What she wanted was a man who listened. And if she said she wanted to be alone, he should leave her alone. Right? Her thoughts were a wishy-washy mess. Which was why she was in no place to be romantically involved with anyone.

Tess saw her mom standing near the front of the line and headed over. "Hey, Mom. You made it."

"Of course I did." She opened her arms to give Tess a hug. "Oh, this is wonderful. Your aunt Sheila told me to tell you that she is so proud. I've already texted a half dozen pictures of this event to her."

Tess grinned. "Too bad she couldn't make it here in person."

"You know Sheila. After years of sitting in this bookstore, she's chasing one adventure after another. She loves what you've done with the store though. So do I."

Tess tilted her head. "Thanks, Mom." Tess was pretty proud of herself too. This book signing was a big deal for Lakeside Books.

"How's everything else going?" her mom asked hesitantly.

Tess had filled her in a little bit on what was going on with Jared's infidelity, but not all of it. "I'm holding my own. I'll come see you soon to catch up," she promised.

Her mom nodded and glanced a little ways down. "Your in-laws are here. You better go say hello."

Tess spotted Mrs. Lane waiting in the line. Heather was with her, looking every bit the glamorous LA actress. "On my way. Thanks again for coming, Mom." Tess moved farther down the line until she was standing in front of Mrs. Lane and Heather.

"I'm so excited to meet a real author. I'm even going to read this book," Mrs. Lane said.

Tess beamed at her mother-in-law. "I hope you do. It has been a godsend for me."

"Oh, dear, you are the strongest woman I've ever known. Jared couldn't have asked for a better wife."

Tess reminded herself to breathe. "Mm-hmm." She looked down until she felt Mrs. Lane grab her hand. "I couldn't have asked for a better daughter-in-law."

Tess's smile was shaky. "Thank you for saying so."

The line started to move forward.

"I better chat with the other customers. Thank you for coming out. This means so much to me that you're here," Tess said.

"Of course," Mrs. Lane squeezed her hand before letting go. "And you'll come to Sunday dinner soon? Maybe bring River with you."

Tess looked down again. River wasn't coming. She had made it clear that she didn't want to see him, and River was the kind of guy who honored a woman's request. Except for that one she'd made at the very beginning of their arrangement that he tell her everything. No holds barred.

Tess swallowed, her throat suddenly dry. She looked back up

at Mrs. Lane. "Yes, I'll come soon," she promised, intentionally ignoring the invitation for River. Otherwise, she might start crying, and this was an important event for her store. Jaliya was a huge author. She wanted more bestselling authors to sign at Lakeside Books. It was one of her goals for the bookshop. Today was a new beginning. For Lakeside Books and maybe for her too.

After the book signing, Tess took Jaliya to the nicest restaurant in town. The Perfect Catch Seafood Restaurant was right on Somerset Lake, overlooking the water where, at any moment one could see sailboats, kayakers, canoes, and all sorts of wildlife.

"I could write a book right here at this table. Do you think they'd rent this table to me for the next year?" Jaliya asked, joking.

Tess reached for her glass of lemon water. "Doubt it, but it never hurts to ask."

"That's my philosophy too."

The waitress came and took their orders. Then Jaliya settled into her chair and folded her hands on the table in front of her. "Okay. Tell me what's on your mind. An objective ear is sometimes helpful."

Tess looked down at the table and back up at Jaliya. "My story could be a book in and of itself. It's kind of embarrassing, to tell you the truth."

"We're friends. Don't be embarrassed."

"Wow. I'm friends with my favorite author. Who'd have thought?" Tess asked.

"Authors are just people too. I've got a million embarrassing stories I can tell you about myself if that'll help."

Tess blew out a breath. "Okay. Here goes."

She told Jaliya about her perfect marriage, or so she thought. Jared's untimely death. Ashley's claim that she was Jared's mistress. She told her about Mia and the paternity test. About River finding out that Jared was in the process of filing for divorce right before his death.

"I didn't find out from River though. It was the lawyer, whose conscience led him to meet with me and tell me. River says he was going to tell me, but I don't know. How can I ever trust myself again after all that?" Tess mused.

Jaliya shook her head. "You can't."

Tess's gaze snapped up to meet Jaliya's across the table. "What?"

"You can't trust yourself to make perfect choices and decisions. That's an impossible standard because everyone makes mistakes."

Tess nodded as she listened.

"So you'll just have to close yourself off and be alone for the rest of your life." Jaliya shrugged. "Then again, you'll disappoint yourself too. And you'll betray yourself because we all do. You'll lie to yourself because we all do that as well." Jaliya frowned. "I don't know what to tell you, Tess. There's no way to protect yourself from ever getting hurt again. It's inevitable."

The waitress came and laid their plates of food in front of them. Jaliya oohed and aahed happily, thanking the waitress, while Tess sat there numbly, wondering at Jaliya's advice. Once the waitress was gone, she cleared her throat.

"So you agree that breaking up with River was the right thing to do? Because I can't possibly trust my instincts. I've proven that they're untrustworthy."

Jaliya picked up her fork. "If you're going to constantly question his motives and compare him to your late husband, it's not the right time. He doesn't deserve that baggage. He deserves to come to you with a clean slate and the benefit of the doubt. If he says he was going to tell you, you have to believe that's true. He's not Jared. He's River. And you're not the same woman who married Jared. You're the one who's gone through the battle and come out stronger." Jaliya popped a shrimp into her mouth and chewed.

Tess sat there processing Jaliya's words. They were true and honest. She'd needed these words.

"I thought you said you read my book," Jaliya teased.

"I have. Several times." Tess reached for her own fork now.

"If he hesitated to tell you about the divorce papers, I'm guessing it's because he didn't want to hurt you. That's the only explanation. So you have to trust that, whatever happens, it's not River's intention to ever cause you harm." Jaliya set her fork down and reached across the table to briefly squeeze Tess's hand. "Honestly, I doubt it was Jared's either. People are people. They hurt each other. They make mistakes. They fall in and out of love. That's just life. You only have control over what you do. It's your choice, Tess. Choose to love with abandon and risk heartbreak. Or choose to close yourself off."

Tess carved a bite of fish with her fork and slid it into her mouth. "You're still single," she pointed out.

"That's because I'm on an adventure of my own choosing. If

I find someone who wants to come along with me, then great. I'm not ready to stay in one place yet. I know myself. I think that's what journaling has given me. I know who I am. What I want. What I'm looking for. And when I find it, believe me, I won't be sitting across from you questioning whether to go after it."

They finished dinner, which was delicious, and the conversation had been thought-provoking. Afterward, Tess headed home with several signed copies of Jaliya's book. One of which was for River, since he hadn't shown up at the bookshop earlier.

Jaliya's words echoed through Tess's mind as she took a hot bath and then changed into PJs. Heather had left a note saying she was out on a date tonight. That was good, because Tess just needed to be alone with her thoughts. She lay back on her bed and closed her eyes. Everything Jaliya had said made sense, especially the part about River deserving better than being compared to Jared. He deserved a clean slate. Tess wasn't sure if she could give him one though.

Chapter Twenty-Seven

On Sunday afternoon, River sat with Douglass, listening to one of his many stories. River was doing his best to smile, but doing so physically pained his face. He felt like he'd been wearing a constant frown since Tess had broken up with him.

"You're heartbroken. I can see it in your eyes," Douglass finally noted. "What happened?"

River's frown settled back into place. "Tess and I broke up. She's not ready. It's too soon."

"Ah. I'm sorry."

"Me too," River said.

"Do you think she will be ready at some point?" Douglass asked.

River absently picked at a loose thread on his jeans. "I don't know. I hope so, for her sake. She deserves to be happy, even if it's not with me."

"You deserve that too. I want that for you. Do you want more of my advice?" Douglass asked.

River glanced over. "Sure."

"You were friends before you were romantic, yes?"

"Briefly. Before that, she hated me," River said with a quiet laugh.

"Well, certainly don't go back to that. But return to being friends. If she's not ready for romance, just be her friend with no pressure or expectations. A person can never have too many friends." Douglass raised a finger. "Unless they all live in close quarters at the assisted living facility. Then they can."

River laughed louder this time. "That's good advice."

"It is, isn't it?" The old man chuckled. "You know, Julie broke up with me once before we were married. She said she wasn't ready. I thought it was over for good."

"I didn't know that. What did you do?" River asked.

"I gave her time to figure things out. I remained her friend. We enjoyed long walks before we were in a romantic relationship. I continued to show up for those. I listened. I waited. I figured out who I was too."

"And it worked?" River asked.

"Like a charm." Douglass grinned over at him.

River liked Douglass's suggestion of returning to a friendship with Tess. Just because her heart wasn't ready for more didn't mean they couldn't see each other. He missed her. Standing, he looked down at the man who'd raised him. "Thanks, Dad."

"Going somewhere?" Douglass asked.

"Yeah. I think I'm going to go meet up with a friend."

"Atta boy."

River gave his father a hug and then headed to his truck in the parking lot. He drove to Tess's house. Her car wasn't there so he headed to the bookstore, which didn't keep hours on Sunday. Even so, her car was parked in the small lot for employees. He walked up to the shop's front door and knocked. Tess headed in his direction, unlocked the door, and opened it to him.

"River. Hi. What are you doing here?"

He shoved his hands in his pockets. "I know we're broken up. I understand that. We're still friends though, right? You don't hate me?"

"I could never hate you."

"Well, you could. You have."

"We're still friends," she confirmed.

"Great. So let's go get some ice cream."

"Ice cream?"

"Mm-hmm. And take a walk along Somerset Lake. No holding hands. No telling you how beautiful you are. I promise."

A small smile curled on her lips. Then it trembled and fell. "I'm not sure I can just be friends with you, River."

"I'm not sure I can imagine a life without you in it in some way. People have a habit of coming in and out of my life, and I've accepted that. But I don't think I can accept it in your case. So do you think you can try to be my friend?" He swallowed, feeling vulnerable and raw.

She finally nodded. "Ice cream and a walk. That sounds nice. I'll just grab my bag. I, um, have a gift for you," she added.

"Oh?"

"Mm-hmm. I'll grab that too."

River expelled a breath. As long as he didn't lose her completely. That was something to hang on to.

She reappeared and handed him a copy of Jaliya Cruise's book. "It's signed. You didn't make it yesterday so…"

"I didn't think you wanted to see me." He took the book. "Thank you for this."

Tess adjusted her bag on her shoulder. "I'm in the mood for coffee ice cream. What about you?"

"Cookies and cream," he said.

She locked the door behind her and followed him down Hannigan Street. "I wouldn't peg you as cookies and cream."

He glanced over. "I'd totally peg you as coffee bean."

"Well, you are Sherlock."

"And you're Watson," he reminded her. "Speaking of which, you offered to come with me when I located a blood relative."

Tess's eyes grew wide. "You've found someone?"

"A sister. She wants to meet. What do you say? Are you up for one more PI adventure?"

Tess smiled. "I could never turn down an adventure with you."

River grinned back at her. Just walking beside her made a rush of emotion swell inside his heart. He loved this woman so much. She was the only one who'd ever made him feel this way, like he could fly if he only just tried. Like he wasn't alone in this life. Tess made him feel whole in a way he'd never experienced. So even if she never wanted to cross that line with him again, he'd take what he could get. Just seeing her smile was more than he probably deserved. If it had to be, it would be enough.

A couple of weeks later, Tess watched as Heather closed the flap of her suitcase and zipped it shut. Heather was returning to LA today. Tess thought she'd feel happy to have her house back to herself, but she didn't. "I'm going to miss you," she said quietly.

Heather looked up from what she was doing. "Aww. We're family. I'll be back for Thanksgiving and again at Christmas."

"Unless some movie role keeps you too busy," Tess said with a sigh. "I never had a sister growing up. I was an only child."

"Yeah, well, I wouldn't trade Jared for anything, but maybe you're the lucky one. He drove me insane when we were young." Heather took a visible breath and looked down at her feet. Tess knew it was still hard for her to talk about Jared. He was Heather's brother, after all, no matter what he did or didn't do in life.

Tess stood and crossed the room to give Heather a hug. "Read Jaliya's book, okay?"

Heather nodded and stepped back. "If only to make you stop hounding me about it."

Tess laughed. "I'll help you get your luggage to your car. You have a long drive ahead of you. You better get started."

"A long drive to listen to an audiobook. My next movie was based on the book so I'll look very smart if I've actually read it." She winked at Tess and lifted one of her suitcases off the bed.

Tess grabbed the other one and followed her out the front door. They hugged one more time outside, and then Tess waved as Heather backed out of her driveway, leaving her to her house again, but not for long. River was coming to pick her up later for another of their many adventures.

She turned and headed inside to shower and get dressed.

She and River weren't dating anymore. They were keeping things as strictly friends. She couldn't say she didn't have feelings for him. She did. She needed time to process her marriage though without the conflict of a budding romance on the side. She was still finding herself remembering moments of her marriage with Jared, identifying the little clues and signs she'd missed that might have told her he was having an affair. She found herself remembering canceled dinners and outings. Jared stepping out of the house to talk on the phone. Why couldn't he talk in front of her? They were small things, but she was weeding through them all.

An hour later, her doorbell rang, and Tess's heart lifted into her throat. She swallowed it back down. Just friends.

She crossed the room and answered the door, doing her best not to think of how handsome River was. "Hey."

"Hey. You ready?" River asked.

She nodded and closed the front door behind her. "I should be asking you that. You're the one who's meeting your sister today." While Tess had said goodbye to the closest thing to a sister she had.

River walked around his truck and opened the passenger door for Tess, waiting for her to climb in. Then he walked around and got in on the driver's side. "I'm excited. I've helped a lot of folks find their relatives in my line of work. I never thought I'd be doing this for myself."

Without thinking, Tess reached across the center console. She squeezed River's forearm. "I'm sure she's going to be lovely."

River looked down at her hand on his arm, but he didn't look at Tess. He visibly swallowed, and Tess wondered what he was thinking. Was he having to keep reminding himself of where they stood too?

Tess removed her hand and laid it back in her lap, listening to the sound of the truck revving. Then River backed out of the driveway and headed down the road. It was going to be an hour-long trip. Unlike with Heather, there'd be no audiobook to make the time pass for Tess though. "Two Truths and a Lie?" she asked.

River chuckled as he drove. "Haven't you realized that I'm awful at this game yet?"

"I'll start," Tess said, ignoring him. "I once stole a pack of gum from the store when I was nine. I punched a boy in the face when I was the same age for calling me ugly. And I cheated on a spelling test in the third grade and never got caught." She lifted a finger. "But I felt so guilty that I confessed to it anyway."

River glanced over and returned his eyes to the road. "Too many details makes me think that last one's true. I think the lie is that some boy called you ugly. No guy with eyes would ever say so."

"That one's true. Turns out he was trying to flirt with me though."

"By calling you ugly?" River shook his head. "Guys can be idiots. Myself included."

Tess smiled to herself. "I never stole the pack of gum. That's the lie. My mother would have killed me right then and there."

River nodded. "Your mom is tough, like you."

"Your turn," Tess said, watching the world pass outside her window.

"I'm nervous about meeting Margie," River said.

Tess waited for him to give two more statements for the game. He didn't. She looked at him again. That statement was obviously the truth, and it was all he had. "You've exchanged emails, right?"

River nodded.

"So you know she's somewhat normal. I mean, not completely if she's related to you," Tess teased.

"She seems great."

"And I'll be there for whatever you need. If she's horrible or crazy, I'll feign sickness, and we can get out of there."

River lifted a brow. "We've already determined you're a bad liar. But thank you. For being here. For coming. For trying to distract me while we drive."

"Of course. I owe you, after all. You helped me with the whole Jared and Ashley thing. It's the least I can do."

"Who'd have ever thought we'd be friends?" River slowed his truck as he approached a stop sign. He took a second to meet Tess's eyes.

She didn't want to blink, didn't want to look away. River's eyes were the safest place in the whole wide world these days. "Not me," she said. She'd never thought she'd be friendly with River Harrison, much less harbor something even deeper for him.

River felt his hands shaking slightly as he put his truck in PARK and turned off the truck with a twist of the engine key.

Margie Thorndike's home was a small white house with

a chain-link fence in the backyard. River could hear a dog barking and announcing their arrival before he even opened the truck door.

"Here goes nothing," River told Tess.

She smiled reassuringly at him. "It'll be fine. You'll see."

"Yeah." Margie had promised to give him the answers to all of his questions when they met in person. Like what was his father like? Had Margie grown up with him?

Tess met River around the front of his truck. He thought that she was about to reach for his hand, but then she shoved her hands in her pockets.

"Thanks for coming with me," he told Tess as they approached the brick porch steps.

"You've already thanked me a half dozen times," she teased.

"Well, I mean it."

The front door opened before River had even rung the doorbell. A woman who was maybe five years younger than River smiled back at him through the screen door. "You must be River," she said, opening the door. She looked at Tess.

"I'm Tess," Tess supplied. "I'm River's...friend."

"And moral support," he told Margie.

"I have moral support today too." Margie winked at him and opened the door, gesturing them inside. "I've made cookies and tea to make this as comfortable as possible."

"Sounds great," River said. "Thank you."

"Of course." Margie led River and Tess to her living room, where a balding man with rimless glasses was seated in a recliner.

"Hi. I'm Rick, Margie's brother," he said.

River felt his mouth drop open a little bit.

"My brother, not yours," Margie said. "Rick is my step-brother. It's complicated, I guess."

River sat on the couch and watched as Tess took the spot next to him. "I guess family usually is."

Margie picked up a tray with cookies and extended it toward River and Tess. "The way I see family, it's the more the merrier. You can never have too many people to love."

River reached for a cookie. "I like that philosophy."

"Do you have a large family?" she asked him.

River cleared his throat. "I'm down to one. So a couple more relatives would be good, I guess."

Margie offered a sympathetic look. "I can't wait to hear all about my new brother."

River took a breath. Margie seemed nice. He'd never had a sister before. He'd never had a real blood relative before either. "Can I ask first...?"

"About our parents?" Margie asked.

"Yeah."

"They died in a car accident when I was in college. Dad died immediately, but Mom hung on in the ICU for a couple days. That's when she told me about you. I've been looking for you," Margie said. "I didn't have a name or anything to really go on. Not until your DNA pinged in the registry."

River listened attentively. "Did she say why?"

Margie's eyes were wide. "She and Dad were young. They had just had their house foreclosed on and were barely keeping themselves off the streets. They stayed at a few shelters and lived hand to mouth. They couldn't support a baby. They knew you wouldn't survive in their care, so they gave you up." Margie lifted a shoulder. "Mom used to light a candle every night before dinner. I never knew why when I was growing up, but now I know it was for my brother. She hoped you had found a good life. She still prayed for you."

River looked down, collecting his emotions. "I wish I could have met her too," he finally said when he looked up.

Margie's eyes were glassy. "You look like her."

River choked out a laugh and glanced at Tess, who was watching him. "I've never looked like anyone in my life. It's a little weird to hear that." He looked at Margie. She looked familiar to him in a way no one else in his life had either. They had the same hair, same nose, same brown eyes. They were family, the kind made of genes and blood. Hopefully, they'd become the kind that his other family was made of too: love and shared memories.

Chapter Twenty-Eight

Three weeks later, Tess nervously wrung her hands. She hadn't thrown a dinner party since Jared was alive. Yet here she was, her dining room table dressed with a fancy spread, complete with candles and flower centerpieces. This was an unconventional dinner party for sure. Her in-laws were coming and so was the woman her late husband had intended to leave her for, along with the child that Jared and Ashley shared. The Lanes had yet to meet their grandchild. This visit was overdue.

Tess had also invited River for moral support. They were still in the role of friends, but her heart harbored so much more than friendship for him. There had been so many times that she'd been inclined to step toward him and press her mouth to his in a kiss, but she'd stopped herself. She didn't want to lead him on, and she didn't want to jump back into something until she was sure. Until she was ready. She was feeling more ready every day though.

The doorbell rang, and Tess straightened. It was too early for the Lanes or Ashley and Mia. She'd told them six thirty. It was only six.

She walked toward the door and opened it, finding River

and Buddy standing there. River was dressed in nice pants and a button-down shirt. His face was clean-shaven, making the scar below his right eye more visible. It never detracted from how handsome he was though.

Tess swallowed past a suddenly tight throat, resisting the inclination to step toward him once more. Instead, she patted Buddy's head as he walked over to greet her.

"Wow. You look beautiful," River said, his gaze falling for just a moment. He'd kept his promise of staying friends. He never went too far with his words or his actions.

"Thank you." She looked down at her long cotton dress. Between casual and formal. "I'm glad you're early. You have a way of calming my nerves."

He stepped over the threshold and presented a bottle of wine.

Tess's lips parted in surprise. "Oh, wow. You didn't have to."

"It's a special occasion."

"It's an odd one, isn't it? Ashley and Mia are joining the Lane family. My family." She shook her head. "I don't resent Ashley one bit. I truly believe that she had no idea Jared was married." Tess turned and took the bottle of wine into the kitchen to chill with Buddy following after her. "I even kind of like her. She has Mia calling me Aunt Tess, which is kind of fun. I'm not an official aunt, but we will be kin in a way." She looked at River. "It's complicated."

"Life tends to be that way."

The way she felt for him was complicated too. Or maybe it was simple. She still loved him. That feeling hadn't changed.

"Thanks for inviting Douglass and my sister tonight too. You didn't have to do that."

Tess shrugged. "I wanted to. I've always loved Douglass, and Margie seems nice. Family isn't all about blood, right?"

"That's right." River's gaze hung on her for a long moment that made her skin warm. "Buddy and I are going camping this weekend." He leaned on the countertop. "I was wondering if you might want to come camping with us?" He looked nervous. "You can think about it. You can say no."

"Yes," she said immediately. "Camping sounds nice."

He grinned back at her. "Great. I'll pack two tents, of course."

"Will you teach me about the stars again?" she asked.

"If you want me to."

Her heart fluttered around in her chest as she remembered the stars he'd named Tess and River. Then the doorbell rang, and she straightened as Buddy took off in that direction. "They're here."

River straightened too. "Relax. They're family, like you said. Nothing to be nervous about with family."

She blew out a breath. "I'm so glad you're here." She headed toward the front door and Mia came barreling in. She spotted Buddy immediately and dropped onto her knees to throw her arms around the dog.

Tess laughed and stepped in to hug Ashley, who trailed behind Mia. "Hi. It's good to see you."

"Thank you for setting this up." Ashley seemed as nervous as she did.

"The Lanes are amazing people. You'll see," Tess assured her. "And you have their first grandchild here. They're going to love you."

Ashley smiled warmly. "Is this weird?"

"Not as weird as I thought it might be." Tess turned and looked at River.

Ashley noticed him now too. "Are you and River dating?" she asked.

River shook his head. "Just friends. Good to see you again, Ashley."

The Lanes, Douglass, and Margie arrived just after, and Tess was a bundle of nerves as she served her pot roast and sautéed vegetables. River followed her into the kitchen every time and helped her with dishes and drinks. Heather helped too. There was wine and laughter, and by the end of the night, Tess didn't know why she had ever been nervous.

"This was so wonderful," Mrs. Lane said on her way out. "Tess, you have outdone yourself. Ashley and Mia, you'll come visit soon. We'll all have dinner at my house next time. You too, River. And your family," she said, snagging his attention.

When everyone was gone, River stayed.

"I'll help you clean up," he offered.

"No. I'll get it tomorrow. I'm wiped out."

River gestured down the hall. "Then you go to bed, and I'll take care of these dishes for you."

She tilted her head and looked at him. "How long are we going to keep pretending?"

"Pretending what?" he asked.

"That we don't love each other. Because I still love you. And I want to be with you, so much I don't even know what to do anymore."

"I've never pretended not to love you, Tess. And I'm prepared to be your friend forever if that's what it takes. It's all up to you and when you're ready for more. *If* you're ready for more."

She sucked in a breath. "I'm ready, but I'm no less scared. Terrified actually." Her chin trembled.

River continued to look at her. "Does it help if I tell you I'm terrified too?"

She shook her head. "No. Not really."

He laughed quietly. "Well, I am. But I've been scared of a lot of things in my life. Standing still because of fear just makes the fear worse. I find that when you run toward the thing that scares you, every step makes it less terrifying."

Tears filled Tess's eyes. That's all she wanted, to run toward River and ignore the tiny voices in her head feeding her worry and lies. She took a step and then another. Then she ran the rest of the way, closing the distance until her hands were pressed against his chest and her face was tipped back to look up at him.

"I didn't mean to literally run, but okay." He grinned.

She burst into laughter. "Well, if I didn't, I might have turned back, and I'm tired of turning back. I want to move forward. With you...I love you."

He lifted a finger and swiped away a tear on her cheek. "I love you too, Tess Lane. Always. Are you sure?"

"Very. I want to hold your hand. Kiss you. Be with you all the time. I want to go camping with you and talk about books. I want it all. No matter what."

River wrapped his arms around her. "I want those same things too. I want a life with you in it. Forever."

Tess didn't want to jump to conclusions with what he meant using that word. *Forever.* They'd just gotten back together. They were taking things slow. Except she didn't need slow anymore. She didn't want to hold back any longer.

"I want forever with you too," she said, looking up into his eyes before leaning in for a kiss.

This was true love. The truest. And yes, it would probably break her heart many times over. But she trusted that it would be worth it in the end. True love always was.

Epilogue

Hello, Somersetters! Here's your daily dose of Reva!

+ Somerset Lake is seeing stars. Our very own Heather Lane landed a leading role in her own TV show!

+ Jana at Choco-Lovers is offering a 4th of July favorite: Red, White, and Blue Fudge!

+ Speaking of the 4th, there'll be live music and fireworks on the green! Bring yourself a date to snuggle up with. I'm looking at you, River and Tess. ICYMI, those two are an item. Maybe they'll be the next big wedding.

+ It's official! There's going to be another book signing at Lakeside Books in October. Romance author Jillian Matthews is heading to town!

+ Listen up, single ladies and matchmakers! The results from my online poll are in. Mayor Gil Ryan just got dubbed

Somerset's Most Eligible Bachelor! Congrats, Mayor Gil.
Get ready to fall in love with some lucky woman!

"I never thought I'd be spending my Thursday night at this tavern," Tess said a couple of weeks later, glancing over at River beside her at one of the tables. All the ladies of the book club were here along with all the men who gathered weekly.

"Well, it's a special occasion," River said. He looked especially nice tonight in a light blue shirt that brought out the color of his eyes.

"A book club baby." Tess winked at Moira, who was seated across from her. Moira wasn't in as good of a mood as the rest of them. Gil Ryan was seated beside her, completely by accident, and she looked stiff and uncomfortable.

"A tavern baby," Gil corrected, listening to the conversation.

"Half book club, half tavern baby." Lucy turned to grin at Trisha Langly-Fletcher.

A waitress appeared with a tray of drinks and started to hand them out, one by one.

"And a Sprite for you," she told Trisha with a knowing look. Trisha wasn't even showing yet. She had just shared the news with everyone last month. "We don't serve alcohol to minors, and that's what you're carrying."

Trisha laughed and offered an adoring look at Jake, who was also drinking Sprite.

"It's time to book your stay at the Babymoon B and B," Lucy reminded them. "Book club ladies get one babymoon stay for free. As my gift to the happy parents."

"Wow!" Trisha gushed. "That's very generous. I'll have to arrange for someone to watch Petey."

"On it," Della Rose called from the other end of the table. She was seated beside Roman Everson, her boyfriend since last Christmas. The two were talking marriage these days. "My boys would love to have a sleepover with Petey anyway."

"Perfect," Lucy said. "I'll get you on the books this week. The B and B fills up fast these days."

Tess waited for a lull in the conversation and then lifted her glass. "All right, everyone. Now that we all have our drinks, we need to make a toast."

Everyone else reached for their drinks as well.

Tess looked at Gil. "Mayor, you want to do the honors? You're the well-spoken one."

Gil grinned widely. Unlike Moira, he was relaxed. The poor man was so obviously in love with the woman beside him though. Tess had caught the way he'd sweetly pulled out a chair for Moira when there was no other seat at the table. He'd scooted his chair over several inches in the opposite direction just to make her more comfortable too. This wasn't elementary school, but one would think Gil had cooties the way Moira acted around him.

Gil raised his glass and looked around the table. "Here's to friends who fall in love, make love, and have babies."

Tess's eyes widened. "I take it back about you being well-spoken," she quipped.

Everyone laughed.

"Well, I for one think he said it perfectly." Jake added his glass to the toasting circle.

"Hear! Hear!" Miles Bruno said.

"Hear! Hear!" everyone agreed. "Cheers."

Tess lowered her drink and took a sip, her gaze moving to River, who was sitting beside her. "Here's to enemies who become friends and then more," she said quietly, just for his ears.

"Here's to Sherlock and Watson," he retorted, tapping his glass to hers.

They both sipped again, the alcohol warming Tess's throat and her proximity to River warming her body.

"So, Gil?" Jake said, getting everyone's attention. "How's it feel to be dubbed as Somerset's Most Eligible Bachelor?"

Gil rolled his eyes. "I think forcing a man into that title is a crime, don't you think, Deputy Bruno?" he asked Miles.

Miles chuckled. "I'm afraid not."

"I don't know. It's bad enough that my mom and aunts are always trying to set me up. With this new spotlight on my relationship status, I feel like a piece of man-meat. How's a mayor supposed to be taken seriously when folks are more concerned with his dating life?"

"Just go on a couple dates and appease the beast," Roman Everson suggested. "Maybe one of your dates will even become your Mrs. Right."

Tess saw the subtle glance that Gil gave Moira and knew that Gil's Mrs. Right was sitting right next to him. At least in his mind.

A slow song came on overhead in the tavern, and Miles stood first, offering his hand to Lucy. "A dance?"

"Why, yes. I think I will," Lucy said.

Then Jake stood with Trisha. Della Rose and Roman got up from the table as well.

River stood and offered Tess his hand.

"I'll never turn down an excuse to hold you in my arms," River said.

"Oh, come on, man. Wait until you're out of earshot to say that romantic stuff," Gil teased good-naturedly.

River seemed to look at who was left sitting at the table. Lara Dunkin had joined them tonight. She'd been coming to book club ever since the first one that Tess had invited her to this summer. It was Gil, Moira, and Lara left sitting.

Moira stopped the next suggestion at the pass like Tess knew she would. "Lara, why don't you have a dance with Somerset's Most Eligible Bachelor?" Moira urged.

Hurt flashed in Gil's eyes for a millisecond. Tess saw it. Then he stood and offered Lara his hand. "I don't bite," he said.

Lara stood as well. "I only bite a little," she teased right back. Then they headed off to the dance area.

"You don't mind if we leave you all alone at the table?" Tess asked, still standing next to River.

Moira made a shooing motion with her hands. "Go. I'd rather be sitting here anyway."

"What does Moira have against Gil anyway?" River asked, once they were on the dance floor.

Tess wrapped her arms around his neck. "All I know is Moira went on a date with Gil's college roommate one night in our twenties." Tess shrugged. "She's been weird around Gil ever since."

"That's it?" River asked.

"I'm sure there's more to it, but Moira won't tell me. She shuts down the subject anytime I bring it up. She'll never reciprocate Gil's obvious feelings for him though."

"Guess he needs to use this Most Eligible Bachelor thing to move on then," River said, taking Tess and giving her a twirl.

She laughed at the unexpected movement and spun right into his chest. Her heart kicked softly as she looked up into his blue eyes.

"How long do we have to stay before we can blow this joint?" River asked.

"We've already had a toast and a drink."

"And a dance," River said.

"I vote we leave now."

"Hear! Hear!" River dipped his mouth to Tess's, brushing his lips to hers. "I like the way you think."

They finished out their dance and headed back to the table.

"Leaving already?" Della asked as Tess shrugged on her lightweight jacket.

Tess nodded. "Afraid so. Back to book club next Thursday for us, ladies."

River stepped over and shook Jake's hand. "Congrats again, buddy."

"I appreciate it," Jake said.

Tess couldn't help but notice how happy he seemed. Trisha was glowing because of her pregnancy hormones, but Jake seemed to be glowing too. And he deserved to be happy. He'd been so devastated after the passing of his longtime girl-friend Rachel right before high school graduation. But now look at him. Time had healed his heart. It had done the same for Tess.

River reached for her hand, and they left the bar, heading through the parking lot to River's truck. He opened the door for her and waited for her to climb in. Then he shut it behind her and jogged around to the driver's side.

"It's still early. My house or yours?" Tess looked at him across the middle console.

"Actually, I was thinking about taking you for a walk along the lake. Are you up for that?" he asked.

Tess smiled. "Yeah. That sounds perfect actually."

They discussed their friends and River's new case as they drove the short distance to Somerset Lake. Then he parked and walked around to open Tess's passenger side door for her once more. He held her hand and helped her step out. Not that she needed help. She just enjoyed having someone to lean on. Someone to share her days with. And to share a moonlit walk on the lake with every now and then.

They held hands as they strolled. After a few minutes, River stopped and pinned his gaze to the ground.

"Oh no," he said.

"What?" She looked up at him. "What's wrong?"

"I dropped something." He squatted and started searching the area, looking a bit panicked.

"What did you drop?" she asked, doing the same.

"Well, it's small, and it's round. Can you help me look?" he asked.

Tess moved her hands over the ground, bending the blades of grass and looking for whatever River had lost. "I don't know what I'm looking for."

River ran his hands over the grass too, and then out of nowhere, he held something tiny and round between his fingers. "Ah. There it is. Found it."

Tess looked at the tiny ring. It had a silver band and a round opal at its center. "What is that?"

"It's the ring I got you after that first night we met here on the lake." He rose back to his feet. He offered his hand and helped her up as well. "After you said you'd lost your ring out here, I went out and got you this one." He held it out to her.

Tess swallowed, emotion swelling in her chest. She took the ring, admiring its simplicity and beauty. "I love it. Can I have it now?"

"It was always yours," he said.

River took it back and slipped it onto her right ring finger. Not her left. This wasn't an engagement ring, and that was good, because Tess wasn't ready for marriage. There'd been a lot of revelations in the past year about her marriage to Jared. She was working through those things, slowly and surely, by journaling, hiking, and falling in love with River.

"Thank you," Tess looked back up at River.

"You're welcome." He cleared his throat. "Not to show up my nineteen-year-old self, but I have something else for you. Another ring," he said, retrieving a tiny box from his coat pocket.

Tess's breath caught. "Oh?" Her heart rate picked up. This was too soon, wasn't it? She wasn't ready.

River held out his palm and the box. "I'm hoping to have my Watson for another adventure. This one might last a little longer than the last," he said. "It might take forever."

Tess's eyes felt wide. She opened her mouth to speak, but no words came out. She didn't want to hurt River by rejecting him. She didn't want to ruin what they were building together.

"Hold on there, Watson. This isn't an engagement ring," he said.

"No?" she asked, exhaling softly. She loved River, more than anything, but she wasn't prepared to say yes tonight.

"No." He lifted the lid off the box, revealing an emerald with tiny diamond accents. "This is what I call an I'm-going-to-love-you-forever-no-matter-what ring. You don't have to marry me now or ever. All I want is you in my life forever."

Tears blurred Tess's vision. "That's all I want too. But I'm not ready to get married just yet."

"I had a feeling." He smiled warmly at her.

"But I am ready to commit to you, River. When I'm ready, it'll be you."

"So can I put this on your finger?" He pinched the band and lifted it out of the box.

"Yes." She fanned her fingers out in front of him, shaking softly. "Whichever one it slides onto."

He slipped the ring on the middle finger of her left hand. "There. It's a perfect fit."

Tess admired it for a beat. She'd always loved emeralds. How would River know that? He was a PI though. Or maybe he just knew her. "Wow. Two rings in one night. I'm one lucky lady."

"And I'm the luckiest man in Somerset Lake. Especially since I'm allowed to use your bookshop's bathroom now," he teased.

She shoved his chest gently. "You're never going to let me forget that, are you?"

"Nope. It's part of our history. It's a good story, IMO." He leaned in. "That means: in my opinion."

Tess laughed unexpectedly. River was always making her laugh. He surprised her, over and over. Every second with him felt like an adventure. "Who'd have thought? The man I loved to hate is now the man I love more than anything." She wrapped her arms around his neck as if they were still on the dance floor at the tavern.

River grinned. "See there? You've always loved me in some way or another."

Tess fanned out her fingers from where her hand rested on his shoulder, staring at her emerald for a beat. Then she looked back up and met River's gaze. "And I always will. Forever, my Sherlock."

He tugged her closer, dancing to the beat of their hearts under the stars. "Forever, my Watson."

READING GROUP GUIDE

Dear Reader,

I hope you enjoyed reading *The True Love Bookshop*! I have always thought, in addition to writing books, that owning a bookstore would be a dream job. How wonderful to spend your day surrounded by books of every subject and written by hundreds of different authors.

Tess Lane has that charming reality, but the rest of her life is a bit of a mess. At least in the beginning of this story. Imagine finding out that the man you vowed to spend your life with was living a lie. That's the spark that ignited this story in my imagination. How well do we really know the people closest to us?

We've all been lied to, let down, and disappointed by a loved one, but hopefully not in the way that Tess has by her late husband. Moving forward isn't always easy, but in true heroine fashion, Tess found the strength and courage, eventually, to let in the last person she ever expected to fall for. I'm glad River was there to pull her through the tough spots along this journey and to show her that love, after heartbreak and loss, is possible. Isn't that why we enjoy reading romantic fiction? To show us that love prevails.

If I did own that bookshop of my dreams, like Tess, I'd want it to be full of stories of hope and happily-ever-afters.

Thank you so much for reading *The True Love Bookshop*!

xo,
Annie

THE TRUE LOVE BOOKSHOP
DISCUSSION QUESTIONS

1. Annie Rains is often praised for writing stories that tug at readers' emotions. Discuss the moments that were the most emotional for you. Which scenes made you laugh? What dramatic moments are staying with you?

2. Tess's attraction to River is intense even though she knows that she should dislike her husband's best friend who tried to prevent her marriage. What draws her to River? How did you feel about her growing relationship with him? Could you sympathize with her? Do you think they can truly be happy together given their past? Do you think that it would have been better for her to get involved with someone else?

3. How did Tess's complicated relationship with her late husband affect her? How would you feel if your spouse cheated on you and then died before you could deal with the betrayal? Did you admire Tess's handling of the situation or did you think she should have done something

different? Do you think that Tess would have been better off not ever knowing about her husband's affair?

4. Even though Tess lost her husband three years ago, she is still suffering from grief. How do you see that grief shaping her character and informing the choices that she makes? Do you think she hired River to investigate Jared because she's stuck in the past or because she's trying to build a better future?

5. What do you think you would have done if you were in Tess's position? Would you have wanted to know about Jared's affair with Ashley? Would you have wanted Ashley to tell you about her child with Jared? Would you have gone as far as inviting Ashley and Mia to be part of the family?

6. River has been keeping Jared's relationship with Ashley a secret from Tess in an attempt to spare her any further pain. Was he justified in doing so? Are there circumstances when it's acceptable to withhold the truth from those we care about and how do we know where to draw that line?

7. River is willing to ask Tess to watch his dog, Buddy. Caring for Buddy is River's last thought before he falls unconscious at the bookshop. Have you loved a dog as much as River loves Buddy? How important do you think having a pet is in someone's life? Should pets be more or less important?

8. Some of the members of the Thursday night book club have not known one another long but they become instant confidants. Has there been someone who was in your life only briefly but had already had a big impact on you?

9. Reva Dawson has taken small-town gossip to a new level with her blog. Do you enjoy gossip and think that it is mostly harmless fun? Or do you think gossip is often harmful and should be avoided? Did you have fun with Reva's idea of local gossip?

10. Jaliya Cruise's book helps Tess recover from her grief and changes her life. Have you read a book that changed your life? What was the book and why did it impact you?

11. Both Jaliya and Tess have felt imposter syndrome. Do you ever feel like an imposter in your own life? In what role? How do you plan to overcome it?

12. Two of the themes in *The True Love Bookshop* are forgiveness and second chances. What developments in the story relate to these themes for Tess? For River? For Ashley? For Heather?

13. Another theme throughout the novel is the concept of hiding your emotions and pretending to be someone you're not. To which characters does this apply most and why? Heather does this literally for a living. Why is she

well suited for a career as an actress? River also does this in ways to succeed at his career as a private investigator. What prepared him to take on roles and hide his emotions? Has Tess been as successful at hiding her emotions?

14. Why do you think River waited so long to find out the truth about his birth parents? Did he do the right thing? Why or why not? How should he have handled things differently? Could you ever imagine circumstances in which you could see yourself giving up a child for adoption?

15. A theme in the book is self-identity. River believes that he is a loner until he falls in love with Tess and reaches out to his birth family. Tess believes that she had a happy marriage until she investigates Jared's absences. In what ways did not knowing about the past help River and Tess? In what ways did it hurt them? How important is it to be aware of our pasts?

16. Did reading this book help you understand conflicts within your own family? Did the story compel you to change your attitude toward anyone or inspire you to do something for those you love? If so, please explain.

17. What constitutes a family is a theme that runs throughout the story. What do you see in the future for Tess and her family including Ashley and Mia? What do you see in the future for River and his new family including Margie?

About the Author

Annie Rains is a *USA Today* bestselling contemporary romance author who writes small-town love stories set in fictional places in her home state of North Carolina. When Annie isn't writing, she's living out her own happily-ever-after with her husband and three children.

Learn more at:
    AnnieRains.com
    Twitter @AnnieRainsBooks
    Facebook.com/AnnieRainsBooks
    Instagram: @AnnieRainsBooks

Acknowledgments

Every time I finish writing a book, I feel like I've completed a marathon. There's so much time and energy that goes into creating a fictional world with fictional characters. I am so grateful for all the people in my life who encourage me and help me in all the ways I need. My family members, of course, are my heroes. Much love and thanks to my husband, Sonny, and my three children, Ralph, Doc, and Lydia.

Much undying gratitude also goes out to my editor, Alex Logan. This book was an uphill climb at times, but I am so grateful for all your help in making it the best book that it can be. I also appreciate all the hard work and effort from everyone with the Grand Central/Forever team. Many thanks to Lauren Shade for giving this book an early read. Estelle, you are amazing. Thank you for helping me spread the word about my books all over social media and beyond. A huge thanks to Mari Okuda as well. I am so fortunate to have you on my team.

Thank you to my literary agent, Sarah Younger. I could not do this without you. And to the newest member of my support team, my assistant, Kimberly Bradford Scott! You are so invaluable and I'm so lucky to have you helping me!

Rachel Lacey, I've lost count of how many books in which I've included you in my acknowledgments, because you've read them ALL! You win the award for best CP ever! And to my #GirlsWriteNite ladies—all my love. I'm so honored to be on this author journey with each of you.

Lastly, but not least, I want to acknowledge my readers. You mean the world to me. I am so grateful to have each of you in my life, reading my books, loving them, and telling others to give them a try. Your kind words through direct messages and emails always make me smile. So thank you for all you do!